Full Measures

A FLIGHT & GLORY NOVEL

Full Measures

A FLIGHT & GLORY NOVEL

REBECCA YARROS

Preview of *The Last Letter* © 2019 by Rebecca Yarros

Entangled Publishing, LLC
10940 S Parker Rd
Suite 327
Parker, CO 80134
rights@entangledpublishing.com

Embrace is an imprint of Entangled Publishing, LLC.

Edited by Karen Grove
Cover design by LJ Anderson
Cover photography by HayDmitriy and paulgrecaud/DepositPhotos
CoffeeAndMilk/GettyImages

Manufactured in the United States of America

First Edition February 2014

embrace

For Jason, you always have been and will eternally be worth my full measure.

Chapter One

Who the hell would be pounding on the door at 7:05 a.m.?

Three tiny knocks on my bedroom door echoed the harsher ones downstairs. Mom was going to chew their butts for interrupting her morning routine.

"Come in!" I called out, scanning through my iPod's playlist before pressing sync. Music made running more tolerable. Barely. Running was hellish, but I'd already calculated how far I had to go to compensate for the Christmas fudge I'd be scarfing down during the rest of my visit home. The thermometer outside said thirteen degrees, and human ice sculptures were overrated, so Colorado at Christmas meant it would be treadmill city. *Yay, me.*

Gus's strawberry-blond curls popped through the small opening of the door, my lab goggles from Chem 101 perched on his forehead. They gave his seven-year-old, puckered-up-in-frustration face a more mad scientist vibe. "What's up, buddy?" I asked.

"Ember? Can you answer the door?" he begged.

I turned down the music coming from my laptop. "The

door?"

He nodded, nearly losing the goggles. My lips twitched, fighting the smile that spread across my face while I tried not to laugh. "I'm supposed to go to hockey, and Mom won't answer the door for carpool," he said.

I put on my best serious face as I glanced back at the clock. "Okay, Gus, but it's only seven, and I don't think you have hockey until the afternoon. Mom never forgets a practice." I'd inherited my type-A nature from somewhere.

He let out an exasperated sigh. "But what if it's *early*?"

"Six hours early?"

"Well, yeah!" He gave me a wide-eyed stare declaring me the stupidest sister *ever*.

"Okay, buddy." I caved like always. The way he'd cried when I left for college last year pretty much gave the kid free reign over my soul. Gus was the only person I didn't mind going off schedule for.

I checked Skype one more time before closing my laptop, hoping I'd see Dad pop online. He'd been gone three months, two weeks, and six days. Not that I was counting. "He'll call today," Gus promised, hugging my side. "He has to. It's a rule or something. They always get to call for their kid's birthday."

I forced out a smile and hugged his scrawny body. It didn't matter that I turned twenty today, I just wanted to hear from Dad. The knocks sounded again. "Mom!" I called out. "Door!" I grabbed a hair tie off my desk and held it in my teeth while I gathered my long hair back in a pre-run ponytail.

"I told you," he mumbled into my side. "She won't answer. It's like she wants me to miss hockey, and you know that means I'll suck forever! I don't want Coach Walker to think I suck!"

"Don't say suck." I kissed the top of his head. He smelled like his orange, Spiderman-labeled shampoo and sunshine. "Let's go see."

He thrust his arms out in victory and raced down the hallway ahead of me, taking the back stairs closest to my room. He slid through the kitchen in his socks, and I snagged a bottle of water from the fridge on my way. The knocks sounded again, and Mom still didn't answer. She must have run off for errands with April or something, though seven in the morning was way too early for my younger sister.

I passed through the dining room, twisted open the top on the bottle, and walked into the living room, opposite the foyer. Two shadows stood outside the door, poised to knock again.

"Just a minute!" I called out, hopping over the Lego star destroyer Gus had abandoned in the middle of the floor. Stepping on a Lego was a special degree of hell that only someone with a little brother could really understand.

"Don't answer it." Mom's strangled whisper came from the front staircase, which stopped only a few feet from the front door.

"Mom?" I came around the steps and found her huddled in on herself, rocking back and forth. Her hands covered her hair, strands of dark auburn the exact same shade as mine weaving through her fingers where she tugged. Something was wrong. "Mom, who's here?"

"No, no, no, no, no," she mumbled, refusing to lift her head from her knees.

I drew back and took a look at Gus with raised eyebrows. He shrugged in response with a see-I-told-you-so look. "Where's April?" I asked him.

"Sleeping." Of course. At seventeen, all April did was sleep, sneak out, and sleep again.

"Right." Another three knocks sounded. They were brisk, efficient, and accompanied by a soft male voice.

"Mrs. Howard?" His voice was distorted through the door, but through the center glass panel, I saw that he'd leaned in. "Please, ma'am."

Mom raised her head and met my eyes. They were dead, as though someone had sucked the life from them, and her mouth hung slack. This was not my Stepford-perfect mother.

"What's going on?" April asked with a massive yawn, dropping to sit on the top step in her pajamas, her bright red hair a messy tangle from sleep.

I shook my head and turned to the door. The knob was warm in my hand. They taught us in elementary school never to open a warm door during a fire. *Why did I think of that?* I glanced back at Mom and made my choice. Ignoring her plea, I opened the door in slow motion.

Two army officers in Dress Blue uniform consumed our stoop, their hats in their hands. My stomach lurched. *No. No. No.*

She knew. That's why Mom hadn't opened the door. She knew.

Tears stung my eyes, burning my nose before the men could even get a word out. My water bottle slipped from my hand, bursting open on the doorframe and pouring water over their shined shoes. The younger of the two soldiers started to speak, and I put my finger up, silencing him before I softly shut the door.

My breath expelled in a quiet sob, and I rested my head against the warm door. I had opened the door to a fire, and it was poised to decimate my family. I sucked in a shaky breath and put a bright smile on my face as I turned to Gus. "Hey, buddy." I stroked my hands over his beautiful, innocent little head. I couldn't stop what was coming, but I could spare him this. "My iPhone is on my nightstand." *In the room furthest from the front door.* "Why don't you head up to my room and play Angry Birds for a bit? It's not hockey, just grown-up stuff, okay? Play until I come get you."

His eyes lit up, and I forced my smile harder. How long

would it be until I saw that in his eyes again? "Cool!" he shouted and raced up the front steps, passing April on his way. "See, Ember lets me play with *her* phone!" he teased as his footsteps raced toward my room.

"What is going on?" April demanded. I ignored her and turned to Mom.

I dropped to my knees on the step beneath hers and brushed back her hair. "It's time to let them in, Mom. We're all here." I gave a distorted smile through the blur my vision had become.

She didn't respond. It took a minute before I realized she wasn't going to. She just wasn't...here. April scooted down the steps, sitting next to Mom. I opened the door again and nearly lost it at the pity in the younger soldier's eyes. The older one began to speak. "June Howard?"

I shook my head. "Ember—December Howard. My mother," I choked out and gestured behind me, "is June." I stood next to her and reached through the banister railing to rest my hand on her back.

He could be wounded. Just wounded. They came to the door for serious wounds. Yeah, just wounded. We could handle that.

The soldiers nodded. "I am Captain Vincent and this is Lieutenant Morgan. May we come in?"

I nodded. He wore the same patch on his shoulder as my father. They stepped in, their wet shoes squeaking on the tiles of the entry hall, and shut the door behind them. "June Howard, wife of Lieutenant Colonel Justin Howard?" he asked. She nodded weakly, but kept her eyes trained on the rug while Captain Vincent ended my world.

"The Secretary of the Army has asked me to express his deep regret that your husband, Justin, was killed in action in Kandahar, Afghanistan, earlier this morning, the nineteenth of December. He was killed by small arms fire in a Green on

Blue incident in the hospital, which is still under investigation. The Secretary extends his deepest sympathy to you and your family in your tragic loss."

My hands slid to the railing to keep me upright, and my eyes closed as tears raced down my face. I knew the regs. Twenty years as an army brat had taught me they had to notify us within a certain number of hours of identifying him. Hours. He'd been alive *hours* ago. I couldn't breathe, couldn't drag the air into my lungs in a world that didn't have my father in it anymore. It wasn't possible. Everything dropped from under me, and unmatched pain tore through every cell in my body, erupting in a sob I couldn't keep contained. April's scream split the air, ripping through me. God, it hurt. It hurt.

"Ma'am?" the young lieutenant asked. "Is there someone we can call for you? Casualty Assistance should be here soon, but until then?"

Casualty. My father had been killed. Dead. Green on Blue. He'd been shot by someone in an Afghani uniform. My father was a doctor. A doctor! *Who the hell shoots a doctor?* They had to be wrong. Did Dad even carry a weapon?

"Ma'am?"

Why wasn't Mom answering?

She remained silent, her eyes trained on the pattern of the carpet runner on the stairs, refusing to answer.

Unable to answer.

Something shifted in me; the weight of responsibility settled on my shoulders, dislodging some of the pain so I could breathe. I had to be the adult right now because no one else here could. "I'll take care of her until Casualty Assistance arrives," I managed to say with a shaky voice, speaking over April's shrieks.

"You're sure?" Captain Vincent asked, concern etching his unfamiliar features.

I nodded. "They keep a binder, just in case this—" I

shoved my knuckles into my mouth, biting down as hard as I could to stop the wail desperate to emerge. I steadied myself again, sucking in air. Why was it so damn hard to breathe? "In case this happens—happened." Dad was a believer that nothing bad happened to prepared people. He'd hate to know he'd been wrong.

The captain nodded. He pulled out a form and had me verify that the information in Dad's handwriting was correct. This was our address, our phone number. Those were our names and dates of birth. The lieutenant startled. "Happy birthday, December," he whispered.

Captain Vincent sent him a silent glare. "We are so very sorry for your loss. Casualty Assistance will be here within the hour, and the care team is ready if that's okay with you." I agreed. I knew the drill, and what Mom needed.

The door shut behind them, leaving our world shattered.

For the next hour, Mom sat silently on the stairs while April wailed on my shoulder. This wasn't real. It couldn't be. I couldn't hold her tight enough to make it stop. The care team arrived around the same time April's cries softened to sniffles. I waved them inside. Armed with sympathetic eyes and casserole schedules, the three women from the family readiness group of Dad's unit took over the tasks that hadn't been done yet. The breakfast dishes were cleared, laundry put in place, the cereal Gus had spilled earlier on the kitchen floor swept. I knew they were here to help—they would smooth things over until Grams could get here—but I couldn't help but feel invaded, taken over like we were somehow unable to care for ourselves.

Who was I kidding? Mom was still huddled on the stairs. We couldn't care for ourselves. One of the care team members took Gus a snack and assured me he was still engrossed in Angry Birds. I couldn't tell him. I couldn't do it.

The casualty assistance officer knocked quietly an hour

later, and I opened the door. April walked Mom to the couch and sat her down, bracing her with pillows to keep her upright. Her eyes changed focus from the carpet runner to the blank screen of the television deep within the recesses of the armoire. She refused to look at any of us. I'm not sure she was capable of understanding what had truly happened. Then again, I'm not sure I was capable of understanding what had really happened, either, but I didn't have the luxury of going catatonic.

"My name is Captain Adam Wilson," he introduced himself. He wore Dress Blues just like the notification officers had, but he seemed uncomfortable in the role he had been assigned to play. I knew I would be. His frame nearly filled the loveseat across from the couch my mother sat upon, and he dragged the coffee table toward him, softly scraping the carpet. "Did you want someone to take notes?" He glanced at Mom. "For when she's feeling up to it?"

"I've got it," a woman from the team said softly, pen and notebook ready.

Captain Wilson gathered a stack of papers from his leather briefcase, and tugged at his tie, making a minor adjustment. "There's another child, correct?" He shuffled through a few of his papers until he selected a form. "August Howard?"

"Gus is upstairs," I answered, taking the seat on the other side of Mom, closest to Captain Wilson. I clutched the black binder I'd gotten out of Mom's office. It was the very last item in the filing cabinet, just like Dad had told me before he left. "I haven't told him yet."

"Would you like me to?" Captain Wilson asked softly. I briefly considered it. Mom was in no state to discuss it with him, and Captain Wilson had probably been trained to deliver information like that. I couldn't do it though, let a stranger alter the universe of my little brother.

"No. I'll do it myself."

April began crying again, but Mom sat as still as ever, vacant, not really here with us. "I want to give him as long as possible before I have to. His world is still normal. He doesn't know that nothing will ever be the same for him." I bit back my own sob. "He's seven years old and everything he knows just ended. So I think I'll give him just another few minutes." *Before I tear him to pieces.* My skin flushed as new tears came to the surface. I supposed that was the way things would go for a while. I needed to get better at pushing them back.

Captain Wilson cleared his throat and nodded his head. "I can understand that." He explained his role to us, that he would be our guide to Dad's casualty process. He would help us through the paperwork, the ceremony, the things no one saw coming. In a way, he was our handler, sent here to be a buffer between our grief and the United States Army. I was thankful for him just as much as I hated his sheer existence.

He would be with us until we told him we no longer needed him.

After he finished his explanation, the barrage of questions began. April excused herself, saying she had to lie down. There was no doubt in my mind that within a few minutes, this would all go public on Facebook. April was never one to suffer in silence.

The questions started, and I opened the black binder. Dad's handwriting was scrawled all over the pages of his will, his life insurance policy, and his last wishes, all the paperwork carefully organized for this exact moment. Did we know where he wanted to be buried? What kind of casket he wanted? Was there anyone we wanted with us? Was the bank account correct for the life insurance money to be deposited? Did we want to fly to Dover to meet his remains while the army prepared him for burial?

Dover. It was like crossing the army's version of the river

Styx.

Mom remained silent, staring at that blank television as I found the answers to what he asked. No question pulled her from her stupor, no tug of her hand, no whisper of her name could bring her back to where I was desperate for her to be. It was becoming blatantly obvious that I was alone. "Is there someone we can call to help make these decisions with your mother?" His mouth tightened as he slipped a discreet glance toward my mother. I was unsure how many shocked widows he'd seen in his career, but Mom was my first.

Grams was a day away. Because she was Dad's mom, I knew the army had officially notified her, just as we had been. No doubt she was already on her way, but until she got here, there was no one else. Mom's parents were dead. Her brother had never been around much in our lives, and I couldn't see a good reason to bring him in now. "There's just me," I replied. "I'll take responsibility for the decisions until she can."

"Ember?" Gus's small voice came from the steps where he stood. "What's going on?"

I placed Mom's hand back in her lap. It wasn't like she noticed I was holding it anyway. After the deepest breath ever taken, I walked over to my little brother. I sat down next to him on the steps and repeated everything we knew in seven-year-old terms, which wasn't anything really. But I had to repeat the one thing we knew for certain. "Daddy isn't coming home, Gus."

Little blue eyes filled with tears, and his lower lip began to quiver. "Did the bad guys get him?"

"Yes, baby." I pulled him into my arms and held him, rocking him back and forth like I had when he was an infant, our parents' miracle baby. I brushed his hair back over his forehead and kissed him.

"But it's your birthday." His warm tears soaked through my running shirt and immediately chilled as I held him as tightly as possible. I would have done anything to take away this pain, to unsay what I knew had to be said. But I couldn't take the bullet from Dad.

Gus cried himself out while Captain Wilson sat, patiently observing my mother and her nonresponse. I wondered how long it would be until words like "medicate" and "psychologist" were brought up. My mother was the strongest person I knew, but she'd always stood on the foundation that was my father.

Once the last of his little sobs shook his body, I asked him what he needed, if there was anything I could do to make this better for him. "I want you to have cake and ice cream." He lifted his head off my chest and squeezed my hand. "I want it to be your birthday."

Panic welled within me, my heart rate accelerating, tears pricking my eyes. Something fierce and terrible clawed at my insides, demanding release, demanding acknowledgment, demanding to be felt. I grimaced more than smiled and nodded my head exuberantly, cupping Gus's sweet face. I turned my attention to Captain Wilson. "Can we take a ten minute break?"

The captain nodded slowly, as though he sensed I was close to losing it, his one stable person in a house of grieving women and children. "Is there anything you need?"

"Could you please call my Grams and check on her? She lost her husband in Vietnam…" It was all I could force out. I inched closer to the inevitable scream that welled up within my body.

"I can do that."

I kissed Gus's forehead, grabbed my keys, and ran out the door before I didn't have the strength to stand any longer. I flung myself into the driver's seat of my Volkswagen Jetta, my high school graduation present from my parents. Dad wanted me in something safe so I could make it home on weekends from the University of Colorado at Boulder. Too bad he wasn't as protected in Afghanistan.

I forced the key into the ignition, cranked the engine, and backed out of the driveway too quickly. I tore down the hill, taking the curves, heedless with my safety for the first time since I got my driver's license. In front of the grocery store, the stoplight turned red, and I became aware of the chill seeping into me, making my fingers tingle. The car read seventeen degrees outside, and I was still dressed for treadmill running. I hadn't grabbed my coat. I parked the Jetta and walked into the grocery store, thankful for the numbing sensation in my arms and heart.

I found the bakery section and crossed my arms. Cake. Gus wanted a cake, so I would get him one. Chocolate. Vanilla. Strawberry. Whipped icing. Buttercream icing. There were too many choices. It was just a damned cake! Why did I need that many choices? Who cared? I grabbed the one nearest to me and headed for the ice cream section where I snatched a quart of chocolate chip cookie dough on autopilot.

I was halfway to the checkout counter when I ran into a small family. They were average: mom, dad, one boy, one girl. They laughed as they decided what movie to rent for that night, and the little girl won, asking for *The Santa Clause*. How was it possible these people were having such a normal day, such a normal conversation? Didn't they understand the world had just ended?

"You know, they'll write on that for you if you want his name on it." The masculine voice broke me from my train of thought, and I looked up into a somewhat familiar set of brown eyes underneath a worn CU hat. I knew him, but couldn't remember how. He was achingly familiar. Of course I would take note of a guy as hot as this one. But in a university with forty thousand other students, there was always someone who looked familiar, and there were very few who I could actually name, or even remember the details of how we'd met. With a face and body like that, I should have remembered this guy, even this shell-shocked.

The guy was waiting for me to say something.

"Oh, yeah, the cake." My thoughts were fuzzy, and I was desperately holding on to what I had left of them. I nodded my head and muttered thanks as I headed back to the bakery. My feet moved of their own accord, thank God.

The heavyset woman behind the counter reached out to take the cake and I handed it over. "Could you write 'happy birthday' on this?"

"Sure can, honey. Whose special day is it?"

Special day? This was a day from hell. I stood there at the counter of the grocery store, with a cake I didn't even care about, and realized this was unequivocally the worst day of my life. Maybe there should have been some comfort in that, knowing if this was the worst day, there was nowhere to go but up. But what if it really wasn't the worst day? What if tomorrow was just waiting around the corner, ready to pounce and bring me to a new low?

"Miss?" My eyes focused back on the baker's face. "Whose name would you like on the cake?"

"December."

"Yes, ma'am, it is December, but whose name would you like on the cake?"

The same griefy-panic threatened to well up again in me, choking my throat. "It's mine. My name is December."

A string of giggles erupted from the baker. "But, ma'am, these are Teenage Mutant Ninja Turtles. It's a boy's cake!"

Something snapped inside me. The dam broke, the river raged, whatever pun came to mind. "I don't care what kind of cake it is!"

"But surely you'd be happier—"

I'd had it. "No, I wouldn't be happier. Do you know what

would make me happy? I would like to go back to bed, and for none of this to have happened. I don't want to be standing in the middle of this grocery store, buying a stupid cake so my little brother can pretend that our dad isn't dead! So, no, I don't care what kind of cake it is, Ninja Turtles or Barbie or Sponge Bob freaking Square Pants!"

The woman's lip began to tremble, and tears formed in her eyes. "Happy...Birthday...December," she said as she slowly dragged the icing bag across the green and blue cake, inscribing my name. She handed the cake back over with shaking hands and I accepted it with a thankful nod.

I turned to see the CU guy with his hand in mid-reach for a pack of blueberry muffins, but his eyes were locked on me, wide with shock.

I couldn't blame him; I was shocked at my outburst, too, appalled that I'd lost it in the middle of the grocery store.

Tears streamed down my face unnoticed as I stood at the register, waiting for the young girl to ring up my cake and ice cream. "Thirty-two nineteen," she told me. I reached for my back pocket, where I normally kept my tiny wallet, but found only the smooth spandex of my running shorts.

"Shit," I whispered, closing my eyes in defeat. No coat. No wallet. Great planning.

"I got this." The brown-eyed guy slid a fifty dollar bill across the conveyor belt to the clerk. I hadn't even noticed he'd been behind me.

I turned to look back up at him, stunned at how tall he was. I only reached his collarbone. The sudden turn made me sway, and he reached out to steady me, his strong hands gently supporting my arms. "Thank you." I dragged the backs of my hands over my cheeks, wiping away what tears I could, and handed him back his change. There was something so familiar about him... What was it?

"Do you need me?" he asked softly, as the clerk rang up

his Vitamin Water.

"What?" I had zero clue what he was talking about.

He flushed. "Do you need me to carry that out? I mean, it looks kind of heavy," he finished slowly, like he couldn't believe he'd said it, either.

"It's a cake." He had to be the hottest awkward guy I'd ever met.

"Right." He grabbed his bag and shook his head like he was trying to clear it. "Would you at least let me drive you home?"

Wow, did he choose the wrong day to try to pick me up. "I don't even know you. I hardly think that's appropriate."

A soft smile slid across his face. "You're December Howard and I'm Josh Walker. I graduated three years ahead of you."

Josh Walker. Holy shit. High school. Memories crashed through me, but that Josh Walker couldn't possibly be the one standing in front of me. No, that one had been a tattooed, motorcycle-driving, cheerleader magnet, not this clean-cut all-American nice guy. "Josh Walker. Right. I used to have a picture of you taped on my closet door from when you guys won state." Shit. Why did I say that? His eyebrows raised in surprise, and I mentally added *or still do, but whatever.* "If I remember correctly, you had your head stuck too far up your hockey helmet to notice any underclassmen." But I had noticed him, along with every other girl in school. My eyes narrowed as I assessed the lean cut of his face, only made more angular and freaking hot by quasi-adulthood. "And you had a lot more hair."

His devastating grin cut through the fog of my brain, distracting me from the pain for a blissful moment. How did a hockey player have such straight teeth?

"See, I'm not a stranger." He handed me my cake, and his smile vanished, replaced by a flash of...pain or pity? "Ember,

I'm sorry about your dad. Please let me drive you home. You're not in any shape to drive."

I shook my head, tearing my gaze from his sympathetic one. For an instant, I had nearly forgotten. Guilt overran me. I'd just let a pretty face distract me from…everything, and it all came rushing back, shredding into me. What was I doing even thinking about him? I had a boyfriend, and a dead father, and no time for this. Dead. I squeezed my eyes shut against the pain.

"Ember?"

"I need to do it. I need to know I can." I thanked him again for paying and headed back into reality.

I slid onto the frozen leather seat in my car and sat in stunned silence for a moment. How could something as simple as seeing Josh Walker again right a little piece of my soul when the rest had been flipped so wrong? The cold of the seat seeped through my running capris, forcing out the warm thoughts of Josh. The cake on my front seat mocked me with stupid, happy, martial-arts turtles. Gus would love it. If Gus *could* love it. God, what was he going to do without Dad? What were any of us going to do? Panic welled up in my chest, catching in my throat before exploding in a cry that sounded nothing like me. How was I supposed to take care of Mom without Dad? How was I going to do any of this when I wanted to curl up and deny it all?

My composure crumpled, and I sobbed against my steering wheel for exactly five minutes. Then I sat up, dried my tears, and stopped crying. I couldn't afford to cry or break down anymore. I had to take care of my family.

Chapter Two

This wasn't my first military funeral, but I had been a kid then, and the death of someone my parents once knew hadn't really struck a chord with me. Dad's funeral slowly tore me apart with each tear I held back. Every time someone hugged me, or told me they were sorry, another piece of me shut down, like my maximum pain threshold had been reached.

Riley, my exquisite, perfect boyfriend of three years, drove down from vacationing at his family's cabin in Breckenridge to be with me. I'm not sure I could really say he was with me, though. He'd been more *with* his cell phone the last few days, and wasn't even here yet. I couldn't really blame him. It's not like I was a joy to be around. Since the notification last week, Christmas had passed with a whisper, the New Year was upon us, and Mom still hadn't responded to... anything. Thankfully, Grams had shown up, all Southern-steel backbone and silver hair, and kept the wolves off the door. No one was threatening to medicate Mom. Yet.

The chapel on post filled quickly. People I recognized and countless soldiers I didn't took their seats in hushed tones. We'd asked for this to serve as the unit's memorial, too. I didn't think any of us could have gone through this a second time. April sat surrounded by a gaggle of her friends, being comforted en masse as she cried, and a small stab of jealousy sliced through me. April was allowed to fall apart. That was a luxury I didn't get to have, not anymore.

"Oh, Ember." Sam, my best friend from high school, pulled me in for a hug at the back of the chapel while I waited for Gus. I sagged a little against her, willing to let her take some of the weight. "This sucks."

She always knew just what to say.

"I'm glad you're here," I said, speaking honestly for the first time today.

"Where's Riley?" The perfect café au lait skin of her forehead puckered as her eyebrows drew together.

I plastered a fake smile on my face. "Not sure, but he said he's coming."

Her furrows deepened, and I saw a flash run through her hazel eyes before she sighed. "Kayla? She's still your roommate, right?"

"She's in Boston with her parents, but she's flying back to Boulder in the next few days." I held my breath and waited for the typical sarcastic quip to come from Sam. There was no love lost between Kayla and Sam, and hadn't been since Sam and I had grown apart last year. I'd gone off to Boulder and become roomies with Kayla, and Sam stayed to go to school here in Colorado Springs. I still loved the heck out of Sam, but it was hard to keep a friendship with such separate lives.

"Right." Organ music started to play, and Sam squeezed my hands. "That's my cue. Ember, whatever you need, I'm here."

"I know you are."

She gave me a weak smile and headed to sit with her mom, who'd been a really good friend of Dad's. I guess that's what happens when you spend years and two duty stations with someone.

"Ember?" I turned to see Mrs. Rose, whose husband had been killed in the attack with Dad. She looked put together in a simple black sheath and matching heels. Her hair was done, makeup perfect and unsmeared. Her two little boys, Carson and Lewis, were immaculately dressed in little black suits.

"Hi, Mrs. Rose. We're glad you came," I answered for my family. "How are you?"

Her hands grazed the shoulders of her boys, like she was assuring herself they were still there. "We're getting by. Your mother?"

My face flushed. "She's having a hard time."

Mrs. Rose nodded. "We all grieve in different ways. She'll come around." She smiled at her boys. "Let's find our seats."

They headed down the aisle, and something dark stole into me, raising my temperature. How could she be okay? How was she so perfectly poised when my mother couldn't hold it together? The unfairness of everything weighed on me. I wanted Mom to pull herself together like Mrs. Rose had.

My cell phone buzzed, alerting me to a new text message.

Riley: *On my way, but running late.*

Ember: *See you soon.*

I slid my iPhone back into my purse as Gus emerged from the bathroom. His suit made him appear older than he really was, another thief stealing his childhood away. He fumbled with the long ends of his tie, which must've come undone while he was in there. Gus only had two ties, both of which my dad had tied before he left for deployment. The knots would slide up and down as we took them on and off Gus's head for church, but we were always careful not to untie them. None of us girls in the house knew how to tie a tie. We'd never given it much thought.

"I didn't mean to do it." His eyes welled up with tears, siphoning my own. I forced a smile to my face, which became just a little easier each time I had to do it.

"It's not a problem, little buddy." I gently wiped away his tears and fixed my concentration on figuring out his tie. A wave of grief overtook me. This was Dad's job. He was supposed to teach Gus how to tie a tie, drive a car, flirt with a girl. How was Gus going to grow up without Dad's example? Sure, my father would never walk me down the aisle, never hold my firstborn child, or the second, for that matter. But I'd had him for twenty years while I had grown to quasi-womanhood. Dad was etched into the very fabric of my being. It wasn't fair that his son only got him for seven years.

My fingers fumbled with the tie, but I couldn't figure out how to make it work. A pair of large hands reached in between us, and I looked over. Shock almost knocked me on my butt at seeing Josh Walker crouched next to me. A sad smile came to his face.

"Hey, Gus, can I get that for you?"

"Hey, Coach Walker. Sure."

Coach? Right, Gus had told me, but I hadn't put it together. The Josh Walker I remembered wouldn't take the time to coach anyone, let alone a hyper group of kids. What had changed him so much in four years?

Gus turned his beautiful smile on me, and I almost hugged Josh for inspiring it. "Ember, this is my hockey coach."

"We've met, Gus." I ruffled his hair and stood up slowly, careful to keep my balance on my heels.

"I went to high school with your sister, little man." Josh made quick work of Gus's tie, deftly looping it around, pulling it through until it resembled my dad's own knot. A surge of gratitude ripped through me. Josh had saved Gus's day.

We took our seats when the chaplain directed. Gus sat next to me, then Mom, Grams, and April. One by one, the speakers came up, giving their best memories of Dad. He had saved so many lives, given so much of himself to those who needed it. He had never failed to inspire me. Well, inspire me in everything but his death. He'd been killed senselessly, helping other people. What was the point, the justice in that? Hysterical laughter bubbled up through my lips, and Grams reached her hand around Mom to steady my shoulder. What, like I was going to figure out the meaning of death and life while sitting here? Preposterous. No one understood the meaning behind war. It was hilarious to think the answer would be bestowed upon me simply because I lost someone I loved. My psych professor would have had a field day with me at that moment.

Midway through the service, a familiar hand squeezed my shoulder, this time from behind. Riley had finally arrived. Rather than feeling comforted, I was annoyed and angry. For someone who professed to love me, I certainly wasn't high on his list of priorities today of all freaking days. No doubt he had a perfect excuse though, some cat caught in a tree, or a stranded stranger with a flat tire.

An officer stood at the podium and began the traditional roll call. *Oh God, here we go.* As he called out the names of soldiers present, they stood in the congregation announcing their presence. All around me, figures in blue popped up like jack-in-the-boxes, alive and well. I thought I was ready to hear it. After all, I knew it was coming. Our CAO had walked us through this many times. They would call my father's name, but he wouldn't answer.

That was the whole point.

"Lieutenant Colonel Howard?" The officer's voice echoed from the silent church. Every muscle in my body tensed and my teeth ground together. "Lieutenant Colonel Justin Howard?" April's keen wail split the silence and tears burned their way down my cheeks. I couldn't so much as raise my hands to wipe them away. *God, just stop calling his name. Please.* But he didn't. "Lieutenant Colonel Justin A. Howard?" One more time. I just had to make it one more time.

"Why do they keep calling Daddy's name?" Gus asked. *To prove he's really gone.*

I couldn't answer him; my vocal cords were paralyzed from fear of what would finally erupt when I spoke. I pulled him closer. "Lieutenant Colonel Justin August Howard?" I knew more was said, but I didn't hear it. Instead, I was back in my memory, watching Dad kneel down so four-year-old Gus could help pin Lieutenant Colonel rank on his shoulders. We'd all been so happy and proud. I guess we were also supposed to be proud today, knowing he'd given his life for something so much bigger than himself. What people didn't understand was there was nothing bigger than my dad in my eyes, nothing worth the cost of his life.

Bagpipes belted out "Amazing Grace." Beside me, my mother finally spoke, whispering my father's name in a broken plea. "Justin?"

I forced my teeth into my lower lip to keep from crying out, slicing into the soft flesh until the pain I caused could stand against the grief tearing through me.

Once the service was over, I felt like congratulating myself for surviving it, but I still had to make it through the burial. We walked down the aisle behind the chaplain, exiting the service through the main door, where a black limousine waited. Grams pulled my mother inside. April followed soon after with her boyfriend, Brett. I waited outside with Gus, knowing Riley would want to come with us.

He came down the steps slowly, dressed impeccably in a suit his mother had picked out, no doubt. His blond hair was parted to the side, and his blue eyes stood out against the black of the suit. Another spurt of hysterical laughter nearly took me. Riley was a living Ken doll. He pulled me into his familiar arms, wrapping me in the scent of the cologne he'd worn since our senior year. He pulled back to kiss me, and his eyes flared. "Uh, babe?" He recoiled, like he was disgusted.

Josh appeared next to me, setting Gus down after a hug. He pulled out a Kleenex and dabbed at the area just beneath my lip. The tissue came away red, stained with the blood I had drawn with my teeth. He gave me a weak smile and backed away quickly, as though he knew he had overstepped a boundary. Whoa. I ran my tongue across my lip and felt the area I'd abused.

Riley rolled his eyes before he realized who it was. "Josh Walker!" He held out his hand, and Josh shook it. "It's been a long time, man. You're coaching my little brother and Gus now, right?"

Josh nodded. "Rory's a great kid. I'll catch you later, Gus."

Gus grabbed onto my hand and tugged. "Can Coach Walker come with us, please?"

Riley answered before I could. "Gus, the limo is only for family."

Gus smirked. "Well, you're not family. Besides, if April and Ember get to bring someone, I can, too."

I couldn't argue with Gus's logic. "You're welcome to join us," I said to Josh, avoiding his eyes.

The limo ride was the most awkward twenty minutes I'd ever spent in a car. On my left, Riley updated his Facebook status. What could he be typing? *Heading to bury girlfriend's dad?* He didn't handle stress well, and I didn't hold it against him. It was simply one of the aspects of his personality that I understood, that I tried my best to complement. After all, that was part of our plan, why we went so well together. I filled in his gaps. "Ah, man," he whispered.

"What is it?" I asked.

He shook his head, scrolling through his phone. "They moved our formal a week earlier."

I didn't bother responding. He wasn't looking for my input anyway. Grams sat stoically, her silver hair pulled into a French twist, her single strand of pearls immaculately appropriate. She'd always had an air of dignity about her, but the way she held herself together in the wake of her son's death was awe-inspiring. Her hands clutched the small picture frame of Dad's basic training she had rested on her knees.

"What's on your mind?" Josh asked, sitting on my right. His phone was out, too; he'd given it to Gus, who was currently destroying small pigs in the *Star Wars* version of Angry Birds.

I subtly gestured to my grandmother with my head. "My grandfather died in Vietnam." I shook my head. "She's already been through so much; this hardly seems fair."

He was quiet for a minute, as though he was carefully choosing his words. "As hard as this must be for her, maybe she's really the only one who can help your mom through this. After all, she's been there."

I watched the way Grams reached out to hold my mom's hand, stroking her skin with her thumb. Josh was right. If anyone was going to pull her back from this precipice she was standing on, it would be Grams. They were equally stubborn women, equally strong, equally capable. "She's going to be okay, eventually."

"So are you." He squeezed my hand gently before quickly pulling it away, careful not to brush the skin of my knee just below my hem.

Riley slipped his phone back into his pocket as we arrived at the cemetery. We stepped from the car and crossed the frozen ground to the plot my father had chosen. At the time, I had thought it was a morbid thing to do, choosing his own funeral plot. Now, I was thankful. It was one more choice I didn't have to make, and I knew he'd be happy. As we took our seats in the front row, facing my father's casket, people walked by. They shook our hands. They leaned down to hug us. They were sorry for our loss. They couldn't fathom our grief. They wanted to know what they could do. I said thank you so many times that it no longer sounded like a word. Selfishly, I just wanted them to stop touching me.

Riley took the seat behind me, keeping his hand on my shoulder, anchoring me as he'd done these last few years. He was my reminder that I would get through this; things would return to normal and our plans wouldn't change. Well, whatever "new normal" was waiting for me.

"Can you make them stop hugging me?" Gus asked, reaching for my hand. I kissed his soft forehead.

"Sure thing, buddy." I ran interference for Gus until everyone finally took their seats. Again, the chaplain began to speak about duty and sacrifice. I fought the urge to stand up on my chair and stomp my foot, reminding myself that I was no longer a petulant teenager. What did they know of duty? My father's duty was here, at home. Now someone else had to step into his shoes, figure out what we were supposed to do from here. It wasn't fair.

The American flag draped Dad's silver coffin. I wanted to see him, to verify with my own eyes that he was really dead. But when his remains arrived from Dover, they came with a cutting little note attached: "These remains are not recommended for viewing." When I got Captain Wilson alone and was able to ask the question, he danced around it until I finally got my answer. Dad was shot in the head, chest, and leg. The asshole had been so thorough there wasn't enough of Dad's face left to see.

The small, childlike part of me wondered if he was really in there, or if there had been some drama-worthy mix-up. Maybe the poor soul in this coffin belonged to another family, and my dad was lying somewhere wounded, unable to tell his real name. But I wasn't Gus. I knew the truth: we were burying my father.

The flag slid from the coffin into the arms of the waiting honor guard. They snapped the flag tight with military precision. That flag had been with him from the hospital in Afghanistan where he was pronounced dead, through Dover where they prepared his body and tailored his uniform, to here in Colorado where we would bury him.

The guns rang out, killing the silence and jolting my heart. The honor guard fired three volleys, each time freezing me until I died just a little bit more. Three volleys for the guns. Three bullets in my father. It was poetic really. Gus began to cry horrible wrenching sobs. I reached for him as the honor guard folded the final corner of the flag into the triangle. Josh leaned forward and pulled Gus over the chair, into his lap, and rocked him like a baby. I nodded my thanks. Across the empty chair I reached for April. She clasped my hand in a death grip as cold as her frozen fingers. We'd forgotten gloves.

A colonel dropped on one knee in front of Mom, grasping the folded flag. She raised her head and brought her chin up, showing a shadow of the spirit I knew she had. "On behalf of the President of the United States and a grateful nation," he said reverently as he handed the flag to my mother's shaking hands. She crossed her arms in front of the flag and pulled it to her chest, lowering her face into the folds as if she could catch Dad's scent on the fabric. Then she began to keen, a low, ugly sound, like her soul had been dismembered.

I held it together until the bugler began to play "Taps." *Day is done, gone the sun.* So often I'd heard it around the military bases where we'd been stationed. There was something familiar, cleansing about hearing it played, as though the song itself was saying this awful event was over.

This was the worst, the lowest we would ever be. *God is nigh.*

Grams shook with grief on the other side of my mother. Now she had truly given all she had for this country. She wrapped her arm around Mom, drawing her to her shoulder; they had each lost the person they loved most.

As everyone left the burial, my family piled into the limo, but I couldn't leave, not yet. The honor guard handed Riley a stack of folded flags, one each for Grams, April, Gus, and myself. Like we needed a memento. War was such a spiteful bitch; she took everything we loved and handed us back a folded flag in return, telling us the honor of their sacrifice was a just and equal payment. It wasn't.

One of Dad's five deployments had begun shortly after Gus was born. In the middle of the night, I had watched Dad pack his bags as Mom rocked the crying Gus to sleep. Even at thirteen, I didn't mind being pulled into my dad's lap. He'd cradled my gangly frame and kissed my forehead in the way only fathers can do. "I need you to take care of your mom while I'm gone," he'd requested. "Take it easy on her; this will be tough, and I need you to be my girl of the house. Can you do that for me? Can you take care of your mom, and April, and Gus?" Of course I had agreed. I would have done anything to please my father, as I knew he would have done for me. Anything but stay.

As they lowered his coffin into the icy ground, I raced forward. "Stop!" The cemetery workers froze, leaving Dad only inches above the surface. I stumbled forward, my heels catching on what was left of the grass. My knees landed in front of the cold metal that marked the entrance to my father's grave. I placed my right hand on the chilled exterior of the coffin and stifled my cry with my left. "I love you," the whisper broke from me. "I miss you, and I don't know what to do without you," I cried. I dragged the frost-bitten air through my lungs. "But don't you worry about them, not

Grams, or Mom, April, or Gus. I will take care of them, I promise."

Riley's familiar arms surrounded me, lifting me off the ground until I was standing. I gave a small nod to the cemetery workers. They began lowering my father again, deeper and deeper into the ground. "I promise."

Chapter Three

"Ember." Gus shook me awake before my 7:00 a.m. alarm could blare. Sleep was great. When I was asleep, everything was normal, and this was the nightmare, but then that stupid alarm would go off, and I was back facing our "new normal."

"Mmmm?" I mumbled, pulling my hair from my face and trying to focus my sleep-deprived eyes.

"I'm hungry." Gus crept closer and laid his head on my pillow, inches from my face. He hadn't brushed his teeth.

"You're always hungry." I tugged him closer, my hand meeting denim where I expected soft pajama pants. "Are you already dressed?"

"I have school today. The bus comes in a half hour at seven-three-zero."

That woke me up. I climbed out of bed, secured my flyaway hair with a tie, and found a smile. "Food it is, bud."

"We're out." He jetted ahead of me, taking the back stairs toward the kitchen.

"Out of what?"

The bright, open windows of the kitchen let in the

morning light, and the tiles were cold on my bare feet. *Coffee. Coffee would be good.* I turned the Keurig on and checked the pantry while it hissed itself awake. *Yeah, I don't want to be up, either.* Gus was right; we were out of cereal, oatmeal, and bagels.

We were out of *everything.*

When had this happened? I pulled out the last of a loaf of bread and checked the calendar on my way to the fridge. January 5. "First Day Back to School" was inscribed in Mom's handwriting on the otherwise empty block. A week from today displayed an ominous message: "Ember back to CU for spring."

I swallowed the panic and, instead of thinking about my departure date, reached past the doors of the fridge to grab the eggs and milk. It was also astonishingly bare. When had the food stopped being delivered? Meals had been coming in and out of this house with such frequency, it never dawned on me to actually go and buy some.

I asked Gus to check on April, and he scurried off, happy to get back to his routine. A plate of scrambled eggs and toast later, I grabbed five bucks out of the change jar for Gus's lunch money and we headed out the door. At the bus stop, the parents were cautious around me. After all, we were now the kids with no dad, but the kids treated Gus no differently than they had before everything changed. He wasn't dad-less Gus; he was just Gus, and it was great.

I kissed him on the forehead and sent him off, then shut the front door, coming back in the warm house. April lounged in front of the television in her pajamas. "What do you think you're doing?" I asked. "You should have been at school already."

"Looking for something good to watch." She had zero intention of moving.

"It's a school day," I said incredulously. She had to get her butt in gear or she wasn't going to make it to first period on time. I knew for a fact it took seventeen minutes to get to the high school from our house.

"I'm not going."

I ripped the remote from her hands and placed it on the farthest coffee table from her. If she wanted to fight me, at least she'd have to get off her butt to do it. "Yes, you most certainly are."

"You're not my mother." Had she seriously used teenager logic on me? Maybe this was payback for all the hell I'd given my mother. "Besides, it's a half day. They don't really expect us to go."

"Well, I'm your grandmother, and you will be going to school today." Grams's hands fastened the last piece of silver hair into her French twist as she came into the room, already dressed and accessorized with her single strand of pearls. Grams believed that class never slept. When April began to argue, Grams cut her off with a single arched eyebrow. "Your father died, not you. Go dress yourself, grab your backpack, and get to school."

April didn't bother fighting with her. We both knew that would get her nowhere. Instead, she got dressed then flew through the kitchen, snagging another five dollar bill out of the change jar as I filled my coffee cup with more creamer than I should have. "Have a good day, darling," I sang to her.

She flipped me the bird in reply and slammed the front door as her punctuation.

Grams reached for the sugar, sweetening her coffee as well.

"Grams, I think we're out of food."

"What do you plan to do about it?" She sipped her coffee and went to catch up on the news. Her point was made; I was old enough to deal with this.

Five minutes and a hundred deep breaths later, I gently

cracked open the door to my mother's bedroom. "Mom?" I called out gently, not wanting to alarm her. Not that much could. She was speaking now, but only when spoken to. She never offered anything to a conversation, nor did she seek anyone out. Mostly, she slept. If she had dreams like I did, the ones where Dad came and told her everything would be okay, I understood. *I'd rather be asleep, too.*

I crouched next to the bed. She looked like hell. Maybe today I could get her to shower or brush her hair. "Mom?" I touched her wrist, which was turned up in sleep, her palm open like a child's. Her brown eyes fluttered open for just a moment. She was there with me. It was the smallest of seconds, less than a heartbeat, but then I saw it take her, the knowledge that he was still gone, that this was real life, and her eyes glazed over.

"Mom, I have to grocery shop today. The house has no food and the kids went back to school." I could tell she processed what I said, but she didn't respond. "I think Gus has hockey this week, but I don't know. January's wall calendar isn't complete." Usually, her calendars were meticulous, her appointments punctual.

I had to try again. She had to respond. "Mom, I don't know if I should use your debit card, or the extra cash lying around, but I have to shop today. Is there anything I can get for you?"

"Sleep," she murmured. "I just want to sleep."

Her eyes closed, and she was gone as soon as she said the words. My fingernails bit into my palms where I clenched my fists. I wanted to let loose a deafening scream, but that would be childish. About as childish as the burning green envy twisting my stomach into knots. I wanted the sweet escape she had.

I pulled her purse off the peg in the mudroom and emptied the contents onto the kitchen counter. Her wallet, sunglasses, keys, and the giant black notebook she lovingly called "The Brain," all appeared before me. I opened The Brain up to January and saw that Gus had hockey beginning again this afternoon. The other dates in the calendar seemed inconsequential, seeing as I wouldn't be here for them. April needed to figure this out quickly.

One more week. One more week here in this grief-ridden house and I could return to college. Kayla had already flown back to Boulder from visiting her parents in Massachusetts. I'd be back at the parties, the mixers, and classes. I wouldn't have to think about whether or not April was up for school, or if my mother had eaten that day. I could be with Riley.

He hadn't been around much. He always apologized profusely, but I knew the awkwardness of this house was nothing he was prepared for, even though he'd been a part of this family for over three years now. He wanted everything to be normal, the way it was in Boulder, and I did, too. The problem was that normal wasn't an option for me anymore, but he hadn't really shown up for me the last two weeks, so he didn't know that.

I wasn't sure normal would even be there when I got back to Boulder.

"Just take her debit card," Grams commented from across the counter. I'd been so lost in my own thoughts I hadn't noticed she'd crept in. "You know better than I do what this house uses, so you take yourself to that store."

I showered, dressed, dried my hair, and grabbed my keys and Mom's wallet on my way out the door. "And December," Grams interjected, "call up that boyfriend of yours and get out of the house tonight. That's an order."

"Uh-huh," I called back absentmindedly.

The grocery store was pretty empty as I tossed a bag of red apples into the cart and hunted for the pomegranates April loved. I moved on to Mom's coffee creamer and included the cookies Gus craved. Item by item, I filled the cart until it took my full body weight to turn it, and then I had to figure out where to put the milk.

Yeah, that had to be enough, because nothing else would fit in the cart. My phone buzzed.

Kayla: *Can't wait to see you next week!*

The feeling was mutual. In ten minutes alone she could make me forget anything was wrong. She was magnetic, vivacious, and my best friend in Boulder.

Ember: *Man, do I need you! Let me know if you have time to swing down to the Springs before start of term. If not, I'll catch you there!*

Kayla: *Will do! Smooches!*

Ember: *Smooches!*

Smooches was a Kayla thing.

I paid for my groceries, smiling as I thought of Josh paying for my cake. I wanted to see him again, but Riley would have a cow. He knew all about the crush I'd had on Josh freshman year. Hell, every girl had had one. Josh had been forbidden, untouchable, and a little dangerous, if those rumors about street racing were true. Talk of him getting kicked out of his previous school compounded with bad-boy racing, a harem of willing girls, and the legend that was Josh Walker was pretty much a given. Not that I had to worry about Josh; he didn't exactly look my way. Ever.

He'd looked at plenty of girls though. I'd seen girls on his arm every day, and never the same one for long. If Josh had been interested in a girl in high school, there was only one reason. Even if I wasn't with Riley, there's zero chance I'd set myself up to be taken down by a player like Josh. Besides, I'd always be with Riley.

I loaded the groceries into the trunk and headed to Starbucks for an afternoon fix.

As the barista filled my order from the drive-thru window, I opened my sunroof and tilted my face back to the warmth. The January air was frigid, but the sun stroking my face felt delicious.

It was the first time anything had felt good since…well, notification.

A smile spread across my face as the scent of my salted caramel mocha filled the car on the drive home. Maybe Grams was right; I needed to get out of the house and remind myself that life still waited out there.

A dozen or so trips later, I had the bags spread out in the kitchen, the contents spilling onto the counter. I heard the door open a scant second before Gus hit the entryway, a cacophony of stampeding feet to the kitchen. "Cool!" he called out, snatching a box of Fruit Roll-Ups from the counter. "Snacks!"

I ruffled his hair and took his backpack, amazed it was already three. "Homework?"

His expression fell. "Yeah." His face puckered up like he'd tasted something sour. "Do I have to?"

"Yep! You have hockey in an hour, so get it done." I poured him a glass of orange juice and set it on the counter before putting away the groceries.

Two grimaces and three broken pencil tips later, Gus finished his homework, and I finished making a sandwich. "Hey, take this up to Mom if you're done."

"Gotta scram!" He snatched the plate and ripped through the upstairs in a flurry of activity. Gus had two speeds: full throttle and asleep.

I cracked open a bottle of water and congratulated myself on a great grocery trip.

The door slammed, accompanied by the swift click of heels on the floor. April sashayed into the kitchen, dropping her backpack, purse, keys, and phone on the island I had just cleared off. I bit back my immediate need for her to clean off her crap. *Hey, was that purse new?*

"Look who I found outside," she sang, arching her perfect eyebrows at me. She took the cold bottle of water out of my hand and headed up the back stairs.

Josh Walker stood in my kitchen, leaning against the counter in jeans, a CU hoodie, and backward black hat. Holy shit, he looked freaking edible. How had I missed how hot he was the last two times I'd seen him? And what was he doing in my kitchen?

"Hey, Ember." He smiled.

"Josh." I was unsure I could say anything else and not jump him, but I went ahead. "What are you up to?" I put the island between us, for his own safety.

"Just grabbing Gus for practice." His smile was lethal, a mix of boyish charm and pure sex. *Sex? Like you'd even know. What the hell is wrong with you? You have a boyfriend!*

"That's…um…really nice of you."

"I figured your mom wouldn't be up for it yet, and Gus has been itching to get back out there." His understanding softened me even further. It was one thing to lust after him, but quite another to find myself…liking him as a person, not just a hot body. After about a minute of me staring wordlessly, he raised his eyebrows in question. "So, what's for dinner?" he asked, motioning to the pile of paper bags I'd accumulated.

"Um…" My mind raced through the ingredients I'd bought. What was I going to make? Chicken? I didn't buy any. Fajitas? No steak. I sighed in exasperation and smiled. "Cookies."

A laugh tumbled from his lips.

"I went shopping, I swear!" I laughed, holding my head in my hands. "I bought all the food everyone likes, but nothing we actually needed!" The laughter wouldn't stop, and my shoulders shook as I let go. "We have coffee creamer, but no coffee, and tortillas but no cheese."

Josh's laughter mingled with mine. He reached over and pulled my hand from my face, giving it a gentle squeeze. "It's good to see you smile, Ember." The nerves in my skin short-circuited where he touched me.

My smile slipped. *Was it too soon? Am I allowed to laugh?* As if on cue, Gus scrambled in from the garage, toting a bag of gear bigger than he was. "Ready, Coach?"

"You got it, little man," Josh answered, slipping his hand from mine. He sent me a smile that made me forget my own name. "Later, Ember." Good thing he reminded me.

I nodded, doing my best not to look too freaking captivated by him. "Seat belt on, Gus, okay?"

Josh didn't mock or patronize me, just nodded his head once. "You hear that, Gus? Seat belt's on you."

The door shut behind them, and I whipped out my cell phone, needing my anchor and a quick reminder that I wasn't allowed to think naughty thoughts about Josh Walker.

Ember: *Hey, honey, what are you up to tonight?*

Riley: *Not much, just missing you.*

A familiar sweet pressure settled in my chest.

Ember: *Feel like springing me tonight? I think I'm ready to rejoin civilization.*

A few minutes passed before his reply buzzed my phone.

Riley: *Man, babe, if I'd known, I wouldn't have come up to Breck.*

Ember: *You're back in Breckenridge?*

Riley: *Up here with a bunch of the guys, thinking of having a party.*

I didn't know how to respond to that one, so I grabbed another bottle of water. A few swallows later, my phone buzzed again.

Riley: *Party is on. Sorry, babe, or I'd come down, but I can't leave these animals with the cabin.*

Riley was having a frat party. A freaking frat party.

Ember: *Don't worry about it.*

Riley: *Love you!*

I shook my head, not bothering to respond. I shot Sam a quick text, but she was up in Denver for the night with her mom.

A freaking frat party. I grabbed the nearest sponge and tore into the mess that littered the kitchen. He couldn't even be bothered with me. Weren't we supposed to have the perfect relationship? Everything had to be pure and white on paper for his "future political career." Where was Mr. Perfect tonight? The kitchen counters received an angry bleaching, and then I attacked the cabinets before moving onto the floors, the refrigerator, and even the shelves of the pantry. No surface was safe from my wrath.

Sweat beaded my forehead by the time I finished almost three hours later, throwing the sponges and gloves into the sink with a little too much zeal. I still didn't feel better.

"It smells like lemons." Gus grimaced, his sneakers squeaking on the wet floor as he hauled his hockey gear back to the laundry room. Mom trained him well.

"Lemons and pizza." Josh laughed, setting down three huge pizza boxes on the kitchen island. "As good as cookies sounded, something told me you were missing a few food groups."

I blew a loose strand of hair from my face, his smile too contagious for my own good. "And pizza has all the food groups?"

He reached out, tucking the strand of auburn behind

my ear, his fingers grazing my neck by accident. Or, at least I convinced myself it was. "Pizza is the exception to every rule." He didn't step back, but stayed within inches of me, and everything in my body became aware of how close he was.

"Of course."

We stood there, staring at each other in a charged silence. There was nothing awkward about being quiet around Josh. No pressure to fill the silence or find something witty to add, but man, the air hummed with electricity.

"Ah, Mr. Walker!" Grams patted him on the back as she came into the kitchen. "My granddaughter needs to get out of the house, and her boyfriend has yet to do anything about it." I heard an *as usual* slip out under her breath. "Could you haul her out of here for me?" Blood rushed to my cheeks, announcing my mortification. It's like she knew he'd blown me off. Or maybe she'd just expected it?

"Ma'am?" Josh asked with a tilt to his head, and a curious gaze tossed my direction.

"She's turning into a hermit, Mr. Walker. I firmly expect cats to begin arriving at the doorstep at any moment. Please, do the world a favor and take her out."

"Where's Riley?" Josh's mouth turned down. Double mortification.

"Breckenridge, throwing some frat party." Oh, was that a twinge of bitterness slipping through my voice?

"Mmmhmm." Grams sighed.

He nodded once, his eyes unfocused. "Right." A myriad of emotions I couldn't place skated across his face, changing the landscape in small, instantaneous, meaningful ways. "Want to crash it?"

A wave of excitement hit me. *Ooh! Surprise Riley!* But common sense and reality got the best of me. "I shouldn't really go that far."

Grams sighed. "Nonsense. Josh, she'll be ready in an hour with an overnight bag. I'm assuming I won't be seeing you until tomorrow. Just grab the key and stay at your parents' cabin."

The cabin had been Mom's forty-fifth birthday present from my father; his one splurge to prove they would retire here, and she wouldn't have to move anymore.

Nausea gripped my stomach at the thought of doing something fun, like I was betraying Dad. I hadn't grieved enough; I wasn't wearing black; I hadn't cried the requisite number of tears. "I just don't want to. I'm not ready."

"Neither was your sister. Did you really think I would go easier on you?" She arched her eyebrows and dismissed me, turning back to the kitchen.

Well, I guess that was settled. Grams had spoken. To the party we were going.

Chapter Four

Two hours later, we wound through the mountains in Josh's Jeep Wrangler. He insisted he drive, but let me control the radio. Given the grimace on his face when I started playing country, I think it was punishment enough.

"I'm glad you don't have the motorcycle anymore. That would have been hell in the snow."

A small smile crept across his face. "What makes you think I don't still have it?"

"They're dangerous."

"They're fun." He swung the Jeep into the oncoming traffic lane, passing the Subaru with Texas plates in front of us. I swallowed a protest at the speed he did it at. It was freaking snowing, but it didn't seem to faze him. He eased off the gas once he pulled back into our lane.

"Is it true?" I asked, sliding a glance at him. "About all that illegal racing stuff in high school?"

A muscle in his jaw twitched, flexed. "I left a lot of things behind when we moved from Arizona. It's the benefit of moving. You get to start over, and what you used to do doesn't define you anymore, or at least it's not supposed to."

Didn't I know it. We'd moved more times than I had fingers to count. His phone buzzed on the console between us, and a discreet glance revealed the name, "Heather." Yeah, I guess not much had changed on the girls-chasing-Josh front. It was a good reminder.

"Looks like you're wanted."

A smirk played at the corner of his lips. "Sure, by the ones not worth chasing." He didn't try to read the text, or even ask me to do it for him. He ignored it completely.

I let out an exasperated sigh. "Why are you doing this, anyway?"

"Taking a pretty girl out on a Friday night?" His hands flexed on the wheel; he knew darn well what I meant.

"Driving over two hours to take me to see my boyfriend." Man, when I put it that way, why the hell *was* he doing it?

"Because it's what you need." His eyes didn't leave the road, so he couldn't notice the way I studied his profile in stunned silence. The cut angles of his face leaned more toward Grecian, less all-American than I originally thought, but that mouth of his...I shook my head to clear it of the thoughts I should not be having, especially with a text from Heather sitting between us. "Why are you with Riley, anyway?"

Well, that sure snapped me out of my Josh-watching. Riley. Right. "Because it's what we do." Once it was out of my mouth, I realized how stupid it sounded. "That came out wrong. That's not what I meant."

"Defensive much?"

I looked back to the road, only visible by the headlights. The snow falling softened everything around us, leaving us secluded. "I just meant that we have a plan, and we stick to it. We've been together over three years, and we have two more before graduation. Then Riley wants to go to law school so he can prep for politics. He wants to get married before law school."

"Seems to be a lot of Riley in that plan."

White hot frustration crept up my throat like acid, and I clenched my fists in my lap. Who was Josh Walker to question our plan? "There's a lot of me, too." Ouch, that did sound defensive. "I mean, I'm the one who wants to get married then, because I can't see us going another few years before we finally have s— " I abruptly cut myself off. Heat stung my cheeks. The car was dark, so he couldn't see, couldn't possibly know I was the exact shade of red as his Jeep's paint job.

"Have what?" he questioned.

I didn't answer.

He snapped his gaze to me, eyebrows arched in surprise. "You're telling me that in three years, you haven't had sex?"

"Eyes on the road!" I countered. He stifled a laugh and turned back to driving. My hands flexed open, closed, open, closed. "I can't believe I just said that. You can't say anything!"

"Are you a wait-for-marriage kind of girl?" There was no mocking in his tone. "It's cool if you are, it's just that three years is a long time to a guy."

I shook my head. I'd already said this much, what was the harm in finishing the thought? Besides, it's not like we ran into each other on campus or anything. "Riley wants to wait for marriage. He says it's for me. You know, squeaky clean and perfect. He promises waiting will be worth it, and it's important to him. It sucks, but everything will be *flawless*... like we planned. I guess he's old-fashioned."

"You don't want to wait?"

This was crossing the line, so I shook my head in response.

His eyes raked down me briefly. "Riley must be a fucking saint."

I hated how good that made me feel. It was Riley's compliments I wanted, right? I'd been careful when I dressed tonight; after all, I'd had a plan, too. I was done waiting. What was the purpose when you didn't know what tomorrow would bring?

My skinnies were tucked into my black boots, and I rocked a lacy camisole under a belted, low-cut gray sweater that Riley liked. My hair was up, the auburn mass quickly piled in a messy bun, but I'd been patient with my makeup. I had to stun him.

But I'd stunned Josh. I'd seen it when he'd opened my door for me. Watching those brown eyes widen with unmistakable hunger lit a tiny flame in a part of me I'd forgotten existed. He noticed me, desired me, and if I wasn't careful, that tiny flame would burn me to the ground.

I cleared my throat, hoping to dissolve the tension and the topic. "So how do you like coaching?"

"It's really been the highlight of these last couple years. Those boys are something else." His lips quirked in a subconscious smile.

That didn't add up. "But how could you be Gus's hockey coach last year when you went to CU?" The two were hours apart.

"I'm a senior at CU Springs, not CU Boulder. I took some time off after I transferred."

"But, I thought you had a hockey scholarship to Boulder?" He jerked his gaze to mine in surprise. "I did pay attention to the gossip of the infamous Josh Walker when we were in school. So why the Springs?"

His lips thinned. "Some things don't work out."

Subject closed. Got it.

I pulled out my phone to see if Kayla had responded to the text I'd sent her as we were leaving the Springs. I really hoped she could come up tonight. No response. That sucked. I could have really used my best friend.

We turned into the town of Breckenridge and made it

through the quaint downtown without hitting any drunken pedestrians. Christmas break brought out the skiers to the slopes and the beer-seekers to the rooftop bars afterward. People who weren't used to the high altitude were usually the first to regret their decision in the morning.

We curved through the town, turning where the GPS told us for Riley's cabin. "This is his str—" My sentence cut off as we rounded the corner and were assaulted by a virtual parking lot of cars on each side of the road. "There's no way they're here for Riley."

As we crept past the cabin with nowhere to park, it was clear they were *all* here for Riley. People milled on the wraparound deck, and I recognized a few of his fraternity brothers. "Hold on," Josh warned before he pulled up onto a large, flat boulder and parked the car.

"Show off." I couldn't contain the laughter that bubbled out.

He slipped from the car and had my door open before I could undo my seatbelt. I looked down to see his arms outstretched for me. From the angle he'd parked, I needed his help to get out.

I swung my legs over, and he grasped my hips, lowering me against him without being suggestive, but awareness of his body caught my breath. This close to him, I only reached his collarbone, which was currently covered by a blue button-up shirt. He jumped off the boulder, lithe, and reached his hands back up for me.

A smile spread across my face before I launched myself into his arms. He caught me with an "umpf!" A laugh escaped him, the sound beautiful and open. "You keep Riley on his toes, don't you, Ember?"

Josh carried me over the snow. "Not really. He doesn't tease well."

He shook his head as he lowered me to the snow-covered

sidewalk. "Well, he's missing out." Snow came down in a thick curtain of white, and Josh picked a flake from my hair.

I took his hand to lead him up to the front door. I shouldn't have wanted to touch him, but I did. I gave his hand a quick squeeze, and let go, telling myself I didn't like it. *Liar.* "Come on, I'll introduce you to—" A drunk girl stumbled down the steps, her girlfriends quick to catch her. "To the people I actually know," I finished.

Dave Matthews Band blared through the house. The neighbors were a few acres away, but I was surprised they weren't upset by the party. We slid past the people lining the stairs up to the deck.

Inside the house was just as crowded as the deck, like someone was trying to break the world record for the most college students crammed inside an A-frame cabin. I headed over to the first group I recognized, a frat brother of Riley's and his girlfriend, whose room was on my floor.

"Hey, Charlotte!" I called out as she jumped up to hug me.

"Ember!" Her beer sloshed over the Solo cup, but I artfully dodged before it ruined my outfit. Her embrace was fierce before she pulled back. "Ember, I'm so sorry about your dad."

"Yeah, Ember," Scott slurred from the couch, his eyes hooded. "That totally blows."

"Thanks," I responded, not wanting to let it in. I was escaping the grief tonight; I couldn't afford to let it take another piece of me. I needed a few hours of respite. "This is Josh."

Josh stepped forward, shaking Scott's hand and smiling at Charlotte, who just about stripped him with her eyes. I couldn't blame her; Josh had that effect on girls. At least, he had in high school, and my guess was not much had changed.

"Josh Walker!" A girl who looked like her breasts were

about to pop free of her low-cut shirt at any moment waved above the crowd.

"Of course you would know a girl here," I muttered in his direction.

He flashed a grin. "Oh, more than one, Ember. Give me a second?"

"Yeah, of course. I'm just going to find Riley."

I watched him cross the room and sweep the blonde up in a giant hug. An unwelcome twinge of jealousy soured my mouth.

"Josh?" Charlotte asked with appraisal, slipping into her boy-ranking mode.

"He's a friend of mine from high school," I answered.

"Yum." She smiled, and I wanted to smack her. "Does Kayla know you're here?"

"No, I sent her a text to see what she was up to tonight, but I drove up to surprise Riley."

"She probably never got it since she accidentally took her phone swimming in the hot tub this afternoon. It's toast."

"You've all been here since this afternoon?" I asked just as a familiar hulking body pressed up against me, his hand reaching around my waist to steady himself. "Hey, Drew."

His breath reeked. "Riley's upstairs, said he needed some quiet."

I nodded and tried to discreetly step out of Drew's grasp. He followed my step. "How was the drive up?"

"Long, Drew—"

Josh stepped smoothly between us, making Drew drop his grip on my waist long enough for me to escape.

"You okay?" Josh asked as we headed up the stairs.

"Drew is a little handsy, but nothing to worry about." More people lined the balcony that overlooked the great room. The whole freaking fraternity was here?

"Ember..." they all muttered, giving me their man-your-life-sucks look. I smiled back as brightly as I could. I wasn't thinking about it tonight, yet everywhere I turned, those who knew me were giving me their brave face. I could keep my thoughts off Dad, but I couldn't control everyone else's.

"Who's your girlfriend?" I asked.

"Girlfr—? Oh, Whitney? Just someone I met up with a time or two." *Met up with. Had sex. The norm.*

"Whoa! Ember!" Another frat brother, Greg, stopped us in the hallway. "Um, did Riley know you were coming?"

"Nope! I'm here to surprise him."

"Just let me tell him you're here..." He moved to step in front of me, blocking the way to the room where I'd slept weekends away for the last few years.

How freaking weird. "Greg, I'm good." I slid past him and opened the door to Riley's bedroom.

"Oh! Excuse me!" I laughed through my shock. I'd walked in on a couple using Riley's bed, and from the motion of the girl taking control, they were definitely having sex. Her jet black hair fell in waves with her head thrown back.

They were so lost in each other that they didn't hear me, and the door clicked softly as I shut it with a giggle. "Oh. My. God."

I turned, leaning my head back against the door as I laughed uncontrollably, and I liked it. I liked letting go and finding something humorous. Once I stopped, the looks of shock on Josh and Greg's face registered. "What?"

Greg blushed scarlet, contrasting with his blond hair. "Ember, I'm so sorry."

"I could fucking kill him," Josh rumbled, low and slow. The shade of his eyes darkened from brown to nearly black, a fierce glint taking over.

"What? Why? Who cares—"

It clicked. Black hair the shade of which I'd only seen on one girl. My roommate. "Kayla." Kayla was in Riley's bed.

With… "No," I whispered, shaking my head in denial.

I whipped around, shoving open the door as quickly as I could manage. This time, I didn't bother being quiet. Kayla was on top, gyrating until she heard the door slam against the opposite wall. "What the hell!"

She turned, giving those of us in the doorway a full shot of her naked breasts, which were easily two sizes larger than mine. I looked past to see the one thing I didn't want to.

Riley was underneath her. *Inside her.*

My breath left me in a defeated rush, and Josh caught me as I stumbled out of the door backward, desperate to get away. Pain, raw and gaping, clawed its way through me, ripping what was left of my heart open to bleed out. I stifled the scream that was frantic to escape, to make my agony known.

"Ember?" Riley scrambled from the bed, and I saw him naked for the first time in our three-year relationship.

I thrust my hand out in front of me, like that could ward him off. This. Was. Not. Happening.

"Ember!" Kayla shouted, wrapping herself in the thousand-thread-count sheets I'd bought Riley last summer.

The shock waned, replaced by boiling hot anger that welled beneath my eyes, flushing my skin with rage and betrayal. "Oh, you do remember me?" I stayed as calm as I could manage as they furiously threw on clothes. "Good to know, because as of this moment, I forget both of you."

I shut the door and backed into the hallway, taking a deep breath. I closed my eyes and counted. Five. Four. Three. Two. One.

Over.

I opened my eyes and nodded my head. This was done. I would not cry, or break down, not where they could see me. I wouldn't be *that* girl.

"Can I get you out of here?" Josh asked. "Before I destroy

that asshole?"

I turned around and smiled. "Yes, please, if you wouldn't mind."

His eyes narrowed as he examined my face, as if he was waiting for a crack to shatter my facade. It wasn't going to happen. He took my hand and led me down the hall, people moving out of our way this time.

Greg stepped in front of him. "Hey, Ember, I'm sorry—"

Josh pushed him into the wall with his right hand in one smooth motion, not even pausing in our exit. I kept my chin up and focused on the lines of Josh's shirt, left untucked but rolled at the sleeves. Greg didn't bother to say anything else.

My focus drifted over to the balcony, where a crowd of Riley's frat brothers overlooked the great room. Pity wafted from them in waves. Did they all know? Was I the stupid one? Music filled the house from the system downstairs, and "#41" came on. My heart broke to the soundtrack of my favorite Dave Matthews song.

But Dave was right as always. *I will go in this way, and find my own way out.*

Charlotte rushed toward me once we hit the bottom of the stairs. "Oh my God, Ember." Her pity only served to fuel the rage burning deep in my chest.

"How long?" I demanded. She dared to stare back at me with this dumbfounded expression that made me want to throttle her. "How long have they been sleeping together?" My voice raised to an embarrassing level before I could stop it.

She blinked repeatedly, her eyes growing larger and larger. "I don't know. I guess a little over a year? That Thanksgiving when you went away with your parents."

"And you *all* knew?"

She shook her head quickly. "No, only a few of us. They tried to keep it quiet."

Tried to keep it quiet in a giant house party? Yeah.

Josh's hand tightened around mine, and he turned in unspoken question. "Right," I responded, feeling a chill come over me. "We're done here."

Josh slid through the crowd, which parted easily for him. It didn't hurt that the guy was majorly built. I followed in his wake until the frigid night air hit my flaming cheeks. The snowflakes should have sizzled as they hit me. He marched through the partiers who had gathered to smoke outside, gently pulling me behind him. Once we reached the boulder, he turned to me with upraised eyebrows. "May I?"

Gone was the physical playfulness he'd shown when we'd arrived. Now his manners were courteous and careful, restrained. "Please get me out of here," I whispered, nearly broken. There wasn't too much of my composure left, but I'd be damned if I let any of those onlookers see me cry, let alone break down into hysterical sobs like I wanted.

Josh swung me up into his arms, and I buried my face in his neck, breathing in his subtle cologne that smelled like sandalwood and safety. He leaned in the open door, placing me on the seat. The fabric was still warm from the drive in. My life had fallen apart in less time than it took the windshield to freeze over.

Riley flew out of the house in jeans and the sweater I bought him last Christmas, jumping over the railing to bypass the crowd. I hoped his feet were bare so they'd freeze to the pavement. "Ember!" he shouted, running down the sidewalk.

Josh cursed under his breath. He balanced on my doorframe, bending over me to turn on the car. "Wouldn't want you to be cold." He stroked the side of my face, buckled my seat belt, and shut the door. I unrolled the window, knowing Riley would want a word.

Josh didn't come around the car, didn't hop in and drive us away. Instead, he casually leaned against the Jeep, his arms folded across his chest, the only sign of the temperature being the visible breath he expelled.

Riley stopped a few feet in front of him, his chest heaving from exertion. Well, yeah, pausing mid-thrust to speed-dress and chase your now ex-girlfriend out of your house probably took a little energy. "Josh, man, let me talk to Ember."

"I'm not her keeper, *man*. The woman does what she wants." He didn't move, but his body radiated coiled tension. I kept my focus on the pulse pounding in Josh's neck, refusing to look up at Riley.

"Ember, please, let me explain!" He took a step toward Josh, but the simple tilt of his head had Riley stepping back. I didn't want to know what Josh's face looked like to get that kind of reaction out of the fearless Riley.

"I'm not really sure there's much you could say to me, Riley." I didn't bother glancing at him. I'd seen enough of his face when it was contorted with lust. "I think I saw everything I needed to know."

"You've been distant this week." What a lame-ass excuse. "I just needed some comfort, and Kayla was there, and one thing led to another. It didn't mean anything!"

I dragged my gaze away from the back of Josh's head, finally meeting Riley's eyes. *I will not cry. I will not break down.* "A year, Riley...?" My voice trailed off because I couldn't speak past the mountain-sized lump that had formed there. "We're done!" I choked it out and bit down on my lower lip, needing to feel the pain.

"You know about..." He shook his head and launched back into his tirade. "I needed someone, Ember! I needed someone to care about *me*! Where have you been? You've been so wrapped up in your family drama that you never stopped to think about what's going on in *my* life!"

"Let's go, Josh."

"You're not taking my girlfriend anywhere!" Riley

shouted.

"She doesn't look much like your girlfriend," Josh drawled slowly.

Riley swung, but only connected with Josh's hand as he caught the attempted punch.

Josh didn't miss. His fist busted into Riley's mouth with a *crack*, the sound nauseating, yet gratifying. Riley flew backward, landing in the snow. Josh stood over him, shaking his head when Riley moved to stand. "Don't get up."

Blood stained the back of the ivory sleeve as Riley wiped his mouth. "What? Afraid I'll kick your ass?"

Josh let loose a wry smile. "Nawh. Afraid I'll end up in jail when I fuck up that pretty little face of yours." Did Riley pale? It looked like it from here. "As December said, we're done here."

A small spark of satisfaction pushed back my wave of tears. Thank God for Josh.

Chapter Five

Anger choked me the whole drive to my parents' cabin, leaving me seething in silence. The trip lasted about fifteen minutes, into a nice but not-quite-as-nice-as-Riley's area outside Breckenridge. Our cabin was more secluded, and the bonus was that Riley wouldn't be there.

How could he and Kayla do this? How could I not see it happening in front of me? They'd had sex, repeatedly, when he wouldn't so much as go beneath-the-belt with me.

Nausea rolled through my stomach as we pulled up the driveway in front of the cabin. My stomach clenched and when my mouth watered I knew it was coming. "Let me out!" I shouted, fumbling, not realizing the door wasn't locked. Josh raced around the Jeep, opening the door and lowering me down in one smooth motion.

The snow came nearly to my knees, but I trudged a few feet away through the heavy mess before I lost my stomach contents. Over and over I heaved, letting go of my dinner, my bile, and the last stable thing I thought I had in the world. I had the common sense to back up a few feet before I fell to my knees, sobbing.

I screamed my voice hoarse while the snow melted into my jeans, soaking my legs in an icy reminder that this was not a dream. No more dreams. They had frozen and shattered the moment I opened that damned door. Every carefully made plan was no more. There was nothing certain left. Not Riley. Not Dad. Not even Mom.

"What else do you want?" I screamed up to whoever wasn't listening. "I have nothing left to give! Are you done with me yet?" I sagged back down into the snow, covering my face with my frozen fingers as I let loose ugly, horrendous sobs.

A warm coat engulfed me, and the scent told me it belonged to Josh. He lifted me easily into his arms, carrying me up to the cabin.

"No." I forced out, and he stopped. "I need to walk." His arms tensed momentarily like he wasn't going to let me go, but he gently set me on my feet.

"I'll get the bags." His retreating footsteps crunched through the snow.

One foot in front of the other, I made it the last ten feet to the door. The snow was packed, leaving a hard crust on top, but I relished the difficulty because it reminded me I was still alive, still here.

Feeling this, the pain, the chill, the strain of my muscles was as necessary as breathing.

I pulled the keys from my sweater and opened the door. Flipping the light switch brought the cabin to life in all my mother's Pottery Barn glory. The door opened into a small mudroom, where our skis still stood propped in their holders from our Thanksgiving trip. I crossed the living room and turned up the thermostat to a respectable level. The stove *whooshed* from the corner as the propane kicked in and the flames came to life. At least the pilot hadn't gone out. That was something, right?

The cabin had a kitchen, dining room, living room, bathroom, and three small bedrooms. I ran my fingers lovingly over the enlarged canvas print of our family on the slopes last year. I stroked Dad's smile as my fingers tingled, feeling seeping back in, hearing his laugh as surely as if he'd been standing there next to me. My mother's eyes were bright, in love. Now she was a hollowed-out shell of the person in this picture.

"What are you thinking about?" Josh asked, dropping our bags on the living room rug.

I didn't bother trying to smile. "This place was my refuge, the promise he made to my mom that one day he wouldn't be in the army anymore."

Josh picked up a framed picture of Gus and Dad smiling, both covered in chocolate from a failed attempt at brownies. "It's good you have it. Another place to feel him in."

I shook my head. "It wasn't supposed to be like this. Nothing is going according to plan. Everything is falling apart around me." I swatted away a tear, the damn things wouldn't stop coming. "Why couldn't he have been a banker? An electrician?"

He put the frame down on the end table, his eyes taking on an odd intensity. "He was needed, Ember. He saved a lot of lives."

"Yeah, all but his."

The silence in the house ached through me, bordering on pain. This was a place of laughter and raucous behavior, where Mom's rules slipped and Dad had no other priorities. This is where they locked their bedroom door on Sunday mornings, and where we learned to make our own breakfasts. This was our haven. Was. Why was everything *was* lately?

Josh distracted me perfectly. "Tell me something about him that makes you smile."

"Like what?"

He shrugged. "Anything you loved."

There were ten thousand things about my dad that I loved. How could I pick just one? But if there was one... "The journals."

"Journals?"

I smiled, thinking back to all the times I caught him hunched over his computer. "He wrote in a journal every day. Well, he typed it. He said he was too lazy to handwrite anything. Personally, I don't think the man could even read his own handwriting. It was atrocious." I laughed at the memory. "He kept everything on his computer. He told me that writing everything down cleared his mind, left him ready to tackle the next obstacle. It was his ultimate superpower, the ability to let everything go by just acknowledging it." I wanted that ability. I wanted the peace he always carried with him.

But more than that, I realized I wanted to read those journals, especially the ones from these last few months. I wanted to know his thoughts, his fears, what it was about his job that made losing his life worth it.

I blinked slowly as if that would clear all the events of the last few weeks from the slate and leave it clean. "Well, since we have all night..." I crossed the floor into the kitchen, climbing easily onto the counter to reach the cabinet above the refrigerator. I brought down a clear bottle wrapped in a green ribbon. "Tequila?"

A slow smile spread across Josh's face, and I nearly dropped my precious cargo. The guy was lethal with that weapon. He streaked his fingers across his short hair, and I saw the blood. "Are you okay?" I asked, setting the bottle on the counter and reaching for his damaged hand.

He shrugged at the sight. "Knuckles are swollen, but that's not my blood."

I pulled him to the farmhouse sink, then rinsed Riley's blood off his hand, watching the fading red tendrils escape down the drain. "Ice?"

"No, I'm fine, really."

I examined the swelling, brushing my fingers over his skin. What would these hands feel like on my body? I glanced up at him, absorbing the way his eyes darkened as awareness spread between us. His eyes followed the motion as I wet my suddenly dry lips before I gave him his hand back.

Oblivion was calling, and I was more than ready to answer. "In that case, grab the limes out of my bag, because I need to get drunk."

"As the lady wishes," he joked as he retrieved the little green gems.

Three shots later, the tequila took effect as heat settled into my belly. I threw another lime wedge into the garbage and hopped up onto the counter in my bare feet and dry pajama pants. I'd long since ditched the wet jeans.

Josh leaned against the counter across from me, keeping up shot for shot. "Feeling better?"

I reached back behind me, opening the cabinet by feel and grabbing a bag of chips. Sour cream and onion were Dad's favorite. "I'm not really sure there's an option of feeling worse." I popped open the bag and shoved a handful in my mouth, offering him the bag. "I'm done dwelling on me. Distract me."

"How?" His eyes narrowed.

Kiss me. Make me forget. "Tell me what happened to badass Josh Walker from high school? I remember you having hair down to your chin—"

"Hockey."

"And that black motorcycle…"

"In storage."

"Why? More illegal fun that's not up for discussion?"

"That was six years ago, December. Besides, would you drive a motorcycle in the middle of a Colorado winter?"

"Good point." He rolled the bag of chips, placing it behind him on the counter. Every movement he made fascinated me. "You're so different now."

His hands flexed on the counter, whitening his knuckles. "How so?"

My eyes closed, and I sank into the memory of a fifteen-year-old girl. "You were popular, a good athlete, and had this whole bad-boy, don't-give-a-shit vibe going for you and all, but I'm sorry, you were kind of an ass." Tequila must have loosened my tongue.

Josh sputtered, nearly soaking me in the shot he was currently downing before he laughed. "Good to know."

"I mean, normally, you were this really hot guy, of course." I opened my eyes to meet his gaze and fell into it. His eyes had turned dark, nearly unfathomable. "But during hockey season, you were more than that. You were a god. Every girl wanted to be yours, and you...let them. You didn't seem to care that you changed them out faster than your hockey tape. You. *Were*. An. Ass."

He dragged the tip of his tongue across his lower lip, catching the rest of the tequila and my full attention. "And now what's your verdict?"

I couldn't pull my eyes from his lips. Mine started to tingle as I wondered what made all those girls run back for more of him. "Jury's still out." He'd been nothing but good to me, too perfect, really, but I couldn't ignore the long line of girls he'd crushed.

"That's fair." He rubbed his hands over his forehead. "I transferred into that school my sophomore year, and it was rough."

I nodded. I knew it well. The upper-class school certainly hadn't welcomed a military brat with open arms my freshman year. But when super-popular Riley showed interest junior year and started dating me, everything changed. Freaking Riley. "Hockey gave me an 'in' to the crowd, but it's not like there weren't tons of rumors about why I transferred in the first place. Funny how the shit you pull in high school sticks with you if you don't move away, huh?"

"Depends. You still sleep with everything in a skirt?" *Like Riley?*

He clutched his hand over his heart. "Out for blood tonight, are we?"

"Truth hurts." Especially lately.

He wiggled his eyebrows and motioned to my clothes. "Hey, I'd totally make an exception for a girl in Daisy Duck pajama pants."

I wanted to laugh, but only a smile emerged. Maybe I'd lost the ability. "Shot?"

He arched those eyebrows in an are-you-kidding-me look. "You sure?"

I did an assessment. Nowhere near sick or pukie but pleasantly buzzed, so round number four it was. Lick. Slam. Suck. The tequila burned sweetly down my throat, firing through my insides. I wished it would burn through my heart and render me unable to feel anything.

"I remember you, too, you know. You were cute back then." His shot glass made an audible *click* as he placed it on the counter. "Your hair was curlier and a little wild, like you were untamed, unbeaten. You were quiet and never looked up when I passed you in the hallway, but I saw you, knew who you were. There was something about you, a fire that was untouchable."

I dropped my gaze to his bare feet. "That fire is dead."

He stepped between my knees, his heat melting through the flannel of my pj's. He gently lifted my chin, bringing me to meet his eyes, and my heart began to misfire. The intensity in his eyes was breathtaking and frightening at the same time. "The fire you have within you is impossible to kill. The first breath you take when you're free of all this, it will come roaring back. That's what is so impossibly beautiful about you."

"Riley didn't think so. I asked him over and over again to touch me, and he would say there was no point starting if he couldn't finish. But he was the one who didn't want me; I wasn't beautiful enough for him." If I hadn't been drinking, I never would have said it. My eyes burned, and a tear slipped down my cheek. Josh brushed it away with his thumb. "What is wrong with me?"

Josh shook his head slowly as he shifted his hands to hold my face. His thumb grazed my lower lip, and my breath quickened. "Not a damn thing."

"Then why would he sleep with her, but he wouldn't touch me?" It was pitiful, and I knew it even as it escaped my mouth, but it just kind of tumbled out.

"Because he's a fucking moron." Riley hardly ever cursed in front of me, but the way Josh said it was almost a caress, and it was the sexiest thing I'd ever heard, jarring me from my pity party. His gaze dropped to my lips, and they tingled in response and parted. "You are the sexiest girl I've ever seen. Always have been."

Then he kissed me. There was no pause, no decision to be made, no slow approach. Josh moved in, and his mouth consumed mine. He tasted like tequila and lime…and something sweeter, darker. His tongue swept out against my lips and I let him in, begged him in. He filled my mouth, stroking the most sensitive spots and retreating only to return.

I couldn't hold back the moan that escaped as his mouth slanted over mine again. I arched into him, bringing my breasts in contact with his chest, and he made a sound like a growl. It was a heady feeling, that power, and I knew I would do whatever I needed to hear it again.

I let go of the counter, wrapping my hands around his back and neck. The muscles that played under his skin intoxicated me with their rippled movements, the heady knowledge that I had Josh under my fingertips. I kissed him back with everything I had, needing it, needing to be as close to him as humanly possible. I needed this, to feel, and Josh was more than worthy of feeling. Josh was worth experiencing, even if only for tonight.

He let go of my face, his hands drifting down my back until they cupped my rear, bringing me up against his very hard stomach. I had to see that stomach, to find out if it looked as incredible as it felt. I pulled my mouth away long enough to tug his shirt over his head. He sucked in his breath through parted lips and raked his gaze over my body. He wanted me. Me!

I gave him what I hoped was a seductive smile and devoured every line of his body with my eyes. Sweet mercy, the guy was built. Tribal tattoos with strange symbols wrapped around his right shoulder and trailed down the right side of his sculpted chest. I traced the tattoo with my fingers. His skin was soft, but the ropes of muscles underneath were so deliciously hard. His stomach was a step beyond washboard, with those lickable muscles carved lower, leading into where his jeans buckled. This was what a man was supposed to look like, and right now, he was *mine.*

I slipped my fingers into the waistband of his jeans and pulled, bringing my body flush against his again. "You..." I struggled for words that could escape the gasping breath I was taking. "You're amazing."

A slow, sexy smile spread across his face, and a rush of pure lust hit me in my lower belly. I'd never felt it with such intensity in my life. "Ember," he whispered against my lips, threading his fingers through my hair as it pulled loose of its pins, and sank back into my mouth.

Yes. Yes. Yes. I wrapped my legs around his waist, locking my ankles in the small of his back. He alternated his kisses between long and deep and small nibbles, scraping my lower lip between his teeth. It was driving me insane. My fingers itched to touch him, so I did, running my hands up into his short hair to slip them down his wide back, dipping into the curves and hollows of his spine. His skin felt smooth and warm, and I wanted to know how it tasted.

I broke away from him and forced his head to the side none-too-gently. His aroused laugh said he didn't mind. The counter brought us nearly equal in height, and I drew his neck down to me, running my tongue up his pounding pulse. He tasted like sin and heaven, all in one man. His breath expelled in a large rush, and I had about two seconds of feasting on his skin before he took control again.

He tugged on my hair, pulling my head back and exposing my neck to the gentle scrape of his teeth. Holy. Shit. He licked and sucked, sending jolts of electricity down my neck, raising goose bumps on my flesh before the chills raced right between my thighs and became something much hotter. I grabbed on to the waistband of his jeans, desperate for an anchor before I melted into a puddle on the freaking counter.

He tugged on the sleeves of my sweater, and I fumbled in my haste to get the thing off. I wanted his hands on my skin. I needed more of the rush, whatever his touch was setting off in me. He dropped kisses along my neck to my exposed shoulders, tracing his way to my elbow, where he licked the inside. I'd never thought of that as an erogenous area, but, um…yes, please.

His hands skipped to my knees and began an upward attack, skimming over the tops of my thighs. Everything within me clenched, waiting for the touch…that didn't come. He gripped the lace hem of my camisole and retreated long enough to gauge my reaction. I lifted my arms above my head; I was more than okay with this. He slowly dragged it up my body, but stopped as the lace covered my eyes, pinning my hands to the cabinets behind me with one of his hands. My breath hitched the second before he covered my mouth with his again. Damn, he could kiss. With my hands captured above me, I had no control. I could only accept what he gave.

He gave me everything. He kissed the breath out of me until I whimpered, arching against him for contact. Blinded by lace, every touch felt more intense, every sigh louder. Then he slipped my camisole from my eyes and laid it on the counter with my sweater.

I sucked air into my lungs in heaves. Thank God, he was in the same state. I launched at him, pulling the short strands of his hair to bring his mouth, his body closer. I wanted everything. Now.

He unhooked my bra with one hand, cradling my face with the other, and the wait to feel his hands on me was torture. He slid both hands under my bra, cupping my breasts, and I shrugged out of the straps. *Finally.*

The bra landed with the camisole, and my head banged against the cabinet behind me as I gave myself over to what Josh was doing with his hands. He put his teeth back to my neck, kissing a path down my chest until he expertly tongued my breasts, and I started to fly apart. I couldn't control the moans that ripped from my throat any more than I could halt what my body was screaming for. I clutched his head, losing myself in every sensation he rocketed through me.

He rose up, kissing my mouth once, twice, before leaning his forehead against mine. We both struggled to maintain our breathing. "God, Ember."

I said the only thing I could think of. "More."

He lifted his head, staring into my eyes like he could see through my soul. "This isn't what you want."

I watched his eyes darken as I dragged my fingernails lightly down his smooth chest, tracing the ridges of his muscles. "Yes, it is. Please don't stop." Was that really my breathless, pleading voice?

He closed his eyes, and the muscles in his jaw flexed. He was fighting for control. His hands stroked down my waist, squeezing lightly before he let go to grasp the counter. He was pulling away. This couldn't stop! Not when I felt this good, this alive. "Please, Josh," I pleaded.

"You don't know what you're asking." He bent his head like he was praying.

"I'm a virgin, not a moron." Virgin. How many girls had steady boyfriends their sophomore year in college and still remained virgins? I shifted my seat on the counter; my insides were throbbing. "Josh, please?" He let out a deep breath, every muscle in his torso contracting. Every word I could think of to describe how incredibly hot he was contained four letters. Damn. I wanted that skin over me, around me, in me. "Please put your hands on me?"

He growled, the sound feral, carnal, and attacked, devouring my mouth and stealing my soul. He wanted me; I felt that much between my thighs when he pulled my rear off the countertop. I squeezed my ankles behind his waist and tightened my grip on his neck as he lifted me by my ass and began walking toward the back hallway. The strength in his arms was incredibly hot, and if he turned me on any more I was going to be clawing my way into his pants before we could find a bed.

"Which one is yours?"

"Second on the left." I went right back to kissing him, this time darting my tongue into his mouth. He groaned and gripped me tighter, sucking on my tongue. Holy. Freaking. Hot.

There was something soft against my back. Oh, the bed.

Yeah, that was right. His weight came over me, and it was the most exquisite pressure I'd ever felt. My neck arched back as he put his mouth to my breasts, his hands stroking up and down my body, igniting fires so scorching I thought I'd combust.

My hands gripped the comforter, twisting it viciously as my head thrashed back and forth and my hips began to move on their own accord. I wanted—needed him to touch me. "Josh—"

"I know." I could have cried with relief when he tugged down my pj's. I lifted my hips and awkwardly shimmied out of them, but I didn't care. They were off! His hands ran up my calves, stroking behind my knees, and then over the tops of my thighs.

He drew his body over mine, our skin sliding in friction so delicious I tingled. Our open mouths met in a brutal kiss as his hand slid down my waist, and finally—finally!—slipped under my panties. I raised my hips into his hand, silently begging, and he groaned against my mouth. He slid his fingers along my core, dipping in to where I knew I was soaking wet. "Fuck. Ember."

An unintelligible sound escaped me when he brushed against my clit, sparks flying through my body. I grabbed onto him, my fingers digging into the taut skin of his shoulders, distorting the tattoo on his right. He felt so good under my hands, necessary.

Again and again he stroked me, until I could taste how much I wanted him. I whispered his name, and he kissed me sweetly as he slid one finger inside me. My hips bucked, wanting more—needing more. He understood my garbled plea, slipping another finger in and stretching me. "You're so damn tight. Perfect." Pleasure webbed through me, low and deep, stringing me up tight until the muscles of my thighs locked and everything within me tensed. In and out, he stroked my body like he was playing an instrument, knowing exactly when to give more and when to hold back.

He dropped his head next to mine, his breathing ragged in my ear as fine tremors ran through me. My fingers clenched his skin. I needed something, anything. I couldn't survive this tense, reaching and straining. "Josh, please—"

He kissed my cheek softly, and then pressed his thumb to my clit as he pinched my nipple lightly with his other hand. I flew apart.

The tension within me exploded, scattering everything in my world except him. He stroked me through my orgasm and brought me down gently, knowing just where to touch to kick back my aftershocks.

It was a full minute before I returned to my senses. "Holy shit, Josh." I turned my head and kissed him between our gasping breaths. "I've never—that was—I don't—"

The sexiest smile I'd ever seen played across his mouth, and the pale moonlight in the room made his eyes seem darker, more secretive. "Yeah." That one word held the answers to every question slipping through my mind.

I reached down his stomach, ready to unzip his pants, which were now bulging out at an angle that had to be uncomfortable, but he stopped my hand, pulling it back to his mouth for a kiss on my palm. Shivers raced through me. "Ember."

No? Surely he didn't mean no. He did not just give me the first orgasm of my life and then tell me "no." "What's wrong?" I trailed my other hand down the rigid line of his tasty abs before he captured that one, too.

"We're not doing that tonight." If it weren't for the sheer determination on his face, I would have tried to sway him. Instead, a tidal wave of humiliation washed over me.

"You don't want me?" I barely squeaked it out. This wasn't happening.

He kissed my fingers and shifted his hips so his erection nearly cut into me. "Trust me, I want you. I want you more than oxygen at this point."

"Then what's wrong?" I looped my naked leg over his hips, and he hissed.

"Fuck, could you make this any harder?" he growled.

I giggled. "That's the plan, right?"

He let out a sigh of exasperation and untangled himself, pulling my back against his chest, careful to keep his hips clear. "I want this; I want you, Ember. But tonight is about *you*, not us. You needed this, and I'm fucking ecstatic to give it to you, but we're not doing this." He pushed his hips against my ass, and I groaned, wanting him inside me. "Until it's about us, and no one else."

Us? I couldn't think about that. There wasn't any more room in my head.

Exhaustion drooped my eyelids. Now I understood why girls said orgasms made them sleep better. At least that's what Kayla had said. Whatever. I sincerely doubted Riley had an ounce of the skill Josh just used on my body.

Josh covered us with the blankets, and with the last of my energy, I reached back around me and slid my hand over his back and under his jeans so I could feel that gorgeous ass.

His laugh nearly broke me into a pit of need again. He slowly pulled my hand out, held it in his own, and wrapped his arm around my body, cocooning me. "Stop trying to take advantage of my virtue," he teased, his breath evening out.

I fell asleep with a smile on my face.

Chapter Six

Bacon sizzled in the pan, popping grease onto my forearm and burning. "Crap." I brushed the oil off me and turned another piece before I gave it the chance to do it again. The clock on the wall said it was ten in the morning, but the time in my stomach said "feed me or die." I was a hungry hangover kind of person. Nothing two Tylenol and a glass of water wouldn't help when they took effect. I just wished I wasn't begging God for them to take effect already. Damn, my head hurt.

I snagged two plates out of the cabinet and loaded them with the finished bacon before I fried up the eggs. The rhythmic *scrape, scrape, scrape* told me Josh had finished snow blowing the driveway and was now shoveling out the walk. Of course, when I'd woken up alone, I figured the guy had made the mad dash out of here because I'd attempted to jump him last night.

Last night. *That* was what everyone raved about when they whispered about sex. Now I got it. I'd always wanted to have sex. I wasn't a prude, but Riley had assured me we'd have plenty once we were married. Why not save it for then? Keep the first years of our marriage hot, perfect? Looking back, kissing Riley was fun, he was *good* at it, but kissing Josh was like a freaking fire caught me and scorched until I burst into flames. There was really no comparison.

Shit. I was burning the eggs. I slid them onto the plates just as the toast popped up. A little butter and we were ready to rock. Right on cue, Josh opened the front door and quickly shut it once he was inside.

I avoided his gaze as he slid off his boots on the entry rug and hung his coat on the peg. I pulled the sugar and powdered creamer out of the cabinet as the coffee finished brewing. Hey, I'd been lucky we'd had eggs here since Mom had been up with Gus and April a couple weeks ago. "Coffee?" I asked without looking at him, stretching on tiptoes and still unable to reach the cups.

"Perfect, thanks," he responded, sliding behind me to take the cups down. I leaned away from him and carried our plates to the table, juggling silverware under them. I'd never really had a "morning after," but I assumed that was what this icky, awkward feeling was. What was he thinking? Was he angry about last night? Had he wanted more? Had he wanted less?

I kept my head down as I walked past him, concentrating on the pattern of the hardwood floor until I got to where Josh had already poured the coffee. Sugar, yes. Cream, more. I preferred a little bit of coffee with my cream and sugar.

"Ember." He was right behind me. The spoon clanged against the counter as I accidentally dropped it. Big breath. "Turn around," he ordered softly.

I had done big girl things last night, and now I had to be a big girl today. I turned, keeping my eyes locked on the way his hoodie settled around his really nice hips. He stepped forward, fitting us together, and my traitorous lower half melted right into him.

He gently lifted my face to meet his eyes, just like he had last night. I was lost. The sun streamed through the window, bringing out the golden flakes in his eyes, a stark contrast to the jet black of his skull cap. "Good morning," he whispered.

I gave a nervous smile that I'm pretty sure came out more like I was baring my teeth. "Hi."

He searched my eyes for long, tense moments, looking for answers I didn't know how to give. "Yeah," he whispered, like he was answering his own question.

He took possession of my mouth in a scorching kiss, cradling my head in his hands and moving his tongue to the same rhythm he'd used with his fingers inside me last night. I went limp in two seconds, flat. He pulled back with a grin, then kissed me softly. Once. Twice. "This is not awkward unless you let it be." His raised eyebrows and smile nearly did me in. "I'm not going to let it be awkward. I want you too much for that."

My eyes darted away. The day after finding my boyfriend, shit, ex-boyfriend sleeping with my roommate was not the time to jump into something new. "Josh—"

"No, no excuses. I want you, and you're not ready for me. You're not ready for anything." He tucked back a strand of hair that had escaped my messy bun.

I shook my head, breaking his grip. "Last night, I don't know what happened. I just needed...I needed..."

"To feel alive."

My gaze jerked back to his. He nailed it right on the head. "Yes, and I guess...I used you." Guilt swamped me as the truth of my words cut through what had been the fog of my thoughts.

He laughed. "Come on. You don't think I knew that?"

"N-n-no." This was not how I'd seen this weekend going. He leaned back against the opposite counter, and I immediately missed his warmth. "You needed to feel alive. Your dad died, and I get that. It's a pretty common reaction, really." His hands rubbed over his face like he was waking himself up. "And after what happened with Riley last night, I wasn't surprised that you needed to feel desired, too."

"So you let me just…" My eyes narrowed. "Why?"

"Because you needed me to. You're so busy taking care of everyone else, you can't see that someone needs to take care of you. So tell me what you need, and I'll be that for you."

Speechless. Somehow the resident bad boy had turned into this…man, and the guy I'd lusted for all freshman year was offering himself to me. I reached for a little snark, something to save me from the brutal honesty he was dishing out, but there was nothing I could find. "I don't even know what I need."

"That's okay with me. The minute you realize that it's okay with you, too, you can start digging out of what's been thrown at you. There's no pressure."

A few weeks ago I'd never have pegged Josh Walker as someone to take care of me. That job belonged to Dad, to Riley. I ducked my head and concentrated on my breakfast. The silence was easy, but charged with what was unsaid. It was a combination I wasn't used to.

"Vanderbilt, huh?" He nodded to the letters plastered across my chest on my favorite, worn-out hoodie.

"Yeah." I pushed the stretched-out sleeves up over my forearms.

"There's a picture in the hallway with you in a Vanderbilt shirt, your dad, too." His tone left answering up to me. I knew he was curious, but not intrusive.

"It's where my dad graduated from, where I always dreamed of going. It was our thing, I guess, since I was born while he was in medical school there. I think my first sleeper was from Vanderbilt." I looked up from my plate and caught his eyes. It was still surreal that Josh Walker was in my cabin, eating breakfast with me. More surreal that he'd kissed me. Touched me.

"Why didn't you go?"

I swallowed back the twinge of bitterness that always accompanied this question, especially when my father had asked me. "Riley got into CU early admission, and that's where he wanted to go."

"Did you get into Vanderbilt?" He leaned slightly toward me over his empty plate.

I moved my eyes back to my disappearing eggs. "I didn't bother applying. Riley didn't think a long-distance relationship would work."

"Did you?"

I shrugged. "Apparently a same-school relationship couldn't work."

"Do you think long-distance relationships work?"

I grabbed my empty plate and stood. "Why the twenty questions, Josh?"

He looked up at me through his lashes, and I almost forgot what I asked. "Just trying to understand you. Do you think those relationships work?"

"I think people who love each other, like genuine love, can make it, sure." I headed for the kitchen and swore I heard him sigh. "But after seeing what my mom went through time and time again, I know it's not what I would ever choose."

He snuck up behind me and gently stole the plate from my hand. "I get that. I can't imagine always waiting."

I watched him methodically wash the dishes, and I took them to dry, putting them back in the cabinet for the next time we'd make it up here. "It's not the waiting that gets me, not anymore. It's the not knowing if he would come home. I won't live like that. I can't put everything in my life on hold, not like she did. Everything she did was about my father, and now what does she have? She's a train wreck." I turned around and found him leaned back against the counter. We were nearly in the same position we had been when he'd kissed me last night. I closed my eyes briefly, failing to rid myself of the images. "Sorry, I didn't mean to go on and on."

He stepped forward, eliminating the space between us. "I told you. You don't need to apologize. If you need to talk, I'll listen."

He caged me in his arms, making escape, if I had wanted one, impossible. I leaned back enough to tilt my head and see him. "You don't owe me anything." Blood rushed to my cheeks. "I'm so sorry about last—"

"Don't you dare finish that sentence," Josh said, his voice was flat, final. "Never apologize to me for something I wanted so badly I could practically taste you before we even left your house." He raised his hand, the back of his fingers grazing down my cheek, leaving chills in their wake. His gaze dropped to my lips and that smile was back on his face, sending "go" signals straight to my thighs. "Oh, and December?" His lips brushed against mine, and every fiber of my being reacted. "Feel free to use me again any time."

Chapter Seven

It was Monday morning and, darn it, I was determined to make pancakes. We always had pancakes Sunday morning, but up until now I'd forgotten. We'd all forgotten. Dad had been gone three weeks now, and we'd already let so much slip. Some things had to return to...whatever this new normal was. I dragged my Vanderbilt hoodie on over my tank top and headed into the kitchen, ready to rock out breakfast before April and Gus came down for school. I'd checked on Mom earlier, but she didn't look any closer to living than she had when I'd left on Friday.

Dad's copy of *The Joy of Cooking* bore an earmark at the pancake page. It was slightly marred by drops of egg and milk. He'd let us help no matter how messy we were. I stroked the dried bits of paper with my fingertips like I could jump back into those moments.

I grabbed the eggs and butter from the fridge, then went to wash my hands. Ugh. Yesterday's dishes were stacked up in the sink. I'd have to leave them for later, once the kids were at school. I folded my sleeves up on my forearm, revealing

Josh's number in permanent marker. I couldn't control the smile that lit my face. He'd taken the Sharpie from his glove box and gently etched his name and number onto my arm. When I'd asked why—I already had his number on Gus's hockey roster—he'd dropped that smoldering look on me.

"Gus has my number because I'm his coach. Now you have it because I'm your whatever."

"My whatever?"

The soft kiss he'd placed on my lips had me leaning in for more. "Whatever you need me to be," he whispered against my mouth. He'd opened my door and brought my bag up the walk. "It's not so easy to wash off," he added, "and neither am I."

My cheeks flushed with the memory, and I scrubbed around the mark, hesitant to wash over it. I called up the stairs to wake Gus and April. Crap, I sounded like Mom. I flipped the spatula in agitation. Of course I sounded like her; I had stepped right into her morning role.

Gus thundered down the stairs in his favorite, faded *Star Wars* hoodie, and I promptly had breakfast on the table. "Ember! You rock!" He was covered in syrup in fifteen seconds, flat.

April walked in, her hair picture perfect, and scoffed. "Like I'm going to eat those carbs first thing in the morning?"

I held my tongue, which took every bit of effort I had. She passed me at the kitchen island, wearing skinny jeans and a sweater. She had lost weight, too much for her slight frame. Yeah, it was all the rage to be skin and bones, but the girl needed a cheeseburger. "If you eat carbs now, you have all day to burn them off," I suggested. She stuck her tongue out at me, and I noticed her righteously awesome pair of new equestrian boots. "Christmas?"

She shrugged, snagged the orange juice from the fridge, and poured herself a glass. I grabbed Gus's Obi-Wan lunch box and packed him up for the day, trying to remember everything Mom did. "Do you have your folder and homework?" He nodded with his mouth full. "Cool. Finish up and wash that face of yours, you sugary mess." I pretended to eat his cheek and was rewarded with giggles. We needed more giggles.

While he and April finished prepping their day, I tried to think of what Mom did on Mondays. It was her "get stuff done" day, I knew that much. I pulled The Brain from the shelf, checking the calendar. Hockey today for Gus. I would see Josh.

Pushing the butterflies out of my stomach, I flipped to the back where she kept her lists. Here we go. Thank God Mom was predictable in her schedules. Mondays were groceries, errands, week prep, and bills. Bills.

I turned to the stack of mail that had sat unopened these last weeks. It consumed the kitchen work desk and was dangerously close to playing a game of fifty-two-envelope pickup. This was going to suck. Time to dig in.

I sorted it into magazines, catalogs, ads, bills, and the dozens of personal cards that had arrived in droves. Bills would be the most pressing. I could make out all the amounts if Mom could manage to sign them. I cut open the first bill, a credit card, and scanned it. Five thousand dollars! I had no clue Mom and Dad even had credit card debt.

Wait. The charges were all in the last couple weeks. To... White House Black Market? Nordstrom's? American Eagle? Restaurants, hotel rooms, they were all adding up. All since Dad died.

"Bus time!" Gus called. I kissed his cheeks, and April sauntered in, with—yep—a new Kate Spade messenger bag across her shoulders.

"I'll take him to the bus," she offered.

"I found the bill." I kept my voice low when I heard

Grams coming down the stairs.

"Oh?" Her eyebrows raised above her widened doe eyes.

"April, you've spent over five thousand dollars. Mom is going to be pissed."

"Mom's not going to notice." She had the nerve to walk away from me.

"It's not right, April!" Damn. When had I become all moral, chasing after my sister?

Her gaze narrowed into a scowl. "Nothing is right. Dad is dead, Mom's a vegetable, and I made myself feel better by shopping. So what? We have the money."

"You stole."

She snorted. "Whatever."

"It's not whatever!" My retort met the door as she slammed it.

"Later, Ember!" Gus hugged my middle and ran out the door, tugging his hat over his ears.

I grabbed the nearest pillow off the entry hall bench and shoved my face into it, screaming. Everything was shit.

"Coffee, dear?" Grams asked, patting the seat next to her.

I nodded my head and took the cup she offered, sinking into the cushions. She would know what to do about this. "Grams, how long are you staying?"

She paused in reflection. "I need to get home. I have a life, too, you know."

I nearly dropped my cup. She couldn't leave. The house wouldn't function. Mom wasn't ready. I wasn't ready. "I don't know what I'm supposed to do anymore, what kind of life I'm supposed to have."

Her delicate arm came around my shoulders, pulling me to her. "Grief, by its very nature, is designed to suck the life out of us because we are so willing to join our dead. It's supposed to be this hard to figure out what to do next, but it's that 'next' that makes us the living, and not our dead." Her soft southern accent drawled on every word.

"Thanks, Grams." What the hell did *that* mean?

She laughed. "Oh, my December, you do what you can with your life, what's in your power. No more, no less."

Do what I can. Yeah.

Housework consumed my morning. I tackled the dishes, vacuum, grocery list, laundry, and hockey gear. At the dining room table with Grams, I wrote out all the bills while she penned eloquent thank you notes for the countless casseroles that had fed us.

Apparently, grief meant busy work, and every time I moved my wrist while writing, I saw Josh's number staring back at me. I really wanted to see him, but I also knew I wasn't ready for what that meant. I was too much of a hot mess to handle myself, let alone any kind of rebound relationship. Was that what he was? My first instinct said no. Josh and Riley were two separate events in my mind, but they were too closely linked.

Around three o'clock in the afternoon, the doorbell rang. I swallowed back the bile in my throat, reminding myself that Dad was already gone; there was nothing to fear from the door anymore. When I opened it to Riley's mom, I wished I'd gone with my first instinct.

"Ember!" She embraced me with one arm, lasagna pan in the other. "I was hoping June might be up for some company now? She hasn't let me see her since the funeral."

Before I could tell her no, Grams stepped in. "She's not at her best, Gwen. However, I certainly think you could remedy that. Why don't you head on up?" She gracefully took the pan. "Thank you for thinking of us."

Mrs. Barton removed her hat, gloves, and coat, hanging them on the pegs like she had countless times since she'd become Mom's friend. Her kind smile and casual greeting told me all I needed to know. Riley hadn't told her. "Let's see if I can't get her cleaned up a bit. Oh, and Riley's just finishing up a phone call and then he'll be in."

Crap. Shit. Fuck.

Grams's astute eyes caught my panic. "Why don't you put this in the refrigerator, Ember?" she drawled.

I nodded and retreated. What the hell could he want? I was pretty sure we'd left everything in Breckenridge. I slid the lasagna onto the refrigerator shelf and heard his deep, remorseful voice behind me as I shut the door. "Hey, Ember."

"Riley." I turned slowly, gripping the granite of the island.

He looked perfect as always: his blond hair was windswept and the blue of his vest matched his eyes. Lying, traitorous, cheating eyes. "We need to talk."

"Pretty sure we don't."

He walked toward me, and I skirted to the right, keeping the island between us.

"I'm so sorry, babe. I didn't know you were coming up."

"That's your excuse?" I whispered through clenched teeth. I didn't need Grams hearing this. She thought Riley was a perfect gentleman.

"I never meant to hurt you!"

"Oh, you didn't mean to fuck my best friend for a year?" Okay, now I was yelling. The coffee cup sliding across the bar in front of the sink told me Grams had heard it. A quick look confirmed, and warm blood rushed to my cheeks. I'd never sworn in front of her. I was about to get it.

Her eyes darted between Riley and me before settling on a graceful smile. "I think I'll head on upstairs and check the bathroom. I just heard there's some trash that needs taking out." With a pointed look at Riley, but not another word, she left us alone.

"Lower your voice. My mom is upstairs!"

"Good, maybe she'll find out what an asshole her son is!"

He tore his hands through his hair, messing up his not-so-casually-made casual style. "It was an accident." I scoffed, but he kept talking. "No, really! The first time you were gone, and we were both lonely, and drunk, and it just happened."

"And it just *kept* happening?" It was his turn to flush. "Yeah. You know what's even worse? You could sleep with her, but you couldn't bear to touch me, no matter how many times I asked you to! God, I must have looked so fucking desperate to you, and the whole time you were screwing Kayla!" I focused on my rage, the accelerated beat of my heart, because if I looked to see where it was cracked and bleeding, I wouldn't make it through this.

"I…" He slammed his hands onto the granite. "Damn it! I wanted to sleep with you, but I couldn't; it would have ruined my plan—our plan. You're the girl I'm going to marry. It had to be perfect!"

Going to, my ass. "And Kayla was perfect? You make zero sense."

"Kayla was easy, available, and a mistake. You are everything I've built my future on. I wasn't risking that by sleeping with you."

"Risk what? This isn't feudal England. Sex doesn't ruin a girl for marriage any more than it's ruined you."

He gripped the countertop, his knuckles turning white. "We agreed to wait until marriage."

"You! *You* were going to wait! I never wanted to!"

"Is that what this is about? Because I'll take you upstairs right now if that makes you happy." He threw out his arm in the direction of the staircase.

"If you think I'd let you near me—" The phone rang. Its shrill tone pulled me out of the downward spiral my emotions were taking. "Saved by the bell," I muttered and picked up. "Hello?"

"June Howard?" Oh, crap. I knew that voice. Mrs. Angelo

from the attendance office at the high school.

I put on my best June Howard impression. "Yes." Mom was in no condition to talk, and I was in no mood to explain the situation to the freaking school. Things were a mess enough already.

"Ma'am, this is Mrs. Angelo from Cheyenne Mountain High School."

"Mrs. Angelo, good afternoon!"

"I'm so sorry to bother you at this time, but will April be returning to us this semester?"

"I'm sorry?" Crap, my impression might have slipped there.

"We haven't seen April back yet. Is she ready to return? I'm so sorry to hear about your loss. We're just trying to keep track of her." Sympathy dripped from her voice.

Crap. Crap. Craptastic crap. "Absolutely, I'm so sorry. Excuse her for me, would you? I'll make sure she's ready tomorrow." April was going to fry for this one.

"Absolutely, Mrs. Howard. Have a nice day."

The click sounded the end of the call, and I put the phone back on its charging deck. Riley was still there, staring, and just like that, the fight drained out of me. "I don't want anything to do with you, Riley. We're done."

"I love you, Ember." Was that panic crawling into his eyes?

"You love yourself. Maybe you loved me when we started dating, but something warped along the way, and you know it's true. If you love me, you never would have slept with Kayla."

"How many times can I say I'm sorry?"

"You're not sorry you did it. You're sorry you got caught."

"Please don't end this." He lunged toward me, and I evaded. "Please. Our brothers are on the same team, our moms are friends. We have a plan, Ember. Just let me get it back on track. I'm so sorry. I can make this up to you."

I threw up my hands. "Stop. Stop chasing, stop apologizing, just stop…being."

His gaze narrowed, focused on my exposed forearm. "What the hell is that?"

I flicked my wrist inward and saw the black marks he meant. "Josh's number."

"Well, that's just fantastic. We have a fight and you hop right to the next guy. I never really pegged you for a whore." Hello, Mr. Hyde.

There must have been parts of me that still loved him, because they shattered in that moment, leaving me naked, bare, cold. "Now we're definitely done. You can leave."

His face relaxed, a soft sigh escaping his lips. Dr. Jekyll was back. "I'm sorry, I didn't mean it. I just saw those numbers…I know that would never happen with you and Josh." He shook his head with a patronizing smile. "You're not even his type, too timid. It's like for hockey or something, right?"

What the hell was that supposed to mean? Too timid for Josh? "And if it's not?" I needed to hurt him, to make him feel just an ounce of the devastation wrecking me. "What if he wrote it there after he spent the night with me in Breck?"

His eyes flew wide for a second before they narrowed into a glare, bringing back Mr. Hyde. "Tell me you didn't fuck him! Tell me that's not how you spent Friday night!"

"The night I caught you with Kayla? You're such a hypocrite, Riley!" I blinked back the threatening tears. "Three years! I gave you three years! I loved you, cared for you, stood by you! I gave up every dream I had and let you plan out our lives by your insane notions that we had to be a perfect couple for you to go into politics in like ten freaking years! For what? To have you doing Kayla on the side for a year of it?" This time *my* hands slammed into the granite, pain destroying my fingers and skirting up my forearms.

The doorbell rang.

"What the hell is this? Grand Central Station?" I snapped. He looked at me like I'd lost it, and maybe I had. "Come in!" I didn't care that Grams might have heard me not greet a guest, or that Mom was upstairs doing whatever it was she did lately.

Six feet and a granite counter separated me from Riley, who I had planned to spend the rest of my life with, but it may as well have been two miles, or two million miles. "Babe, I love you. I know we can fight for this. I won't see her again, I swear. Once we get up to Boulder, everything will return to normal, I know it. I'm the only one for you." His gaze ran past me, and he stepped back reflexively before glaring. "What the hell are you doing here? It's a little early for hockey."

Josh came up beside me, put an Ember-labeled Starbucks down on the counter, and met my gaze, melting my tension instantly. My posture relaxed as he unzipped his black ski coat, revealing jeans that hugged low on his sculpted hips and a soft gray Henley. He couldn't have been more different from Riley's carefully chosen polo. "I'm not just here for hockey."

"Well, you're not fucking welcome to anything else in this house," Riley fired back, coming around the island. "It's not like you actually want her! I remember the girls you went after in school, and Ember isn't on that level."

Not on that level? What the hell? The man I'd thought was the love of my life didn't think I was enough to merit Josh Walker's attention. He thought so little of me. How had I never noticed it before?

I glanced up at Josh. "Whatever I need?" He gave a small nod, and I pounced. I threw my arms around his neck and fitted his mouth to mine. I knew this was for Riley's benefit, but the moment Josh's lips touched mine, I forgot all about Riley.

Josh grabbed ahold of my rear and lifted me against him. I lost myself in the feel of his mouth and the plunge of his tongue as he slanted over me. My body remembered his, softening against him. Oh, yes, I remembered exactly what his body could do to mine, and I wanted it again.

"Are you serious?" Riley's shout broke through my haze. Josh kissed me gently, brushing my mouth with his one last time before setting me back on my feet.

It took all of my concentration to turn back to Riley. "Get out. We're done, and I'm not saying it again."

"We'll fix this when we get back to Boulder, Ember. I'm not walking away this easily. I don't care what happened with this guy." His face was a mottled red. "Remember, we have a plan! I know you want the same things I do."

The phone rang again. "For the love of God!" I ripped it off the charger and stabbed the talk button. "Hello?"

"May I speak with December Howard?" a polite female voice asked me.

"This is she." I was so not in the freaking mood to deal with anything else today. Josh and Riley sized each other up across the island, and I was afraid that any moment there would be an all-out brawl in my kitchen.

"This is Ms. Shaw from the registrar up here at CU Boulder. One of your classes"—papers swished in the background—"Psych 325: Early Childhood Trauma, has been cancelled. Was there another class you'd care to put in its place?"

"Cancelled?"

"Yes, miss."

Josh turned, his eyes softening, and took a step toward me. Riley crossed his arms and leaned forward onto the island.

It wasn't a choice between them. I would never make a choice this big on a guy...right? But Gus needed me, April was floundering, and Mom wasn't functioning. What the hell was I supposed to do?

You do what you can. Grams was right. I could only do what was in my power, and everything else I had to let slip. But this? This was in my power. "No, thank you."

"You wouldn't like to add another class?"

Past versus future, but with the options in front of me, I couldn't tell which was which. Both were familiar, both were a sort of home, but there was only one place I was needed. I met Riley's sullen gaze. "No, ma'am, I won't be returning to Boulder. My father died over break, and I'm needed at home. Could you withdraw me from all classes? I'll be transferring here to CU Springs."

Riley's face lost all its color, and he shook his head quickly. His mouth opened and shut like a fish caught out of water.

"I'm sorry to hear about your father, and to lose you, December," the clerk said with sympathy.

I looked up at the slow smile that spread across Josh's face and said, "Thank you." I hung up, knowing she was right: when it came to the people at Boulder, Riley and Kayla, it was their loss.

I just wasn't sure it was Josh's gain.

Chapter Eight

"The dorms were full," I explained to April as she helped lug in the last of my boxes from the car. She'd jumped at the chance to see my new apartment. "Besides, Sam's roommate flunked out last semester, so it's pretty perfect." It had only taken a week, but I'd moved from Boulder, enrolled at UCCS, and managed to avoid Riley...and Josh.

I didn't even want to think about either of them right now. I couldn't be the girl who switched colleges over a guy. Unless you included Dad, then I guess I really was that girl.

"Does this mean I can crash here on weekends?" She flung herself onto my bare bed.

I chucked my pillow at her. "Only if Mom okays it. I'm not your hideout." It was nice to have a moment where I could be her sister and not her mother.

She picked up a picture of our family, the one from that last afternoon at the Breckenridge cabin, from the top of an open box. "If she ever recovers from her lobotomy." She absently stroked her thumb over Mom's smiling face in the family photo. It was the last one we'd taken before Dad deployed. That made it our last one, period.

"She'll come around," I promised what I had no right to.

"Right. She doesn't even realize you've transferred schools." She rolled her eyes and changed the subject. "How did Kayla take you moving out?"

Ouch. I didn't expect that to hurt, but it did. "I went while she was still in Breckenridge and moved my stuff out. It's not like she didn't know the reason."

"Riley's an asshat." I didn't argue with her language. She eyed the mini-fridge and TV I'd pulled out of our shared dorm room. "Did you leave Kayla anything?"

A wicked smile flashed across my face. "Every picture I had of Riley and me, with a note that said, 'He's all yours. Smooches!'"

"Badass!"

She crossed her feet, revealing another pair of new shoes, and I couldn't hold my tongue. "April, I paid off that credit card bill, but you have to give me the card, and Mom has to know. What you're doing is illegal, and wrong, and hurtful—"

"Jesus, stop lecturing me." She pulled the card out of her back pocket and tossed it onto my desk as she hopped off the bed. "Bathroom?"

I stepped into the living room and pointed the way.

The apartment was perfect. Located on the north side of town, it was close to campus, but not too far to get home when I was needed. I'd wanted to live at home for the semester, after all, that was why I'd left Boulder, but Grams would hear nothing of it.

"You're moving forward," she'd told me. "Not stepping back."

I picked up a picture of Sam and me on graduation day. We were both so happy, her with a megawatt grin and the keys to a new car, me with a sappy smile and Riley's class ring on a chain around my neck. If this was moving forward, why did it come attached to so much past?

The door slammed, and Sam waltzed in with an afternoon fix. Her killer body wasn't hidden under the bright miniskirt and sparkly Uggs.

She juggled three mall-sized shopping bags and as many Pikes Perk take-out coffee cups, balancing the cups under her chin while she opened her bedroom door. The bags hit the ground, and she danced into the living room. "This is going to be great!" she said with way more enthusiasm than I was feeling as she passed me my coffee.

"Everything is moved in. I just need to unpack."

"Did you register for classes?" She sank onto the microfiber couch.

"Yup, funny what they'll wiggle you in for with a dead-dad card." It had been torturous to explain to the registrar without breaking down, but I'd made it. "A lot of the good ones are gone, but I got into the American History class I need."

Sam read my mood pretty well. "Once you get settled, this will be easier."

I nodded my head absently.

"Time to pick up Gus and get home?" April asked, emerging from the bathroom.

"Yeah," I grabbed my keys. "Sam, want to come? We'll be back in time for a run later."

She nodded mid latte-slurp, and then spoke. "Yes to coming along, hell no to the run. You've gone insane with that crap."

I looked around the mass of boxes and knew we'd be up all night if I wanted to get a workout in. We had two days until classes started to finish up the apartment. There was a giant fake expiration date on my allowed-grieving time, and then I had to function.

The bleachers for the practice ice at the World Arena filled quickly. We grabbed a couple seats on the cold metal bleachers and waited for Gus's practice to let out. Their over-padded figures ran a scrimmage for the last five minutes, and Gus was going all-out. He'd never been particularly sports oriented, but the minute Dad strapped skates on him a few years ago, his niche was found. The kid loved it.

But as cute as Gus was out there, my eyes were drawn to his coach. Josh dressed was in simple warm-up pants, a jersey, and helmet, all on top of a pair of black hockey skates that he wore like an extension of his body.

His movements were powerful, quick, graceful, and freaking hypnotic. I couldn't look away as he moved from one blue line to the other, correcting players and getting the heck out of their way. Funny, but if this had been four years ago, I'd have found myself in exactly the same place, entranced by watching Josh Walker skate.

"Earth to Ember!" Sam waved her hand in front of my face, jolting me. "Do you need a napkin for the drool?"

I tore my eyes from Josh and focused back on Sam. "Nonsense."

"Girl, I have seen that face. Do you forget all those games we stalked so you could salivate over Josh Walker?"

I couldn't control the laughter that snuck out of me any more than I could keep the backs of my thighs from going numb on the bench. "Remember when you pretended to be my mom so we could get excused from class for that away game?"

Sam did her best impression of my mom, and we both sank into giggles. April turned from her seat lower on the risers—heaven forbid she get caught sitting with me—and glared at us for making such a scene. Sam and I may have grown apart over the last eighteen months, but a few hours together and we were right back to senior year.

Warmth streaked through my heart, washing away a little more of the crust of crap that seemed to have settled over me.

I wiped the laughter-induced tears out of my eyes and focused on the ice, watching Gus steal the puck and pass it to his teammate. He was bouncing back, and I envied him these moments.

The only time I successfully escaped thinking about Dad, was when I was with...

I raised my eyes and caught Josh giving me a head nod and single wave. My breath expelled in what sounded too much like a sigh.

"What is that about?" Sam asked, nudging my side.

"OMG," a girly voice whined behind me. "Josh Walker just waved over here. Do you think he noticed I have his number painted on?"

She what? My head snapped back before I could call up the willpower to keep my eyes forward. The girls were annoyingly gorgeous, airbrushed, and straightened to sorority perfection. And one of them had a number thirteen painted on her cheek in blue and gold. Josh's number, if he'd kept the same since high school.

"He's been looking over here for like ten minutes," the other girl said.

I wiped the horrified look off my face and forced my gaze forward to the ice. "I guess that hasn't changed. Fan girls and all." I tried to keep my comment light, but failed. I couldn't help but be disappointed that girls still chased Josh.

I bet he still liked to get caught.

"Things change," Sam whispered so the girls behind us wouldn't hear. "And something tells me he wasn't looking above you."

Josh skated over to the glass in front of us, turned, and

blew his whistle, ending practice for the day. The boys skated for the locker room. He turned around, pulled off his helmet, and locked his gaze to mine. A slow smile spread across his face, and I couldn't help but give it right back.

He nodded his head toward the door, and I nodded in agreement before he skated off. The girls behind us let out a collective "Hmmpf."

"Damn," Sam whispered. "Have you jumped him yet? Because if not…"

"Shut it, Sam." I paid close attention to my feet as I climbed down the bleachers. Falling on my ass was not on my agenda for the afternoon. I passed Riley's mom, who was waiting for Rory, and gave her a half smile. She looked like she wanted to say something to me, but I wasn't up for hearing it. Once my feet were on the ground, I took a quick peek for April, who was practically sitting on the lap of a guy who was not Brett. *What the hell is she doing?* I did my best to ignore her and give her the privacy she wanted. Following the glass around the side of the arena led me to the door where Josh waited, running his fingers over his slightly sweaty, still incredibly sexy hair.

"December." He smiled, stopping every thought I had in my head.

"Josh." It was the best I could do without sounding like an idiot, especially knowing what I had to tell him.

He pulled me to him by my waist, and I rebelled against every instinct I had to melt and give in. I stepped back and shook my head. "I can't."

His eyes narrowed. "Riley?"

"Oh, hell no."

That brought another heart-attack grin across his face. He closed the distance between us without touching me, whispering in my ear. "You like it when I touch you."

Boom. Turned on. Shit. Was this guy exuding pheromones,

or did I simply see him and think, *yes, sex is good. Now.* I couldn't stop the smile that sent mixed signals, but I took another step back. "Yeah, that's the problem."

"What's up? Do I get an explanation? Or is it just creepy to want your brother's coach? I happen to think the coach aspect is pretty hot."

"Hot? Everything about you is hot. It's just..." Crap. When he cocked his head to the side like that, he exposed the side of his neck. I knew how that neck felt under my teeth, how it tasted. I knew how *he* tasted. My lips tingled and parted.

"Don't look at me like that and tell me no. That's not fair." His voice strained behind the teasing.

I shoved my hands into my coat to keep from putting them on him. "I just dumped Riley, and moved back here, and there's my family, and a new school..."

"So no new flame to add to that?"

I flushed, despite the freezing temperatures inside the arena. "I just need to sort myself out." His face fell. *Crap, I did* not *just it's-not-you-it's-me him, did I?* I stepped closer, despite my better judgment, putting my feet between his skates. They made his impossible height even more gigantic to look up at. "It's not that I don't want you." The skin of his neck was begging to be touched, and I gave in, running my hands over his stubbled jaw before I stroked my fingertips down his neck. "Because I want you more than I should." The whispered admission tumbled free before I could stop it. "I just don't want to drag you into the incredible wreckage of my life." And I wasn't sure I'd survive if I turned out to be just another one of the girls chasing him. Was he worth that risk?

He laughed through his confusion. "So you're saying slow? Or no?" He raised his arms and put his hands back against the glass. "Because you're killing me here."

"I need you separate," I tried to explain, focusing way too much on his mouth for my own peace of mind. That mouth had been on my skin, all over my body.

"Separate from?" He kept his hands on the glass like they were glued to the surface.

"Separate from the crap. Separate from all the bad shit that's happened in the last month." How could I explain what I didn't understand myself? "I don't want a rebound, or a quickie in your dorm room."

"I don't live in the dorms."

"Not the point, Josh."

His eyes were dark. I knew that look. That look would have me peeling off my clothes in spite of the crowd around us. "Forget what I just asked you, because I don't want an answer." His voice dropped, and his head bent toward me. "I want you. Not a minute ticks by that I don't crave the sight of you, the feel of you. But I get it."

"You do?"

A wry smile came across his face. "I don't want to screw this up, either, December."

"Why do you do that? Call me December? Everyone except Grams calls me Ember, since before high school." I craved the sound of my name on his lips. He made it sound like pure sex and the sweetest prayer.

He leaned down, brushing just close enough to my ear that I could feel his breath, but he wasn't touching me. Chills raced down my neck to my spine and set my body on fire. "Because it means I have a part of you no one else does. Like my own little secret side of you."

He had just about every part of me as it was.

"Josh!" the living Barbies called to him from the nearest bleachers. "We came to watch you play!" They waived a huge blue and gold paw in the air.

He gave them a head nod. "Thanks, girls."

He was still playing? "You play for the Mountain Lions?"

"We have a game tonight. Want to watch?"

The hopeful tone of his voice nearly broke my resolve. Almost. "I need to get Gus home and check on my mom."

"Okay." He reached out and brushed a stray strand of auburn hair back behind my ear. "Another time."

I couldn't say anything that wouldn't come out *touch me now.*

"You're swimming in a pretty big shit fest. Just don't forget to ask for help when you need it. Don't carry this all on your own."

Why couldn't he be an ass? Why did he have to say the most perfect things? "You'd better get going."

He searched my eyes for a moment, but I refused to break. I would not rebound on Josh Walker. I would not run from one guy to the other. He cleared his throat. "Practice Monday?"

"We'll get him here," I promised.

He stepped away from me, toward the girls who waited like groupies. I flipped to my back, leaning up against the cold glass and knocking the back of my head on it. I squeezed my eyes shut so I wouldn't be tempted to watch him walk away with those girls. Who the hell let Josh Walker walk away?

"December."

My eyes snapped open to see his fathomless brown ones leaning over me. His mouth was scant inches from mine, and I would have been willing to commit murder to close that distance without guilt. "Josh." It was a whispered plea.

"We're taking it slow until you say so, because I can't bear to hear a 'no' from you. But here's your only warning: I'm going to chase the fuck out of you." The promise dripping from his voice was enough to set my thighs on fire.

He pulled away, leaving me a heart-thumping mess against the glass. He waved to the girls and walked right past them without another word, but then turned back around. "Oh, and Ember?" I blinked in response. "I'm still your whatever, for whatever you need."

We dropped Sam off for dinner with her mom and pulled into our driveway. Gus made a big deal about carrying his gear in by himself, so I let him, despite stifling my laughter at the Josh-sized bag. He struggled ahead to the door, and I pulled April back.

"Hey, what was with that guy at the rink?"

"Who? Paul?" She innocently brushed imaginary dirt off her arm.

"Yeah, Mr. Not-Brett. You looked pretty close to the guy."

"And you were nearly clawing off Josh's clothes, so what does it matter? Not that I blame you. That guy is so sexy."

The wistfulness in her tone made me sputter. "It matters because I don't have a boyfriend! Also, you don't get to call Josh 'sexy.' He's six years older than you."

"Whatever. Look, I'm glad you're home and stuff, but don't stick your nose into my business like you haven't been gone these last couple of years." She huffed into the house.

I felt like some kind of absentee landlord, trying to mop up damage I hadn't witnessed. She was right. As close as we'd been growing up, leaving for college changed things. We'd both matured separately, and now there was a distance between us.

Inside the foyer, the scent of garlic bread and scallops enveloped us. "No way," April muttered, haphazardly tossing her purse into the entryway.

"Mom?" I hung up my coat and cautiously approached the kitchen.

She stirred the contents of the steaming pot on the stove. Her hair hung wet down her back, and she wore clean clothes without my prompting. Her eyes may have been red-rimmed and swollen, but she was *here.* "Ember, would you grab the dressing out of the refrigerator for the salad?"

I looked at April and Gus, and we all shrugged with wide eyes at one another. Grams stirred the pasta and gave us a subtle nod.

"Come on, guys, you know the drill. Ember, salad dressing. April, pour the drinks. Gus, grab the silverware." Mom gave out orders like she hadn't been bed-bound for the last four weeks. Another heartbeat passed. "Now." She pointed toward the dining room with an Alfredo-sauce-soaked spatula.

We jumped, scurrying to our assigned roles. No one spoke, afraid of shattering the fragile normalcy. We brought our assignments to the table, and took our usual seats for the first time since…yeah. Grams pulled an extra chair from the side of the china cabinet to sit next to Gus.

She left Dad's seat empty.

"Gus?" Mom prompted and bowed her head.

Gus's sweet voice filled the air as he said grace, but his voice stuttered after he asked to keep our daddy safe during his deployment. He was just so used to saying it. I jerked my eyes to Mom in panic that it would set her off. She paled, but held still and silent until he finished.

"I think that was perfect, Gus." Grams kissed his temple.

"Now who's hungry?" Mom raised her head with a weak smile.

Just like that, the tide of grief receded enough to breathe as we passed the dishes around. The clatter of plates mixed with Gus's excitement over his day and his ability to share it with Mom. I stole glances at her in between bites; she was smiling down at Gus, listening to what happened with his day. Her smile didn't reach her eyes, but it was there.

April's head drooped next to me, and she quickly

brushed off a tear. I reached the small distance between us and took her hand with a gentle squeeze. Our eyes met, and something intangible passed between us, something that felt dangerously like hope.

She clung to my hand as desperately as I gripped hers. With a trembling lip, I raised my eyes to Grams's. She gave me a slow smile and a single nod, and there it was again, hope coursing through me, the taste sweet in my mouth. I was scared to acknowledge it, to think it even, in case it jinxed us in this moment, but I couldn't ignore my optimism.

We were going to get past this. We were going to be okay.

"You're not at school," Mom stated as she stared at the calendar. "Has it really been that long?"

"I'm at UCCS now." I looked back to the living room where Grams sat in the corner stitching, but she simply nodded her head back toward Mom. I was on my own.

"Right," she muttered. "I remember you saying that. Kind of." She shook her head like she was trying to clear it. "You moved home."

"Not exactly. I live with Sam now. We have an apartment up toward campus, but I'm close enough to grab Gus and stuff when you need help."

"You came home because of me."

I didn't reach out for her. We weren't exactly a touchy-feeling, mother-daughter duo. "I came home because we lost Dad, and nothing was right in Boulder. This is where I'm needed, and I made the best decision I could with what's been going on."

"You've kept the house going, you and Grams. Thank you."

I didn't want her thanks. I wanted her to pull herself

together and promise she wasn't going to retreat into that cave of a bedroom. I wanted her to take care of Gus, and April, and mostly, herself. I wanted not to be the only adult in the family anymore.

Where did this anger come from? Shouldn't I just be happy she was here for the moment? She was functioning? I didn't want to feel this way, so I ignored it as best I could.

I gave a closed-mouth smile before my stupid thoughts came out and ruined what progress she'd made. "Mom, are you…you know, okay?"

"Everything hurts," she whispered, sounding like Gus. She tore her eyes from the calendar with a shake of her head. "Do you want to go back to Boulder? I don't want to keep you here, from your friends and Riley."

"Riley isn't exactly missing me."

"Oh, Ember. What happened?"

"Turns out he doesn't do long distance well." I put my hand up to ward her off when she stepped toward me. I didn't want sympathy from her, not when she needed all the energy she had to keep herself together. "Yeah, so I live with Sam, and the number is on the fridge next to my class schedule. Just call and I'll be here."

"Ember, I'm sorry you've lost so much."

"What doesn't kill you makes you stronger, right?"

"Right. Whatever doesn't kill you." She went back to staring at the calendar.

Chapter Nine

I slung my messenger bag over my shoulder and snatched my coffee off the roof of my car. Thank God there was a Starbucks between the apartment and school, or I might never have gotten going this morning.

Arranging the apartment had been more physically exhausting than I expected, but it turned out perfectly. It was incredibly freeing to have a place off campus with no rules, regulations, or random room checks. Plus, Sam as a roommate was an added bonus. For every detail that had changed about us in the last eighteen months, there were at least two that hadn't.

I pulled out my schedule as I walked into the building, checked the room number, and slid inside the class without spilling my coffee all over my white sweater. Score.

A quick scan of the room showed a few open seats in the front row. I set my coffee on the desktop and slid my bag off my shoulder to take out my books and pens. I couldn't wait to fill the pages of the empty spiral notebook. History got me in the same way some girls dug nail polish or shoes. I'd pegged my major early.

I shook my head at the obnoxious giggles from the back of the room. A leggy brunette perched on a desk in front of a guy, and if he couldn't see past the facade dripping off her, then he deserved whatever he got out of that one. She threw her head back in laughter.

Shit. That guy was Josh.

His eyes widened as they met mine, and that grin stole my breath. I ripped my gaze away and took my seat, concentrating on the white board. Stupid freaking hormones. Did he really have to look that good at 8:30 in the morning? Who was I kidding? The guy was pretty much sex personified twenty-four hours of the day. I couldn't blame the girl for sitting on his desk. Hell, she showed restraint. I'd have been in his damn lap.

I didn't need to look over to know that he had taken the empty seat next to me. *Keep your eyes forward.* I would not look over. I would not get lost in those brown eyes or remember exactly what those hands were capable of on my body. Nope.

"I'd been dreading this class, but seeing you this early in the morning makes it worth getting out of bed, December."

"You and the 'December'..." I muttered, not willing to admit how much I liked it. "You can't just call me 'Ember' like everyone else in the world?"

He leaned over, his mouth closer to my ear. "I only do it when no one else can hear, and besides, I'm not just everyone—not to you."

Did his voice have to be so smooth? I glanced to the back of the classroom, tapping my pen on the empty notebook that would soon be full of delicious historical facts. "I think your paperweight is missing you."

The brunette was sulking in her back-row seat, and I couldn't blame her.

"Want to take her place?"

His mocking tone brought my gaze right to his, and I was a goner. I couldn't stop the smile that erupted on my face when he waggled his eyebrows and patted the top of his desk. I shook my head and forced my focus back to the front of the room. "I'm not sure it's a good idea to get that close to you," I reminded him with a smile.

"I'll sit on my damn hands if it means you'll wiggle up here."

Speechless. I couldn't even think of a retort for that one.

The prof saved me by handing out his syllabus and starting the lecture. I paid attention, really. Well, not really. I wrote down copious notes, but felt Josh's eyes staring, which reminded me too much of his hands on me. I snuck a glance and found those brown eyes locked onto mine. Hot. Freaking on fire.

I crossed and uncrossed my legs, reminding myself that class was not the place to jump a fellow student, and paid more attention to the details. Papers, I could handle writing papers, taking notes, and concentrating on the Civil War. What I couldn't handle was my self-imposed slow-down on Josh, not when I was ready to jump him in the middle of class.

It was the longest and shortest hour of my life. I was almost as desperate to get the hell out of that room as I was to stay there as close to him as I could get. Our prof dismissed us, and I scurried out the door like my chair was on fire. Monday was a light day, and I didn't have another class until the afternoon, so I could get a jump-start on the reading if I headed home right now.

I was nearly to my car when Josh caught up to me. "What? No good-bye?" he teased, not even out of breath from his jog.

I opened my door and tossed in my bag, cringing when the books slammed to the floor on the passenger side. "Good-bye, Josh."

"Cold."

I turned to look, but his eyes held the humor his tone didn't. I rolled my eyes. "Seriously."

"Seriously what?" He leaned against my car. "I'm not kissing you, not calling you, since I don't even have your number. Maybe a guy just needs a study buddy."

"Study buddy?" My voice cracked, and I cleared my throat to cover it. I shoved my hands into my pockets to keep the chill off my fingers and my fingers off Josh. That seemed to be the only way.

He leaned in, just inches from my mouth, and even though I'm the one who drew the line, my body wanted him to cross it. "Something tells me we'd be really good at doing it together."

My mouth dropped open. "Josh!"

An impish grin stole over his face. "What? We would be good at studying together."

I swatted his chest with the backside of my hand and laughed. "Ugh!" Then again, he'd been right. We'd do a lot of things...*well*...together.

Dave Matthews rang out from my back pocket, and I reached for my phone, thankful for the distraction. A quick glance at the screen and April's picture elevated my heart rate. She was supposed to be in school.

"April? You're supposed to be in third period by now." God, I sounded like Mom.

"You might want to get over here. Uncle Mike just showed up and there's a news crew and Mom doesn't want them in the house and it's a big mess."

"Slow down, April. You're talking too fast." I reached into the car and started the ignition to warm the engine. "What's going on?"

"Uncle Mike showed up as I was leaving for school, and then about a half hour ago, a news crew showed up. Mom's wigging out."

"I'll be right there." I hung up and turned to Josh. "I have to go, there's major shit going down at my house with my mom's brother."

His flirtatious look was gone, immediately replaced with concern. Too bad that was almost sexier than the flirting. "Do you need me? Help? Do you need help?"

I bit back my instinct to say yes, that I wanted him with me. I couldn't depend on another guy, not this soon. "No, I'd better handle this alone."

His face fell, and he swallowed quickly with a curt nod. "Yeah, okay."

"Thanks for asking, though. It means a lot."

I made the drive to the south side of town in twenty minutes, pulled into our subdivision-standard driveway, and threw the car in park. Sure enough, some huge news conglomerate was parked outside our house.

I'd called Captain Wilson on the way home. He'd warned us something like this might happen, especially with the incident being Afghan military on American, but when the funeral had passed and nothing had happened, I'd hoped it wouldn't. Apparently it did.

"Mom!" I threw open the door and tossed my keys into the entry hall basket. Then I hung my coat onto the pegs. "Mom!" I called into the kitchen, but there was only Grams.

"She's upstairs."

"Grams, what the—" I stopped myself before I ended up with an old-school bar of soap in my mouth. "What's going on?"

"Your mother's brother arrived earlier and brought some guests. Some rather uninvited guests." She sipped her tea calmly, but there was a slight tremor in her hand.

"Right."

I took the back steps two at a time, coming around the corner at my bedroom door and running smack into a cameraman.

"Oh, excuse me, ma'am," he muttered.

"You're damn right, excuse you. Get out of my way." I pushed past him and two guys with long, metal rods until I found April cowering in the hallway.

Her breath expelled, and she hugged me to her. "They're in Gus's room."

"I'll take care of this." I had no idea how I was going to do it, but I was. I ruffled Gus's hair where he was plastered against April's side. He should have been in school. *He shouldn't have to see this.*

I cracked open the door to the *Star Wars* shrine Gus called a room and walked straight into an argument.

"I don't want this, Mike!" Mom shouted at her younger brother. Yoda's giant face on the bedspread separated them.

"They're willing to pay you, June. This is a legitimate story, and our family should have a public say about what happened to Justin."

"Uncle Mike?" I shut the door behind me and took my place next to Mom. If she didn't want this, I wasn't going to allow it.

"April, I told you, this is between your mother and me. Run along now and go to school."

"I'm Ember, not April, and not as easily dismissed. If my mother wants these people to go, they'll go." I looked him up and down, from his dark suit to his expensive-looking tie. "And you're shorter than I remember."

He flushed. "Of course you're Ember. I misspoke. It's been years since I've seen you."

"Yeah, like fifteen or so. I hardly think that entitles you

to any opinion about what's going on here." I had vague memories of Uncle Mike, and they usually revolved around my mom's parents who were now dead.

"I'm here to help my sister."

"Right, which is why you were so thoughtful during the funeral and everything?" There might as well have been crickets in that room.

A woman cleared her throat, and I turned to Gus's desk behind me. A leggy brunette I vaguely recognized stood and offered her hand. "You must be December. So tragic, losing your father, and on your birthday nonetheless."

My head snapped back like I'd been slapped, and my eyes narrowed. "Yes."

A camera-ready smile erupted onto her face. "Excellent! I'm London Cartwright, and we'd love your reaction, since I understand you held the family together?"

"My mother would like you to leave, and I'll have to ask you to do the same, Ms. Cartwright."

The smile didn't falter. Eerie. "I'm sure once you understand what we'd like to do…"

"And what the hell is that?"

"They want to expose the Green-on-Blue killings, Ember. Really delve into what our continued presence is doing, and why our soldiers are being killed, victimized by the men they were protecting and training."

What. The. Fuck. "My father wasn't a victim. He was at war."

"We just want to give you an opportunity to share your feelings." Ms. Cartwright crossed the room and stared at the wall behind Uncle Mike.

Mom shrank back. "Mom?" I asked. "What do you want me to do?"

Her eyes went vacant. *No. Not again.* I grabbed her shoulders, ducking my head to look into those eyes. "Mom?

Stay with me." I pulled her to the doorway. "April, take her downstairs to Grams. You, too, Gus." April led Mom and Gus downstairs, and I made sure they were clear before I turned back to Mike and Ms. Cartwright.

"Do you see how fragile she is? What are you thinking?"

"Your dad deserves to be remembered and the American people should know that he didn't die in vain." Her voice dripped false sympathy. Maybe a weaker person would have fallen for it.

"It's a war. No one dies in vain." I shook my head and nearly laughed. "Hell, everyone dies in vain. My father is not your headline."

Uncle Mike leaned forward with his car-salesman smile. "Ember, this could be really good for the family. People are moved by what's happened, and we know college isn't cheap. We could all use this."

My face fell slack, unable to even process that he'd suggested we profit from Dad's death. A very bitter taste filled my mouth. "You're out of your mind if you think—" I sucked in my breath as I saw the pennant Ms. Cartwright pinned to Gus's bulletin board. West Point. "Get. That. Thing. Off. His. Wall."

"We thought it would be a good touch, army family and all. You'd be representing the army, so to speak." She made it sound so reasonable, like I was the one off my rocker.

"Dad went to Vanderbilt, not the Academy." Words slipped through my clenched teeth. I was afraid to give full rein to my temper. "Gus doesn't want to go to West Point, and he's not going to."

"Be fair, Ember. Gus should be proud of the military legacy in this family." Uncle Mike pulled a West Point shirt out of Ms. Cartwright's bag. "Besides, people will eat it up when we interview him in this. Who knows, maybe one day he'll be the military man in the family."

Something within me snapped. The fine web of civility I'd woven around myself after Dad died and Riley screwed Kayla shredded around me. They were not going to use Gus. I clamored over the bed and ripped the shirt from Uncle Mike's hand. "Get out!"

"Ember—"

"GET. OUT!" I gripped the shirt, longing to shred it, but it wouldn't be enough. I shoved through them and tore the pennant from the bulletin board. The thumbtacks went flying under the bed, skidding along the bare hardwood. "No story! No pennant! No West Point!" I held the offensive crap in front of me and herded them out of Gus's room. "Now *get out*!"

They scurried from the room, Ms. Cartwright's stilettos frantic on Mom's cherished hardwood floor. I chased them down the back steps, the camera and sound guys getting caught up in their wave of retreat. "Get out! Get out!" It was my mantra, and it was all I could think.

They bottlenecked at the kitchen door before popping through, scattering across the tile floor. Mom sat at the dining room table, a cup of coffee in her hand. Grams stood guard, wearing a look fiercer than I'd ever seen. I pitied that news crew. For a second. Maybe.

"Ember—" Uncle Mike started toward me, and I backed around the island to the kitchen sink.

"Don't! How dare you bring this in here! How dare you even think of putting such an idea into Gus's head! The army? West Point?" I shook the shirt and pennant as if they were his neck.

"It's just a symbol—"

"No! There will be no army for Gus, no West Point, no interview! Are you insane? Why would we ever want him to…to… No! This family has bled enough, and I will not let you walk in here and cut us any deeper!" My voice cracked.

I couldn't handle the images that pennant put into my head. Gus in a uniform. Gus laid to rest under an American flag.

I threw the pennant and T-shirt into the empty kitchen sink, then tore open the drawer to the right, pulling out the lighter Mom used for birthday candles. A click later, the flame burst to life, and I set the West Point shirt on fire.

"Ember! What are you doing?" Uncle Mike stepped forward, but the warning in my eyes must have been enough because he quickly retreated.

"That is what I think of your cute notions of dressing Gus up like a future soldier and parading our grief around for profit!" The flames rose from the sink as Captain Wilson came in, flanked by two other soldiers. "Now get the fuck out of our home!"

"Ember?" Gus's small voice broke through my rage. My gaze snapped to his worried eyes peeking backward over the sofa where he sat cuddled next to someone else, someone I couldn't bear to see me like this. Someone whose brown eyes were locked onto me and my insanity.

The smoke detector wailed, finally sensing the danger. At that moment, I seemed more hazardous than the fire. I reached around the flames and flipped on the faucet, using the spray attachment to drench the burned mess and wishing it would put out my rage as easily.

My heart raced, threatening to jump out of my chest, and my cheeks flamed as hot as the shirt I'd just destroyed.

Captain Wilson escorted the team out. "Don't bother contacting the Rose's. They've been warned. This family has signed no releases, and you are not authorized to use anything you heard or filmed here today."

"June, I hope you'll reconsider." Uncle Mike put his hand on Mom's shoulder.

"Not a chance, Mike."

Whoa. Mom spoke up, a hint of her usual stubbornness I

knew so well peeked out. What a relief.

"Please—"

Grams rose from her seat, her backbone stiff. "I believe my daughter-in-law asked you to leave, sir. Please don't abuse her hospitality by making her ask twice."

Uncle Mike shot one more pleading look at Mom. Her single, arched eyebrow said he wasn't getting anywhere with her. I hadn't lost her to the void if she could still fight back.

Before I could make more of an ass out of myself, I walked out the kitchen door and stood on the porch. The mountains rose up before me, consuming my vision, but all I could see were the flames I'd just doused. I leaned over the icy, wooden railing and let the chill seep in.

The door slid open on the track, and I cringed.

"Hey, you okay?" Josh's voice washed over me, bringing a wave of comfort I didn't need, didn't want. He'd just watched me go completely freaking postal.

"I told you I had this. You didn't need to come."

He leaned back against the railing next to me. "It's okay to lose it every once in a while."

"Every once in a while is more like every day right about now, and I don't want you seeing it." I took a deep breath to stop any more stupidity from leaking out of my mouth. The freezing air burned in my lungs, but it felt good.

"I don't mind."

I gave up examining the grain of the railing and lifted my head to meet his dark, understanding gaze. "Don't you get it? *I* mind, Josh! That's why I told you to stay away, to give me space and time to sort this shit out!" Deep breath. I had to stop yelling or he'd really think I was a nutcase. Instead, I started laughing, only solidifying my insanity. "Man, I never used to yell, and now it's all I do."

He reached out and ran his hand down my back, and I hated how delicious it felt. I jerked away from the touch and didn't miss the wounded look that crossed his eyes. "You can't be here. You can't see me like this, because if you do, it's all I'll think about when it comes to us. You can't save me all the time."

He crossed his arms in front of him, his breath visible in the freezing air. "For fuck's sake, December! You're carrying everyone in that damn house! Someone has to carry you. I can't just watch you suffer and do nothing."

"Stop watching! I told you not to come here! I told you to stay away, and you're everywhere! You're at hockey with Gus, and in my class, and you're…you're…just everywhere!" I couldn't let him see this. I couldn't be this weak, this insane. The man had watched me set a fire in my kitchen sink. Crap. Shit. Fuck.

"December."

"Go."

I didn't have to tell him twice. He sighed, shook his head, and walked away. The only sound I heard from his retreat was the door sliding open and shut. I slumped against the railing, using the ice to cool my flushed cheeks.

The door slid open again, and I nearly screamed in frustration. "I asked him to come." Gus laid his head on the railing, turning those trusting eyes on me.

"Why? How?"

"I have his phone number, duh." He seemed so much older than he was. "Mom was mad. It's better than sad, I know, but still. April called you, so I called Coach Walker. He told me I could whenever I wanted to."

Well. Crap. I stood and took him into my arms. "Sorry I yelled, buddy. Things are just complicated right now."

He burrowed into me. "Because Daddy's gone? Or because Riley isn't your boyfriend anymore?"

I kissed the top of his head. "Both, little man."

"You hate the army that much?"

I squeezed him tighter. "No. I don't hate the army. I just don't want anyone I love in it anymore." I couldn't lose another person I loved.

"The fire was cool."

Leave it to a seven-year-old to catch the basics. "Yeah, but don't do that, okay? I gotta go back to school. I have a class later."

He nodded. "Can you take me, too? I don't want to be here. It's sad here."

Pain rushed through my chest, but no tears came. Maybe I was finally past the point of crying.

Twenty minutes later, I had Gus and April dropped off at school and was headed back to the apartment. I didn't want to be the person I was at home. I didn't want to feel responsible for everyone. I wanted to be selfish, to sleep until ten and skip class, to focus on the weekend party schedule instead of the pee-wee hockey schedule. Just being twenty would be nice.

But I wasn't just twenty anymore.

I hauled my bag out of my car, cursing when I snagged a pocket on the gearshift. Would freaking anything go right today? I took the stairs to the fourth floor, needing to burn off some of the salted caramel mocha.

I reached our door and fumbled with the key. My fingers were still half numb from riding without the heat, but I wanted it cold. It slipped from my hand, hitting the carpet. I rested my forehead against the door and closed my eyes for a moment to keep from cursing at the lock. Like it was the damned problem.

I bent and picked it up, then slid it home, opening the door with a twist. Before I stepped through, a familiar frame filled my vision. Josh stepped off the elevator and headed toward me. My impulse was to run, jump, and kiss an apology into his mouth. I craved his hands on my skin, his mouth on mine. He had the power to make me forget for just a minute.

Which was why I couldn't. I wouldn't use him that way.

But what the hell was he doing here? Again?

"Josh, seriously?"

He glanced up from the messenger bag he was looking into and an incredulous look crossed his face. "Seriously, what?"

The guy was so aggravating. "You can't just follow me from my house to my apartment! I told you I need some damned time!"

He laughed, full-out, making me doubt his sanity. At least mine wasn't in jeopardy at the moment. He shook his head and walked toward me...and past me, stopping at the next door and slipping a key into the lock.

"Nice to meet you, neighbor." He gave me a mock salute, then opened and closed the door behind him, leaving me standing in the hallway like a moron. Crap.

"Ember? Is that you?" Sam called out from inside our apartment.

I walked in, dropping my bag in the front hall, and plopped down into the massive arm chair. She put down her laptop and watched me. "Chicky? What the hell is wrong with you?"

I shook my head. "Oh, I'm a hormonal, self-involved wench. You?"

She tossed her pint of Ben & Jerry's at me and I devoured it without checking the calories on the label.

Chapter Ten

Awkward. That was the only way to describe what it felt like to sit next to Josh Walker when he wasn't talking to me. It didn't matter that I didn't want him to talk to me. Right?

His gaze burned into me, but when I turned my head to catch him, he was staring back at the professor. By Friday evening, I was ready to eat myself alive with guilt.

I'd been a total bitch. The guy came when my little brother called, which pretty much elevated him to godlike status in the guy department, and he couldn't help that we'd moved in next door. Turns out he'd been living there two freaking years. If I could have disappeared through the floor in utter embarrassment, I would have.

"Hey, you there?" Sam caught me staring off into space in the general direction of the Dave Matthews poster in the living room.

"Yeah, I'm just distracted."

She pulled her robe snug around her body and adjusted her towel turban. "The girls and I are headed out in a couple hours. Why don't you come? You could use some rebound action."

I surveyed the mountain of school work on the coffee table in front of me. "I wish." Well, not the rebound, but the rest. "I could really use a drink, but Gus has practice early tomorrow and I told Mom I'd take him."

"Did she ask you to?"

"No, I offered." When she remained silent, I looked up from my childhood education text. "What?"

"It's been a month, Ember."

Like I needed someone to tell me how long it had been since I'd lost my dad. One month, two days, and eleven and a half hours since notification. "Yeah? And? She needs help."

"I'm not saying she doesn't. Look, I really admire what you've done. You've given up a hell of a lot more than any other kid would. I'm just saying maybe it's time to trust her a little more. Maybe you could start waiting for her to ask, instead of assuming she can't handle it all."

"You don't understand."

She sat next to me and pulled my hand off my notebook, holding it in hers. "You're right. I don't. No one really does. But I've seen your mom in action, through both of these last deployments, and in Kansas, too. She's tough. Just make sure you're not selling her short. Besides, isn't your Grams still watching out for her?"

"Yeah, she keeps saying she's leaving soon, but it's like she's waiting for something, some green light that we're okay. I'm just thankful she's still here, otherwise I think I would have moved back home." I smiled, realizing what Grams had saved me from. "Besides, Grams knows nothing about hockey."

A wicked smile sprung onto Sam's face. "Maybe Josh is the reason you wanted to take Gus?"

Blood rushed to my cheeks. "I have to apologize to him."

"Then go apologize." She stood up and toweled off her

hair. "Girl, the guy lives next door. Get your ass over there and say you're sorry. I have to go get my sexy on." She sashayed into her bedroom. Not like Sam needed any help in that department, but I knew whatever getup she'd choose would accentuate every asset the girl had.

I glanced at the clock: 7:15 p.m. The nervous pit in my stomach told me I was really going to do this. I put down my books and got my butt off the couch. Was I really going over there in jeans and a zip-up hoodie? Yup. It wasn't like I was trying to impress him, right? This sent the appropriate stay-away message. Plus, I hadn't put on makeup or shaved my legs. Who the hell would shave their legs for an apology?

Before I lost my nerve, I slipped out of our apartment, barefoot, and walked next door to his. Three knocks later, I held my breath and waited to make an ass out of myself again.

The door opened, and a lean, extremely hot blond guy answered. "Hello there," he drawled as his eyes drifted over me appreciatively.

"Hi, I'm Ember, your neighbor?"

A very sexy smile lit up his face. "Hello, Ember, my neighbor."

"Yeah." I peeked around him. "Does Josh happen to be here?"

His face fell. "Ah, shit. Did he already call dibs? You don't really look like the Josh type."

I arched my eyebrow at him, and he stuttered, "You're hot as hell, he just usually goes for the…"

"Barbies?" I was well aware of what "type" Josh went for.

"Exactly." He opened the door, making room for me to slide past him into a hallway that mirrored our own layout. "Walker! You got company!" He turned back to me. "Just in case he isn't what you're looking for…" He flashed a killer smile. "My name's Jagger."

I tried to ignore that he was hitting on me. He was really

good at it. "It's nice to meet you, Jagger."

"Oh, it's my pleasure." He held his tongue between his teeth, flashing a tongue ring.

"Jagger, back the fuck up off Ember."

My breath stopped, and then expelled in one huge rush.

Josh leaned against the wall, one ankle crossed. A pair of gray flannel pants hung low on his hips. One tug was all it would take. One tug.

My mouth dropped open before I could close it. He wasn't wearing a shirt. All that soft, inked skin draped across those muscles, and God, I remembered how it tasted. The thought of tasting it again had more than a spark raging through my thighs. Just being in the room with him turned me on in a way that had me seriously considering Sam's suggestion of a rebound.

"And another one bites the dust," Jagger muttered and left us alone in the entryway.

Josh didn't budge, waiting on me to make the first move. I didn't blame him since my signals blew so hot and cold. The guy never knew what he was in for.

I closed the gap between us, until I was close enough that I had to lean my head back to look in his eyes. Close enough that I caught the faint scent of sandalwood coming off him. I stood there, staring up while he held my gaze, unable to say what I needed to. How could I explain what I didn't understand? Those brown eyes burned right through me with an intensity I couldn't fathom, but wanted more of.

He reached out, cupping my face in one hand. "December?"

I stayed silent, not trusting my mouth. After all, what my mouth wanted betrayed what my head was preaching. My heartbeat sped up and my breath caught. I leaned into his palm, turning slightly to catch more of his incredible scent. Little droplets of water clung to his skin. He was straight out of the shower.

Fuck. I wanted him. I wanted him over me, weighting my body into a bed, a couch, a freaking kitchen counter. I needed this man. Not anyone else, just Josh.

I attacked, bringing his head, his lips to mine. There was no preamble, no gentle request this time. We met in a fury of open lips, both ready for the other. I sucked his tongue into my mouth. He growled. His hands sank down my back, skimming my ass before he gripped it and pulled me against him. He spun and pinned me to the wall.

Yes. This was what I wanted.

My fingers gripped his wet hair, desperate to bring him closer. He tasted like strawberry ice cream, and my brain sent hot images of me dripping it onto his stomach and licking it off. I couldn't help the moan that escaped into his mouth any more than I could stop the movement of my hips against him.

Those hot flannel pants hid nothing on this man.

He released my mouth, only to run his tongue down my throat. I let go of his head to unzip my hoodie. He lifted me higher, the muscles of his arms bulging, the tattoo rippling with his movements, and brought his mouth to my collarbone. The back of my head hit the wall as I arched my neck, rattling a few of the pictures on the wall. From the higher angle, I looked down on him, watching him take nips at my skin and then soothe with a soft kiss. When he looked back up at me, his eyes were so dark I could barely make out his pupils. He wanted me.

Good to know we were on the same page. I cupped his face with my hands, reveling in the softness of his freshly shaven skin. "Josh," I whispered.

His eyes widened, and I sank further into them, if that was even possible. He lowered me, rubbing my body against his in a delicious friction that made me want to shove his pants off with my feet. He conquered my mouth, stealing away all of my thoughts.

Kissing him was so fucking addictive. He changed pace, sped it up, mellowed it out, but kept me wondering what he was doing next. He gave me control and then took it back. Josh robbed me of every logical thought in my head except the quickest way to get him out of those clothes. I wanted to see where the lines in his abs headed. My hands slid down his chest, tracing along his stomach until I reached his pants. I skimmed under the elastic, needing to get my hands on him, to feel that soft skin under my fingertips.

He groaned against my mouth, which was the sexiest sound I'd heard since he'd made the same one in Breckenridge. "December." He panted against my mouth, resting his forehead against mine. "I'm fucking desperate to carry you to my bedroom, but I don't think this is what you want."

Wait. What *did* I want?

Oh my God. I'd basically assaulted him in his hallway. After I'd told him repeatedly to slow it down. What the hell was wrong with me?

I covered my face with my hands. "What am I doing?"

He gently pulled my hands away. "What *are* you doing?" His eyes had changed from lustful to compassionate. I couldn't battle this Josh.

"I came to say I'm sorry for the way I've been treating you. Sorry for the mixed signals." I laughed. "But apparently I jumped you instead, and now I'm sorry for that, too."

"Sorry for jumping me?" His grin sent another hum through my stomach.

I lost all pretense. "No. I'm not sorry for jumping you. I'm sorry about my god-awful timing."

His grin faltered. He stroked his thumb over my lips. "I told you I'm here for whatever you need, Ember. Jumping, apologies, whatever."

Whatever. I needed him, but was too frightened of what

that meant to acknowledge it, because more than anything, I needed myself. Why did it always feel like the part of me I needed was buried inside Josh?

"I'd better get back to studying." My excuse sounded lame even to my ears.

He stepped back. "I'd better get in the shower."

"Didn't you just...?"

His eyes sparkled with intensity, and I had to control every muscle to keep from diving for him and his offer of the bedroom. "Yeah, but I think I need another one at a different temperature."

Josh Walker was taking a cold shower for me? Maybe I could jump in behind him and warm up the water... "Oh. I'm sorry about that, too." Not really.

A slow, sexy smile spread across his face. "I'm not." He backed me into the wall again and leaned down, hovering right above my mouth. I was not going to give in again; I wasn't strong enough to step away twice, and I wasn't ready for a relationship. "If you apologize like that, feel free to treat me like shit any time you want. I will be your personal doormat."

He pressed a soft kiss to my lips.

"I have to go." I breathed unevenly. I had to get away... before I didn't.

He opened the door for me and watched until I was walking into my apartment. "Hey, December?"

I didn't want to turn around. I didn't want to see his half-naked body on display, or the lines of the tattoo I craved to trace with my tongue. "Yeah?"

"I hope you sleep better than I do."

The change in topics threw me. "You're not sleeping?"

He slowly shook his head. "Knowing my bedroom backs up to yours, that you're only a wall away, lying in bed, makes that pretty fucking impossible."

Every muscle in my body loosened, tingles of energy rushing through me. Could a girl orgasm from words? A charged silence passed between us.

"'Night."

It was my turn to stare until he shut the door behind him. I stumbled into our apartment, shutting the door behind me, then sinking to the floor. Sam popped around the corner, her hair styled and makeup half done. "Did you apologize?"

I could have denied what had happened, but if I was going to choose a friend to trust, then Sam was the perfect candidate. She'd never betrayed me once in our five years of friendship. "If by apologize, you mean nearly swallowing his tongue and debating if I should remove his pants with my hands or teeth?"

"Nuh-uh!" She pulled me off the floor and wrapped her arm around me. "Oh, girl, you'd better dish." She plopped me down on her bed and went back to the vanity, watching my reflection as she expertly applied her makeup.

"I'm not even sure what to say."

She turned in her seat. "How about you start with how you finally got the guy you drooled all over freshman year?"

Freshman year. I hadn't just drooled all over him, I'd fantasized about him, written his last name attached to mine in the back of my English notebook. He'd been total teenage girl drool material, but it hadn't been the eight-pack abs from the weight room that got me. No, his devil-may-care grin was what drew me to him, the way he never seemed to care what social norm dictated.

"Earth to Ember."

"Hmmm?"

"Lost in Josh-land?"

"Just thinking about how things have changed. Five years ago I never would have had the guts to even speak to Josh." Oh no, our social orbits were nowhere near each other. He had been the sun, and I had been somewhere like Pluto, trying, but still not even a planet.

"Remember when I dared you to ask him to Sadie Hawkins?" She applied her mascara like the cosmetic expert she was.

The memory swept over me, and I laughed. "Thank God I found out Vickie Brasier already had! Could you have imagined the utter embarrassment?"

"Well, now you're hooking up with him!"

I grimaced. "Not exactly hooked up. More like...half hooked up?"

She waggled her finger at me. "You let that man get away without snatching a piece?"

"He kind of turned me down." Could she hear the sheer mortification coming through the high pitch of my voice? I sure could.

"Huh."

"What's that supposed to mean?"

She went back to her mascara. "It's just that he has kind of the same reputation here as he did in high school. The girls chase him, and he lets them 'catch', if you will. He's the perfect rebound guy for you, actually. He doesn't tend to go back to pastures he's already grazed. Hmmmm."

"Sam, spit it out!"

Her eyes locked with mine in the mirror. "I don't know. I don't really hear about him turning hot girls away."

"Great, so I'm broken."

"Why don't you ask him about it at hockey tomorrow? He's never had a problem with his reputation."

"Oh yeah, that sounds logical and all. 'Hey, Josh, why didn't you sleep with me when I threw myself at you?' Is that something you would ask?" I zipped my hoodie to the neck, suddenly feeling a little cheap.

"You threw yourself at him?"

"The night I found Riley and Kayla."

We hadn't really broached the Riley/Kayla topic. She knew why I left, voiced her disgust at Kayla and all, but had never said I told you so. "What exactly did he say?"

I pulled my knees up to my chest. "He wasn't having sex with me until it was about 'us,' and not just about the damage on me."

Her mascara tube hit the vanity, and her mouth gaped open. "Holy shit. You got to Josh Walker."

I was too scared to smile. "Not as much as he's gotten to me."

Chapter Eleven

There wasn't enough caffeine in the world to justify Gus being on the ice at seven a.m. It took about a half hour for him to gear up, fifteen minutes to drive to the arena, a ten minute well-check on Mom, which I promised I'd finish after practice, and a half-hour drive to Mom's house to pick up Gus. That had me getting up at five on a Saturday morning and forsaking my morning run. The alteration in my schedule had my skin crawling, but Gus was worth the adjustment.

The seven minute pit stop at Starbucks made this possible. No caffeine, no wakey. That's how my body worked.

I finished tightening his skates, kissed his curls, and sent him to the ice with a playful swat on his backside. "Go get 'em, Tiger!"

"Ha! Never heard that one," he threw back.

Two more weeks of the season and then playoffs. I could keep this up for that long. Besides, even though Mom had been awake, she hadn't really been there. Fake smile, fake laugh, but real pancakes. One day off from Sunday, but the effort was there, and much appreciated. I hesitated to hope that she was getting better, but maybe if I carried her just a little further, she'd come back to us for real.

My mocha warmed my hands as my backside absorbed the chill from the steel bleachers. I nodded to the two blond girls I'd seen here last week and attempted not to let my eyes bug out of my head at what Tweedledee and Tweedledum were wearing. It was way too freaking early to show that much cleavage at a kids' hockey game. I kind of hoped they froze their assets off. I squashed my mean thoughts and searched the coaches, but Josh wasn't here, yet. It wasn't like him to be late when hockey was involved.

I took my book out of my bag and went back to studying my mind-numbing childhood education texts. If I could knock this out this morning, I had the rest of the weekend to indulge in my history reading.

Every few pages, I lifted my head, telling myself I was checking on Gus. I was really looking for Josh. Maybe I should have apologized for what happened last night, but look how that apology turned out. If I tried to say I'm sorry now, I would probably start humping his leg like a horny dog.

"I guess no Walker brownie points today," one of the Tweedle twins muttered behind me.

I locked my gaze on Gus, refusing to turn around and blatantly stare at the stalkers behind me. It didn't stop me from listening, though.

"I know." Tweedledum sighed. "Totally makes getting up so damn early a waste of time if we can't go out to breakfast with him."

"I guess we could take Jagger out," Tweedledee muttered. I hadn't noticed before that Jagger coached with Josh.

"You've already slept with Jagger."

"Only because Josh wasn't interested."

I sputtered, nearly sending coffee out my nose.

"Yeah, he's been kinda off for the last few weeks, you

know? He's turning *everyone* down." Tweedledum sounded annoyed. "And sorry, but Jagger may be hot, but he's no Josh."

He was turning down everyone. I bit back my smile and tried to tune out of their conversation and focus on my work when Gus wasn't on the ice. By the time the game was over, he'd scored one goal and had an assist for the win. Each time, he'd pointed to me in the stands like such a big man. I was so proud of him.

Dad would have been proud of him, too.

The familiar ache settled in my chest. The pain wasn't lessening; it was still sharp at moments and dull at others, but it was sinking in my heart, making room for other things, too. I had room to smile at Gus's goal, to find joy in his grin.

I blew him a kiss after the team fell on each other in a melee of black and gold. He needed this. Hell, *I* needed this.

Gus waved at me, but it was Jagger who faked receiving the kiss and blew one back. I couldn't stop the laughter that bubbled out of me.

It didn't go unnoticed by the Tweedle twins.

"Hey, you, Red!" Tweedledum shouted down to me.

I gathered what composure I had and turned. "Yes?"

"Was Jagger Bateman kissing at you?" Her eyes narrowed and her lips turned in an insulted sneer. Great.

I took a deep breath. This was how those crazy hockey-parent YouTube clips started. "I'm his next-door neighbor. He was just goofing around. I'm sorry, is he your boyfriend?" I damn well knew the answer to that one.

Did she flush? "No, I just know him." Her voice dropped suggestively. "Really well."

The other girl narrowed her eyes. "Yeah, and I'm really close to Josh, his roommate."

What. A. Bitch. "Ah, well, to me he's just my neighbor and my little brother's hockey coach. Which one is your brother?"

Now they both flushed scarlet. "We just come to support the team."

"Yeah," I dropped my gaze at their exposed cleavage and raised my eyebrows. "Those puppies definitely need all the support they can get at seven a.m."

The kids cleared off to the locker room, and Jagger motioned me over. "See you later, girls. Don't catch a cold!" I snagged my bag and empty tumbler as I hopped off the bleachers. I couldn't get away from them fast enough.

"What's up?" I asked Jagger as he waited by the locker room doors. "Gus okay?"

He gave me a killer smile, but it didn't make me want to strip him naked and pounce the way Josh's smile did. Good to know I was discerning with my horniness. "Yeah, he was a star out there today. Just wanted to tell you he lost a snap when he took off his helmet, so just in case he forgets to tell you, he needs that fixed before practice on Monday."

"Awesome. Thanks, Jagger." He might have been all jokes and smiles, but I liked that he was serious when it came to the kids.

"No problem." He leaned back against the wall, changing gears. "I know you're really here for Gus, but you're here for Josh, too, huh?"

There was no point lying to Josh's roommate. I nodded my head slightly. "Pathetic, I know."

"He's different around you," he admitted, looking at me through assessing eyes.

"He's different around every girl!" Tweedledee sang, popping over. "Hiya, Jagger."

Jagger smiled at the girls, "Heather, Sophie, nice to see you." Darn, now I knew their names. I liked my version better.

Wait one second. *Heather*? Was she the one texting Josh?

"So where's Josh?" Heather, aka Tweedledum, asked.

"Yeah, did he go and disappear again?" Tweedledee, Sophie, chimed in.

"He's busy this weekend." Jagger shot me a look I couldn't interpret. "Ember, I'm sure I'll see you around. Gus should be out in a sec. Don't forget about the helmet, okay?"

I nodded to him, keeping my breathing even and my back to the girls who laid obvious claims to the boys next door.

"You know Josh disappears every few weeks, right?" Heather asked me, stepping into my vision. "Not that you'd need to know the schedule of your...neighbor." She looked me up and down and then smirked like my jeans and zip-up Tigers fleece weren't good enough for her.

Sophie chimed in. "Every few weeks he just needs to...go blow off some steam."

"Yeah, like with a new girl," Heather muttered under her breath, but I heard her. She meant me to.

I'd never been so thankful to see sweat-covered curls as I was when Gus came out of the locker room. "Ember! Did you see that rockin' goal?"

I took his stick, but he was picky about carrying his own gear. "Yeah, you're a star!"

"Ladies." Gus gave the girls the head nod. He'd been spending too much time with Josh.

"See you next stalking opportunity?" I asked with a sweet smile. They glared, and we walked out. "I think this victory deserves donuts!"

"Score!"

Forty-five minutes later, armed with mochachinos and a dozen donuts, we made it home. I juggled the coffees while Gus manhandled the donuts, but they made it in the door surprisingly in one piece. Mom and Grams sat at the dining room table. Mom gave us a forced smile as we came in.

Gus slid the donuts onto the table and didn't bother getting a napkin or washing his hands before he stuffed a chocolate-glazed into his mouth. He was always famished after games.

"How was the game?" Mom asked me, gawking at his face.

"Great, they won, three to one, and Gus scored a goal and an assist." I handed out the coffees, leaving April's in the holder. She probably wouldn't be up for hours, but at least she wouldn't bitch that I'd forgotten her on the coffee run.

"Good job!" Grams cheered.

Gus wiped his face with the back of his hand. "Thanks, Grams! Mom, do you think you can come next week? It's parents weekend and our last game before playoffs."

Her smile faltered, and I almost jumped in for her. "We'll see how this week goes, okay?"

No one mentioned that she hadn't left the house since the funeral.

"Cool!" He reached for the box again, and Mom snapped the lid shut.

"Not until you shower the stink off you and put your sweaty duds in the hamper, mister."

"Yes, ma'am," he grumbled, but headed for the laundry room and back stairs.

She'd disciplined him. She'd cared. She'd noticed something outside herself for real, no faking. I couldn't help the smile that spread across my face as I slipped into my seat. Flanked by Grams and Mom, the heaviness eased, like some of the weight I'd been carrying was lifted off my soul.

The phone went and wrecked it while I was mid-Boston-cream bite. "Hello?" I swallowed, hoping I didn't sound too garbled.

"December? This is Captain Wilson."

I knew it was routine, and he was just checking up on us, but my stomach still plummeted. There wasn't a single pleasant event I could associate with that man. "What's up,

Captain Wilson?"

Mom's head snapped to attention, her gaze burning into me.

"Some things came in for you. Would it be okay if I dropped them off in about fifteen minutes?"

"Yeah, no problem. See you in a few." We hung up, and I looked to Mom. "Captain Wilson will be here in about fifteen minutes. He has a few things to give us."

Panic walked in and sat on my chest. I swallowed with difficulty. What was so important that it couldn't wait until Monday? Papers? More insurance work?

"How kind of him to give up his Saturday morning," Grams commented when Mom couldn't.

I didn't want to know.

I pushed back from the table and headed upstairs to wake April. I swung open her door, and the scent of alcohol and vomit assaulted me. "Holy shit." I covered my nose with the sleeve of my fleece and shook my sister's still-dressed body. "April, wake up."

She mumbled incoherently and dug deeper into her nest of blankets. I tried again, gently moving her shoulders. Then she breathed on me, and I almost wished I hadn't moved her.

Death. She smelled like death that had been rolled in crap and a bottle of Cuervo. I grabbed ahold of her covers and yanked back with one hard pull, leaving her sputtering. "What the fuck, Ember!"

"Get your ass up and into the shower! Captain Wilson is on his way, and Mom is going to need us." I threw her blankets into the hamper. They smelled suspiciously like puke.

"Give me back my blankets and leave me alone. I don't feel good." She burrowed into her pillows.

I calmly walked across the hall to the bathroom, poured a large glass of water, and snagged two Tylenol from the cabinet. I lowered myself to her bed and rubbed her head.

"I know you don't feel good, honey. Take these." *You stupid, stupid girl.*

She sat up and gave me a sleepy acknowledgement, swallowing the Tylenol and hitting the mattress with a thud. "Thank you. Now leave me alone."

I stood quietly and took stock. She was pale, clammy, stinky, and hungover. Grams would have a field day in here, but I couldn't do that to either of them. I lifted the glass of water high into the air and poured it down over her face. She came up spitting and shrieking. "You bitch!"

I shook the final droplets out of the glass and set it down on her nightstand. "Yup. Now get your ass out of bed." I threw the latches and slid open her window, letting the rancid room breathe the frigid Colorado air. "You want to drink like a big girl? Then you deal with the big-girl consequences. Now get in the shower, and for the love of God, brush your teeth!"

I waited until she marched out of her room and into the bathroom, flipping me off as she closed the door behind her. Too damn bad. She could be pissed; I really didn't care.

Gus was already in the dining room and on his third donut before I made it downstairs. He was freshly washed and covered in chocolate. "Em-buh?" he called out with his mouth full.

"Yup?"

He swallowed. "Can I have your strawberry glazed?"

I looked at the donut I'd bought because it reminded me of how Josh tasted last night and nodded. "Go for it, buddy. Do me a favor and go watch a movie in your room? It's not going to be fun down here for a bit."

He nodded, already consumed with his strawberry donut, and headed up the stairs. With the three of us at the table again, there was no noise except the ticking of the pendulum from the grandfather clock.

It started to sound like the clicking of a roller coaster,

dragging me up the first hill. The problem was that I didn't know what was coming, how far or fast the drop to the bottom would be. How far my heart would fall out of my chest again.

But there was beauty in not knowing what was coming my way, in being unable to brace for impact.

The doorbell rang, and I jumped, despite knowing he was coming. We all three stood, and this time, Mom answered the door. "Captain Wilson."

"It's good to see you, ma'am," he answered, removing his cover as he entered the house. "Where would you like it?"

She pointed into the living room. Two soldiers walked in tandem, carrying a large, black Tough Box. Then another pair of soldiers did the same. They set the black boxes in front of the couch, on either side of the coffee table. What the hell?

The men stood back, shifting their weight awkwardly as I took a closer look. On the top of the boxes, white writing stood out in dark contrast. "Howard. 5928."

These were the things my father had taken to Afghanistan with him.

Chapter Twelve

No. No. No. How much more could we take?

Grams sat Mom down on the couch. She'd deserted us again, retreated into her mind and left me to stand in her place. I swallowed the bitter pill and stepped up. "This is all my dad's, right?"

Captain Wilson nodded. "It came in late last night, but I didn't want to make you wait any more than you had to. Would you like to go through his inventory?"

"Just let me sign for it."

"December, it would be best to verify that it's all here," he urged.

I snatched the clipboard from him. "Unless you have Dad in there, it doesn't matter what the hell is in these boxes." I furiously scribbled my name over yet another government form that threw Dad's death in my face. I signed, dated. Flipped to another page. Signed. Dated. Flipped again. Signed. Dated. I could have been giving April up for adoption for all I knew. I didn't bother reading anything anymore.

"Would you like us to open them, or leave the

combinations with you?"

Mom was in no position to answer.

Grams raised her eyebrows, asking me. It was always freaking up to me.

I raked my hands through my hair and took a breath, getting control back. "Open them now, please. Let's get this over with."

Two soldiers stepped forward, careful not to jar Mom and Grams, and opened the locks with nearly simultaneous pops. Without further preamble, the hinges squeaked as they ripped off the scabs we'd fought so hard to grow and opened up new crates of grief.

"Is there anything else?" I asked the captain, unable to take the vacant look on Mom's face for another minute.

"No, ma'am. These are all of his belongings sent home by his unit."

All of his belongings meant his journal! "His laptop is in there, right?"

"Yes, ma'am. We had to wait for the computer to be cleared, which is why it took so long." He looked down at the floor and I grasped his meaning.

"Cleared his computer?" I asked, trying to misunderstand him. "You mean checked for viruses, or classified data, right?"

He grimaced and took a breath. "No, ma'am. Official policy states we have to wipe the hard drive before returning it to the family."

You had to be fucking kidding me. "You wiped his hard drive?"

"Yes, ma'am." He was having trouble holding my gaze.

"His pictures? His journal? Everything we had of him? You just erased it like you were taking out yesterday's trash?" My fingernails dug into the palms of my hands, desperate to draw any blood they could. Even mine.

"Please understand—"

"No! You stole from us! You took something you had no right to!" I shook my head, trying to dislodge this nightmare. "We've done everything you've asked for! Everything! Why would you do this to us?"

"It's policy."

"Screw your policy. You erased what was left of him! His thoughts! This is wrong, and you know it!"

Mom's low wail ripped through me, finally letting loose the very sound bottled inside me. Her misery echoed my own, and I dismissed Captain Wilson by turning my back.

Mom knelt in front of one of the boxes, one of his army-tan T-shirts held up against her face, breathing him in on the inhale, screaming on the exhale, calling out his name. My throat closed up, but I found my voice. "Get out."

I didn't need to say it twice.

The soldiers filed out into the fresh air and left us trapped within our own grief.

"What's going on?" April struggled down the stairs, and I didn't have the energy to yell at her about her hangover anymore.

"Dad's stuff," I answered, gently lifting Mom to the couch by her arms. Grams rocked her like a baby as she kept the shirt against her nose, soaking it in tears and gut-wrenching sobs. She hadn't cried like this before, not that I'd heard. She'd been too numbed, too full of shock to grieve like this a month ago. I almost wished I could shove her back into her catatonic state and spare her all of this.

I picked up another T-shirt and brought it to my nose. It smelled like him, like rainy days and reading on the couch. It smelled like hugs and scraped knees and comfort over first heartbreaks. It smelled like him so much that he could have been wearing it. But that was impossible. He was buried twenty minutes from here and couldn't wear this shirt again.

I would never have another hug, another laugh, another Sunday crossword.

All I had was this damned shirt, and I understood Mom's wailing. It echoed the screams building in my heart that I didn't dare let escape. Instead, I took another breath of Dad's scent and wondered if they had been thoughtful enough not to wash it.

"What do we do?" April's voice shook next to me.

I'd seen Mom do it for every deployment, and this was no exception. "Get the Ziploc bags. The big ones."

She came back a moment later with the gallon-sized bags. Soon, these shirts wouldn't smell like him anymore, and we really would have lost every part of him. "Start smelling the shirts. If it smells like Dad, bag it."

"Why?"

I swallowed back my tears. "When you were two and Dad deployed, you had night terrors. No one knew why, but Mom couldn't get them to stop." I nearly laughed. "God, they told me this story over and over. Anyway, Mom never washed Dad's pillowcase, so she slipped it over your pillow. It smelled like him, and you slept. Once that smell wore off, she unbagged some of his shirts that she'd saved and covered your pillow with those."

Silent tears tracked down my sister's face. "Okay."

I squeezed her hand. No words would do.

While Grams let Mom cry it out, April and I sorted the things that smelled like him from the things we knew had been washed, bleached, or never worn. After the second box, we had seven shirts that smelled like Dad.

I gathered up the bags and took them upstairs and into Mom's walk-in closet. The bottom drawer of the tall dresser was empty. It's where he'd kept all these shirts. I slid them into the drawer and shut it.

I stood, taking stock of the top of the dresser where he

kept his treasures, as he had called them, the little things we'd made for him over the years out of rice and macaroni and egg cartons. My handprint in plaster from his first Father's Day sat next to a picture of all three of us we'd given him for his last.

My knees gave out, and I sank to the floor. I gave myself ten minutes and cried out everything I could, letting the sobs rack me and wreck me, giving in to the utter misery of losing him. This had to be it, right? This had to be the last big moment of pain.

How did we get here? We'd been doing so well, healing, moving forward, and now it was back to square one, feeling like the army walked in and notified us today. Why couldn't there be a clear path out of this mess? Why did everything have to be so garbled and undefined and utterly fucked up?

Would this end before it broke me into unmendable pieces?

I wanted someone to hold me, to tell me it was going to be okay, to assure me that my life hadn't ended with Dad's. I wanted solace, and comfort, and not to think about it for a while. Wasn't there anyone else who could help carry the weight of this house?

More than anything, I wanted Josh's arms around me, and that alarmed me more than any of my other desires. But as scary as wanting him was, at least I knew wanting him would never bring me here, he'd never be a soldier, never be draped in a flag.

"Ember?" Gus's voice came into the bedroom, breaking me out of my pity party.

I wiped the tears from my eyes, thankful I'd started wearing waterproof mascara since Dad was killed, and walked out of the closet. "Hey, little man."

"Mom is crying again."

"We got Dad's stuff this morning, and it's hard for her

right now."

He nodded slowly. He held out his hand, and I took it, walking downstairs with him. Dad's things were stacked neatly on the furniture, waiting for Mom to tell us what to do with them.

I found his patrol cap on the coffee table and fought with myself momentarily before I placed it on Gus's head. It didn't mean he was going to be a soldier, and I knew that, but it hurt to see the multi-cam pattern on his sweet face.

The diamond of Grams's wedding band caught my eye in the sunlight. She had lost both her husband and son. Tears watered her eyes, but she didn't let them fall as she rocked Mom back and forth, like she was trying to absorb some of her pain. I didn't see how Grams could have room for any more than what she already carried.

I sat down next to my mother, who'd begun hiccupping now that the wailing had stopped. "Mom, do you want us to sort this out or just put it back in the boxes? We don't have to do this now."

Her eyes skipped around the room until they landed on the boxes. Then she made her first Dad-related decision. "Return the army gear to the boxes, leave the personal stuff out. One thing at a time, right?"

I forced a smile. "Right."

We loaded the scrubs and uniforms back into the boxes but left out the pictures he'd taken with him, his shaving kit, and the odds and ends. The computer would make a great door stop. I picked up the hardback copy of his favorite book, Kahlil Gibran's *The Prophet*. He nearly had the whole thing memorized, and the cover was worn in spots from his hands. I thumbed through the pages, smiling at my favorite passages, feeling the rush of pain as I came across his.

Papers fluttered to the floor before I could catch them. I closed the book and picked them up. Sealed envelopes with names on them: June. April. Mom. August. December. "Mom?" I showed her the letters.

She sucked in her breath and stretched out her shaking hands. I gave the letters to everyone. He'd managed to send a piece of himself from so far away. I heard ripping and tearing as everyone dug into them.

Everyone but me.

If I opened it now, that would be it, and I would never hear from Dad again. I couldn't accept that.

I tucked mine into my back pocket and went to help Gus. "I got it," he replied, and took his letter to his room. Everyone had pulled away, experiencing a private moment with Dad.

I finished packing up his things and took the rest to Mom's room. She might not be up for it now, but eventually she'd want to know where these things went. She'd pulled herself out of this before, and I knew she'd do it again. Until then, I'd stand watch like Dad would want.

I called Sam and stayed the night with my family, curled up in my bed. The sun rose; snow settled in and came down in thick blankets of fluffy white madness.

I walked downstairs to the smell of sausage frying in the pan, and Mom singing. Mom. Singing. I peeked my head around the corner ninja-style, wondering if she'd been snatched and replaced during the night, but no. She was singing "Les Misérables," which was pretty dang ironic, flipping sausage while Grams scrambled some eggs.

"Good morning, sleepy," Mom said with a wave of her spatula.

I took a seat at the bar, and Grams handed me a fresh cup of coffee, doctored just the way I liked it. I was afraid to drink, or pinch myself. I was afraid to wake up and find Mom catatonic in bed again, unable to move.

"Looks like we're getting some snow," I said harmlessly, testing the waters of normal conversation.

"We're supposed to get seven inches today, but the airport should be back open tomorrow," Grams said with a wink. "I booked my flight for tomorrow evening. Would you mind taking me?"

I shook my head. "Happy to do it." Happy to take her, devastated that she was leaving. I took a long sip of my coffee and watched Mom. She moved with practiced ease, maybe a little stiff in places, but she was here. Her eyes were puffy from crying all day yesterday, but something had changed when she read the letter.

Mom was coming back to us.

By five o'clock, there was still no getting out of our subdivision. Not in my little VW. I really wanted to get back to the apartment. There, I could study, lose myself in campus, pretend none of this was really happening.

Now I understood why Grams had been so adamant that I take the apartment with Sam and not move home. I might have suffocated in my grief here.

Grams gathered up her sewing basket and sat on the couch next to me. She took out the service flag, the one that had hung in our window for years. I knew the tradition. Those with a son or, as tradition wavered, a husband deployed to war hung a simple white banner, outlined in red with a blue star in the middle. It was a matter of pride, announcing you had given something for this country, that the family had done their part.

But when a soldier was lost, those blue threads of the star were replaced with gold, proclaiming his sacrifice and the grief of the family. I watched, entranced, as Grams threaded the needle with shiny gold thread and began to stitch.

"This is what you were waiting for, right?" I asked. "Before you left to go home, you wanted to be here when they brought his things."

She looked over her sewing spectacles at me. "Yes. I knew this would hit your mother, tear her apart. But whatever my Justin said to her in that letter seemed to pull her out of it a little. She's surprising me, and I think she's ready to begin living again. So am I."

"I'm scared for you to go," I quietly admitted, scared Mom would hear me.

"December, you have to trust your mother. You have held her up for so long, but you need to let her walk on her own now. Gus and April aren't your responsibility anymore. Live your life, sweet girl." She looked back to the flag and continued her work. "Your father died. You did not. I did not." She ended on a whisper. "It is the business of the living to keep on doing so. We are no exception. We are not the first family to lose a man to war, and I fear we will not be the last. But we will be resilient."

Through. Pull. Push. Through. Pull. Push. Over and over she drew the needle through the flag, leaving the blue outline of the star, all that was allowed to remain of him according to tradition. She stitched on the gold star, its shiny, reflective threads changing the definition of my father's life from one of service to one of sacrifice. That stupid gold star declared this one event in his life, his death, more important than all of the nineteen years that blue star had witnessed while hanging in our living room window.

Somehow, in the circus of the last month, everything with Riley...with Josh...Dad's death had overshadowed his life, and that made me angrier than anything else.

Chapter Thirteen

Environmentally friendly or not, I wished Colorado would have salted the roads. The red-gravel crap did nothing to increase traction. It was a hell of a drive to school on Monday morning.

I slid into my seat at class and took out my book and the chapter outline I'd done while reading. I'd been so rushed getting up north for school that I'd forgotten my student ID and hadn't even had time to grab coffee, which did not bode well for my day.

A steaming cup of heaven was set down on my desk. I looked over to see Josh smile and take his seat. "I saw Sam this morning, and she said you'd stayed down south because of the snow last night. I figured it was probably a white-knuckle drive in today."

I nodded. "It was a little hellacious."

"I would have driven you. One phone call and you would have been cozy in the Jeep." He pointed to the cup. "Coffee and all."

I had to suppress my smile. "I told you, I can handle

myself without you rushing in to save me. Besides, I heard you were busy this weekend." A twinge of bitterness slipped into my tone. I couldn't help but wonder who he'd been with.

"From who?"

I took a long drink of the delicious caffeine and ignored his question as our professor started class.

He snuck sideways looks at me all class long, and I diligently kept my head down. I could concentrate on the Civil War. Yeah, that's what I'd do. The problem with that logic was that I spent the whole hour thinking about not thinking about Josh. Epic fail.

Where had he gone this weekend? Who was he with? Why the hell did I care? I'd made it clear to him that we weren't in a relationship, so what right did I have to even know the answers? None.

Class could not get out soon enough. By the time the prof dismissed us, I'd already packed my bag so I could lunge for the door. I made it out of the building and into the crisp air before Josh caught up to me, matching my pace.

"Was the room on fire?"

Yes. I was going up in freaking flames. I blushed. "Nope, just busy today."

"Right. Want to snag a late breakfast before you head off to study?"

I paused in the middle of the snow-covered courtyard, and he stopped. "We shouldn't. I mean, I can't. I mean... crap."

He laughed, attracting the attention of nearly every girl on the quad. "I guess that's a no?"

I hated being this flustered. "Yes. I mean no, because we're not dating."

"I'm quite happy where we're at." A look of heated intensity came over him as his gaze dropped to my lips. "Problem is you keep telling me we're somewhere else."

But that didn't change the facts here. "I'm so sorry about Friday. Some apology, huh?"

He stepped close enough that I caught his sandalwood scent. I wished I could put my hormones in time-out. In the corner. Far away.

He gently lifted my chin and brushed his lips over mine. "Ember, I adore the way you apologize."

Crap. Was the man's voice directly linked to the throbbing between my freaking thighs? I called on every ounce of strength I possessed and stepped back from him. I didn't miss the appraising stares we were getting from the other kids on campus.

"Nothing has changed, Josh." I had to repeat that enough so I'd believe it. "You're...you, all Josh-y and perfect...now, but I know it's just a matter of time..."

The muscle in his jaw flexed. "A matter of time until what?"

"You know." I glanced around us, keeping my voice low.

"No, Ember, I'm afraid I don't." He raised his voice, uncaring of prying eyes.

On cue, Tweedledum waved as she walked by, giving her ass a deliberate sway. "Hiya, Josh. Maybe I can see you later?"

His eyes didn't stray from mine. "Not a good time, Heather."

I pointed to her back as she shimmied away. "Right there. You know girls will always be lined up for you, and it's not like you to turn them down. I'm me...and you're...you, and it's only a matter of time until you realize the chase isn't as fun when the rabbit is caught. Especially when the rabbit isn't exactly all put together."

He clenched and unclenched his teeth until he took a deep breath. "Listen up. Forget whatever it is you think is 'like me.' I haven't so much as *touched* another girl since that night in Breckenridge. And it's not because they're not asking. It's because they're not *you*." He raked his hands through his hair, tugging on the strands. "Have some faith!"

"Faith gets you screwed over, Josh, and Riley wasn't even a quarter as sought after as you are. You're Josh-freaking-Walker!"

"And you're December-freaking-Howard, and you happen to be the only girl I'm interested in. I'm not Riley! When I make a choice, that's it. I don't back down. I didn't get where I am in hockey or school by backing down, and I choose you."

"I'm nowhere near ready to be anyone's choice." Not ready to risk my heart.

His eyes narrowed, but he let my jab slip. "One day you will be, and I'll still be here, no matter how hard you push me away." With a sigh, he turned to leave.

"Why?" I called after him. "Why are you doing this?"

He looked back, his knuckles white with restraint on his bag. "Because I'm masochistic enough to care about you, and someone has to, Ember." All hint of teasing was gone.

I stopped at the university gym and ran six miles, trying to outpace everything that seemed to be chasing me. I lost myself in my iPod and the rhythm of my feet against the treadmill, refusing to think of anything but my breathing.

I needed a plan. I needed to know what the heck I was doing.

Once I made it home, showered, dried, and dressed, I unpacked my bag.

Dad's letter slipped out onto my desk.

I picked it up and sat on the bed, tracing my finger over his curt scroll. I wanted to crawl inside the moment he'd penned my name, as if there was a way to reach out and touch him through the ink. I lifted the envelope to my nose, seeking some trace of him, some proof he'd really held this. No such luck; it smelled like plain paper.

The envelope was crisp and white, not like the ones that had been through the overseas mail system to make it to us. This letter had never seen the outside of his book. When had he written it? Which deployment was this penned for? Did he always write one? I stared at the sealed envelope.

Dad, did you know you were going to die?

"Ember? You here?" Sam's voice rang out from the entry, accompanied by the sounds of her book bag hitting the floor.

"Yeah." I stashed the envelope on the top of my bookshelf, between a picture of Gus and one taken during our last trip to Breckenridge. Time to act normal.

"Awesome, because Kappa Omega is having a party on Friday and we scored an invite!" She waved the golden envelope in the air like a trophy.

"No way. Frat boys are the ones who screw your roommate when you're not looking."

"Promise? I'd love to get a piece of some Kappa Omega boys." She breezed past me into my room and flung open the doors of my closet, and I couldn't help but laugh. "Girl. You know you're twenty, right?" She pulled out a ribbed turtleneck. "Twenty, not forty-five."

I grabbed it out of her hands. "Hey, that's Ann Taylor!"

"That's ancient librarian." She grabbed my modest neckline and yanked it lower, exposing a crazy amount of cleavage for ten a.m. "Whip out the girls, because we're finding you a rebound. If you won't jump Josh," she muttered, "because you're insane, then we'll find you a hot little frat boy."

Josh was off limits. I wasn't bringing him into the shit-fest my head was at the moment, but I couldn't see myself hooking up with some random guy either. "Maybe this isn't such a good idea."

Sam was already pulling me through our apartment into

her room. She opened her closet and started throwing clothes into my arms. "This is a brilliant idea. Hey, put that phone away! What are you doing? We're planning your social debut here!"

I ignored her and dialed Mom's cell. It was Monday, and I had to check up. "Hey, Mom?"

"Ember? What's up, honey?"

"Just checking that you got Gus's helmet fixed." If not, I still had time to pick up a new snap before tonight's practice.

"All done. We're heading to the rink after school. Did you want to come watch?"

The rink, where Josh would be. Where I'd have to listen to the Tweedle twins discuss him. Where Mom would think I was watching over her because I couldn't trust her.

I needed a little distance from Josh to sort myself out, and I needed to trust Mom.

I had to start somewhere.

"Actually, I'm going to get caught up on some homework. Kiss Gus for me, okay?"

I heard her sigh of relief through the phone. "Absolutely. Remember, playoff game is Saturday morning, and you know he'll be looking for you."

Yeah, they'd both be looking for me. "No problem, Mom."

Chapter Fourteen

Snow Bash was the sought-after party invite of February. Sam dressed me in a blue, strapless cocktail dress and pinned my hair up. Friday night came with the agenda of finding a rebound guy.

She handed our invite to the plebe at the door, flashing him a killer smile before yanking me inside. Her sequin-covered dress lit up like a disco ball. We fought our way through the crowd to the bar as memories of Riley bombarded me. He'd loved his stupid frat parties.

A cute blond guy with dimples came over with two red solo cups. "Would you girls like a drink?"

"No thanks. We're headed to the bar." I flashed him a smile to take the sting out of my words. I wasn't rejecting him, just the drinks. No chance in hell was I taking a drink some stranger had poured, or poured something into.

Sam clutched my hand and hauled me toward the bar, weaving in and out of the people both dancing and just hanging out. A DJ was set up in the corner, and Bruno Mars's "Locked Out of Heaven" blasted on the speakers.

Sam squeezed up to the bar, ordered us two Sam Adams, and popped the bottles. "Here's to rebounds."

We clinked our bottles, and I took a long pull of the Cherry Wheat. Rebound. The goal tonight was to find a suitable guy. Someone who would take my mind off Dad, and April's crap, and Mom, and Riley, and...and...Josh. Yeah, right.

The awesome thing about grief was that it took precedence in my heart, consumed every other pain until I chose to let it in. Dad's death overshadowed Riley's betrayal like a broken leg to a stubbed toe.

I just wondered which one would leave harsher scars over the long haul.

"What about him?" Sam pointed to a frat boy with dark brown hair and a nice smile.

"Too short."

"Okay...him?" She gestured toward another guy. Good build, good height.

"No smile."

She sighed and turned. "Hmm...him?" This time it was a blonde. Perfect build, dressed like an Abercrombie model.

My stomach lurched. "Too Riley."

"Point taken." We leaned against the bar. Sure, there were a lot of guys girls would drool over. It didn't take long to peg my problem.

None of these guys were Josh.

A smokin' hot dirty-blonde, wearing the frat's polo, tapped his bottle on the mouth of Sam's, causing beer to spill out everywhere. "Hey!" she shouted, jumping back to keep her shoes from being ruined. "Deacon! Why do you have to be such a jerk?"

He grinned and popped a peanut from a nearby bowl into his mouth. "Sam, you're looking mighty fine this evening."

"It's not going to happen." I knew that look on her face.

She liked him, but not enough to go after him. She smiled as another guy with gorgeous Hispanic features walked over. "Have you guys met Ember?" She tilted her head my way. "Ember, this is Deacon and Mark."

Mark's smile was kind and welcoming. "Nice to meet you, Ember."

Deacon's green eyes scanned over me. When I thought about choosing someone who wasn't Josh, a wave of uneasiness churned in my stomach, but I pushed it away. If I was going to hunt for a rebound, someone to lose myself in for a while, then Deacon might fit the bill.

He gave me a slow smile and reached for my hand. I hesitated, but gave it to him. Instead of shaking it, he lifted it to his face, flipped it, and pressed a kiss to my palm. "It's a delight to meet you…" He paused, raking his eyes over me again. "Ember."

Um. No. The violation of my space by that kiss locked my muscles in revulsion for an instant. I swallowed, willing myself to relax. As soon as my panic wasn't obvious, I withdrew my hand, forcing the smile to stay on my face. "You, too, Deacon."

Jagger slid between Deacon and Sam. "Watch out, Deke. Josh has dibs on this one."

Annoyance itched at me. "Josh does *not* have dibs on me. We're not dating."

Jagger's eyes narrowed. "You sure about that?"

Was I? We had to be only friends, at least until I wasn't such a wreck. I'd already made that decision, right? Right. "I'm sure."

"In that case." Deacon closed the distance between us and tugged me up against him. "Wanna dance?"

Sam gave me the head-nod urge, and Jagger grimaced, no doubt disappointed in my choice. This was what I was here for, what I'd decided to do. Stick to the rebound plan. "Sure."

Deacon pulled me onto the floor to something a little dirtier. Rihanna's "S&M" came over the speakers, and everyone around us got even closer, if that was possible. Deacon crooked his finger at me, and I slid up next to him, ecstatic to lose myself in the beat. Dancing was one area I could let loose.

He yanked me closer, pushing his pelvis into mine. *Whoa, buddy.* His hands drifted over my back, gripping my waist and headed south to my hips. I repeated the "this is okay" mantra in my head. After all, if I rebounded with a guy, I had to let him touch me. I had to enjoy him touching me. Yes. I could do this.

He moved against me, turning himself on, but I just couldn't relax. I couldn't let myself go like usual. I cringed every time he moved his hips against me. *Put that thing away already.*

His hands gripped my butt, pulling me up higher on him as he ground against me. "Damn, baby, you're gorgeous," he whispered in my ear. His hot breath reeked of beer.

It was the final straw. I raised my hands and pushed back against his chest. "Deacon, no."

That was all I got out before a giant body came between us. I caught his familiar scent before hearing his voice. "Back the fuck off, Deke."

"Whoa, she said she wanted to dance, Walker." Deacon stood a head shorter than Josh, and nowhere near as intimidating.

"She didn't say she wanted her ass grabbed, did she?"

I stepped around Josh's back and slid between them, facing Josh. "It's over, Josh. Nothing to worry about."

He kept his focus on Deacon, and if looks could kill... Yeah. "Go the hell away, Deke, and don't come near Ember again."

Deacon put his hands up like he was under arrest, gave

me a shrug, and walked away.

"Seriously, Josh?" I jabbed my finger into his chest. "I had it handled. You didn't need to go all caveman." But I was glad he did. Hell, I was glad to see him. "What are you doing here?"

He smiled and pointed to the frat letters embroidered on his shirt. "How did you think you got these tickets?"

"I didn't peg you for a frat boy." A twinge of disappointment caught me off guard.

He brought his face down to mine, rubbing his nose along my cheekbone to whisper in my ear. "You can't peg me for anything."

I pulled away to save my own sanity. I wanted that mouth on more than my cheek, and that's why I couldn't have it. Not with him. "Thanks for the rescue."

"Why were you dancing with Deke?"

"Because I wanted to."

His eyes narrowed. "Right. I figured that out. Why Deke?"

Because you scare the shit out of me. "He was there."

He pulled me against him, and my body caught fire. Why couldn't I freeze up around him? It would make everything so much easier. "Lie to everybody else, December. Not me. I see right through it. Why were you dancing with Deke? What are you looking for?"

I debated lying to him, but what was the use? He'd seen me at my worst. He deserved the truth. "I thought I could rebound." My face flushed, even with the heat of the party. "I just wanted to forget, to lose myself for a while in something that doesn't hurt. Everything still hurts."

His eyes bored into mine, stripping my soul raw. "Dance with me." It wasn't a question.

"I can't use you."

"It's not using if I want it. Besides, it's just dancing, and

I think that's covered under the whatever-you-need clause of our unwritten contract."

"Contract, huh?" I couldn't stop my smile.

His was slow and downright sexy. "Contract, vow, promise, whatever. It all means I'm your whatever, and whatever means dance. Now."

He was perfect, and I was helpless. I slid up to him and moved to the music. Pressing myself against him, I forgot everything but the beat pounding through me and the movement of my hips with it.

Big mistake, looking up into those gorgeous brown eyes. Going. Going. Gone. The need to touch him, to feel his hands on my body clawed through me. I nearly groaned remembering what he could do with those hands. "Whatever?" I asked, testing my boundaries.

"I'll never tell you no if I can help it."

Locked into his eyes, I reached my hands out, stroking over his muscled shoulders. I ran my fingers down his biceps and arms, savoring the tingles in my fingers and the spark in his eyes. When I reached his hands, I couldn't manage a seductive smile, so I simply grasped his hands and put them on my waist. "Is this okay?"

He pulled me close to his body in answer, fitting my legs so that I straddled one of his, and then moved me in perfect synchronization. Two seconds in Josh's arms, and I was ready to forget any rebound plan had ever existed. My dress rode up higher on my thighs.

He held me to him, and I let go. Where I moved with the music, he followed, his hands moving up and down my back, skimming over my skin where the dress ended and sending shivers through me. Two songs, three, and the sweat beaded between my breasts. Thank God my hair was up. I turned around, pressing my back into him. He kept up with me move for move. His head slipped to my shoulder, and he kissed the skin there. My head fell back against his chest as he pulled me against him tighter. His tongue stroked over my neck just before his teeth grazed across me, and his hands moved lower to my hips. The loud music camouflaged my moan to the other dancers around us, but he heard it. His fingers bit into my skin in response. I was crossing the line, but I pushed back against him, needing to feel that he wanted me.

He did. I shamelessly moved my hips against him.

"December..." My name was a whispered plea on his lips.

I turned in his arms, but kept my body as close as before, rubbing against him in every place I could. A familiar ache stirred in me. I needed to feel his mouth on me. I ran my hands up the smooth line of his back, wrapping one around his neck while the other grabbed onto his hair and pulled him to me. "Josh?" I asked. I wouldn't force him into something he didn't want. *Please, please want me.*

His gaze dropped to my raised, parted lips, and after a breath, he plunged. With one movement, he was on me, his tongue in my mouth, stroking, enflaming. I kissed him back just as fiercely. This was exactly what I needed, exactly *who* I needed. Josh.

Fuck the plan.

I leaned into him on my tiptoes, my heels still not bringing me level to him. His hands moved from my hips to my ass, and without strain, he lifted me against him, right where he somehow knew I needed him to be. There. God, yes. There. "Josh..." I groaned against his mouth, giving up every pretense of dancing.

His tongue moved in and out of my mouth, stoking the fire that was threatening to burn my body alive. I barely remembered we were on a dance floor. Kissing Josh robbed every logical thought from my head and left me with a base need: his body on mine. The ache between my thighs built with every onslaught of his mouth, like he had a direct line to my core.

He pulled his mouth away, his breathing hitched in a way that had me wanting to push him for more. "Fuck... December..."

Now that sounded like a plan I could go with. "Upstairs?" I asked, too turned-on to be embarrassed by what I was asking.

He leaned back, looking into my eyes. "Here?"

I brought his lips to mine, speaking against their softness. "You said whatever I need, right?" He nodded. "I need you to make this ache stop, Josh. You're the only one who can."

Without another word, he led me through the crowd. People reached out for him, calling his name, but he only acknowledged with a nod. A smile of feminine satisfaction spread across my face. His mind was only on me.

He pulled me up next to him at the steps, keeping his hand on the small of my back as we nearly ran up the carpeted staircase. He steered me to the left when the hallway split, entering the first room on the right. The noise from the party was muffled as he shut the door, the only light in the room coming from a lava lamp in the corner. That was all I saw before he spun me, pressing me back against the door. "Whose room?" I got out breathlessly, not really caring.

"Mark's. He won't mind."

Josh's eyes were dark, intense. He was as turned-on as I was, and I loved it. This time I attacked, bringing myself up to his mouth and sweeping my tongue inside, tasting nothing but the addicting flavor of Josh. He reached behind my knee and lifted my leg to curl against his hip, then ran his hand down the back of my thigh, under my dress, to my rear. My dress slid up my thighs to my waist. Good. Better access.

I rocked my hips into him as he ground against me. If he moved just a few more times like that, I was going to come against the damn wall. Yes, please. His mouth left mine to stroke his tongue down my neck, nipping and sucking as he went.

A sound like a whimper escaped my throat when he kissed his way across my collarbone and buried his nose into the valley between my breasts. "So damn sweet," he muttered. His hands gathered the fabric around my waist and he tugged, popping my breasts free of the neckline. He nudged the line of my strapless bra down and flicked his tongue over my nipple.

He groaned, or I did. Whatever.

I held his head to me, needing more. Deeper. Like he read my mind, he obliged, pulling my nipple into his mouth and sucking. "Josh…" His name was ripped from me.

With my breast in his mouth, he carried me, turning toward the bed. He sank to the surface with me. His weight was perfect, holding me to the earth when I was ready to fly away. I slipped my legs down his hips, and he repositioned himself exactly where I needed him, pressed against the throbbing ache that seemed to grow more intense. I wanted all of him against me. I needed to feel his skin.

"Shirt," I mumbled as I jerked up the ends of his button-down. He pulled away from me long enough to rip the shirt and undershirt over his head, leaving his bare chest above me. "You're so incredible." I ran my fingers down the planes and angles of his chest, over the swirls of ink, stopping to stroke the carved lines of his sexy abdominals. It was no wonder half the student body was panting after Josh Walker.

So was I.

"December." Desire raged through his eyes along with another emotion I was almost scared to name. Tenderness? Caring? He stroked the sides of my face, lowering himself to capture my mouth in a gentle kiss. "You have no idea how perfect you are."

I dragged my nails down his back, and he drove his

hardness against me. I grasped his mouth-watering rear at the same time he claimed my mouth again, bringing me higher and higher. I would never get enough of this frenzy he put me into. I would never get enough of him.

I moved my hips against him, seeking relief from the pressure. "I'm on fire," I admitted, any embarrassment swept away with the need coiling in my body.

His eyes locked onto mine with a gaze so hot I was amazed I didn't spontaneously combust. "Me too." He kissed a path down my chest, stopping to suck on my breasts one after another as his hands worked their way up from my knees, skimming the insides of my thighs. *Yes. Yes. Yes.* The wicked grin that came across his face told me I'd just said that out loud. He skimmed over the debauched neckline of my dress, to where the hem met my waistline, and then he kissed the soft, exposed skin of my stomach. I arched off the bed.

His hands stroked up my thighs until he reached the edge of my panties, and then the frustrating man paused. Paused! Didn't he know I needed him to use those hands? I needed his fingers on me. Now. I rolled my hips in a silent plea. "What do you need?" he growled against the skin just above my panty line.

"Josh…" I begged.

"Tell me what you need, Ember. I'll do whatever you want."

I'll do whatever you want. The words bounced around my brain like a pinball, lighting up every sex-starved cell in my body. Josh Walker, who I'd fantasized about all through high school, was not only in bed with me, but offering himself on a platter. "You. I need you. I only want you." The last part slipped out in a whisper before I could stop it, revealing way too much about what was really going on in my heart.

He must not have heard it, because he growled against my skin, and bit into the soft silk of my panties. I lifted my hips, and the man dragged them down without breaking my gaze. Holy. Fucking. Hot. He slipped them off my heels, slid his way back up my body, stopping to lick and suck the area right behind my knee. My breath labored to keep up with my hammering heart.

He brought his head up and stared at me for three breaths, like he was contemplating something. "I have to taste you," he whispered. His head dipped, his tongue stroked over my clit.

"Josh!"

I'd heard stories of how this could feel, but nothing prepared me for the lightning streaking through my body, concentrating where his mouth worked me over. He slipped one finger inside me and stroked in time with the swirling motions of his tongue.

Once.

Everything built, pooling low, tensing the muscles in my legs as my feet dug into the bed.

Twice.

He slipped a second finger in, and my head thrashed on the pillow. My fingers tore into the sheets, and my body coiled tighter and tighter.

Three times.

I saw the stars. My body trembled and bucked against his mouth as bliss poured through me, stretching from my head, through my fingers, to my toes. He gently brought me down, stroking out every aftershock he could with his tongue.

When I finally drew a ragged breath, he moved up my body and kissed me deeply. He tasted like him, and…me. "You are fucking exquisite. Addictive."

"I don't even have words for that, what you just did." My lungs heaved for air.

The smile that came across his face was heart-stopping and gorgeous. "I've been dreaming of that for…" His brows furrowed, like he was keeping himself in check. "A while."

My hands slipped down the ridges of his abs, to the waistband of his jeans where his hardness strained. One flick, and I had the button open. Go me!

Josh pulled out my hand and refastened it all in one movement. "Not here."

Was he rejecting me? Again? "I want this. I want you."

He dropped to the bed next to me, burying his face in my neck. "God, I want you. But I'm not going to take your virginity in someone else's bed during a damn party."

I wiggled my naked hips against him. "I want you to."

He slid his mouth up, kissing my jawline. His breath was ragged in my ears. "Not until you're in my bed, Ember. Mine. No one else's."

A sound like a foghorn came down the hallway, followed by a shriek. "What is—"

"Fuck." Josh snagged the bottom of the comforter's side and jerked it over the two of us, rolling until he was on the other side of me and we were cocooned in darkness. My face pressed against his chest, completely covered by the blanket. As he tugged the blanket up to cover my hair, the door burst open and a foghorn sounded. I slammed my hands over my ears until it stopped.

"Playing through!" A drunken group of frat boys stormed the room, and it sounded…like they were putting? Oh yeah, the ping of a golf ball against a club was unmistakable.

Josh pulled me in closer to him. "What the fuck! Emory! Caleb!"

"Ah, shit! Walker! We totally thought Mark was in here!" Oh yeah, they were toasted.

"Well, apparently he's not, so get the hell out!"

My cheeks burned against Josh's chest.

"Who ya got under there, Walker? You know Jessica Kirtz is looking for you."

Of course some girl was looking for him. A girl was always looking for him.

He sat up, careful to keep me shielded. "Out. Now!"

"Playing through!" they shouted again. With another shot of the foghorn, they retreated, leaving the door open in their wake.

I sat up, lowering the blanket just past my eyes, and caught a peek of plaid shorts, sweater vests, and pom-pom-adorned berets on three of his fraternity brothers. Those boys went all out.

Josh ripped his hand through his hair. "Fucking freshmen!"

I couldn't help it, the laughter burst out of me, anything but ladylike. There were even a few snorts. After an incredulous look, Josh joined in until I collapsed against his bare chest, laughing so hard tears watered my vision. It was minutes before I could get myself under control.

I wiped away the last of my tears with a smile.

"I guess you can see why I choose not to live in the house."

"It's certainly entertaining." I leaned up and kissed him softly before any awkwardness could set in. I thought about jumping him, but something about the open door and another foghorn sounding talked me out of it for the moment.

He kissed me back, lingering.

I ran my fingers over the ink of his tattoo, over his chest, curving with his shoulder and onto his arm. When I felt a scar the length of my pinky finger, I smiled. "Bar brawl?" I asked, bending to run my tongue along it.

"Ferocious lizard attack," he joked.

"Oh thank God!" Sam shouted, barreling into the room like the devil was after her.

"Playing through?" I asked, trying to keep my face serious and failing miserably. Josh and I burst out laughing again.

Sam's mouth dropped open. "I would almost think this was funny if I didn't just catch your little sister in a room down the hall with Tyler Rozly."

"What? April is here? How the hell did she get here? She's underage!" Lame, but it was the only thought I could get out.

"She's naked, Ember, and those boys have a camera."

Chapter Fifteen

"Oh, God." Everything in my head shut down for a millisecond. Those boys could have naked pictures of my sister. She was only seventeen. Seventeen with naked pictures. If they got posted on the Internet she'd never escape them.

"Sam, give us a sec." Josh pulled his shirt over his head as she nodded and shut the door.

April didn't have time for me to freak out. I pulled my bra up and tugged the neckline of my dress to where it belonged. Untangling from the covers, my heels fell to the floor, and I slid my dress down from my waist. "Where are my panties?" I panicked, throwing back the covers.

Josh held up the purple pair, and kneeled down so I could step into them. He slipped them over my thighs, and though I knew sex wasn't on his mind, it was still pretty damn hot when he met my eyes.

"You okay?" I couldn't believe I'd left him in this situation again.

He nodded. "Let's help your sister."

I rearranged my dress again, then flung open the door.

Sam leaned back against the wall. "This way." I secured loose pieces of my hair as I followed her down the hall. Three, no, four doors down, she pounded on the door. "Open up!"

"Go away!" a gruff voice answered.

"April?" I called into the door, trying the knob anyway. It was locked. Too bad they hadn't locked it in the first place. Then again, Josh and I hadn't, either. I shoved the handle again, like my sheer determination to get my sister out of there would magically open the damn thing. "April!" I shouted, pounding on the door.

"Get the hell out of here!" The guy yelled again. I didn't know Tyler Rozly, but if he had my sister in that room, he was on my shit list.

A pair of hands gently pushed me aside. Josh was here. He pounded once on the door. "Tyler, open the door now."

"Hell no!" The giggle that accompanied the declaration was enough to tell me April was in there.

"Tyler, it's Walker, and if you don't open this goddamned door in twenty seconds, I will get your ass thrown out. *Now.* She's a minor." The veins in his neck pulsed.

A muffled curse made its way through the door, and I mentally counted each of the seconds Josh threatened Tyler with. In eighteen seconds, the lock clicked, and the door swung open to reveal a shirtless guy I assumed was Tyler. "What the hell are you cock-blocking me for, Walker?"

I slid between Tyler and the doorframe. "April?"

My sister sat up in the bed, clutching the sheet to her bare top. "Ember?"

All of my rage toward April turned on Tyler. "That's my little sister!"

Tyler crossed his arms, but standing next to Josh he couldn't pull off intimidating. Josh dwarfed him. "She didn't seem too 'little' to me."

Josh stepped in front of me before I could get my hand

across Tyler's smirking face. Asshole! "She's seventeen, dude. Last time I checked, you're twenty-one, which makes her jailbait."

Tyler paled. "No, you're wrong. She looked young so I asked to see her UCCS ID when she came in. Her name was on the list and everything."

April sat silent in the bed, giving me a guilty look I knew all too well.

"You took my ID."

"It's not like you needed it." She went from contrite to accusatory in a breath.

"You're December?" Tyler blanched, all of his earlier bravado discarded on the floor with April's underwear. Shit. Her underwear was on the floor!

"Apparently. And you're an asshole for sleeping with my seventeen-year-old sister." Before I could launch any further, the foghorn sounded down the hall. I'd almost forgotten. "Josh?"

He nodded. "I got this." He slid past Sam and took off.

April still hadn't moved. "Put. Your. Clothes. On." I seethed on each word. She grimaced like she was going to argue with me. "What? Do you want more naked pictures?"

"Naked pictures?"

My fingernails bit into my palms. "Those guys had a camera!"

That got her moving.

Tyler slid down the back of his door, defeated. I couldn't blame him, not really. He'd questioned her, she'd given him my ID. She'd duped him.

"Hell no, Walker! The pics are ours!" The shouts came amid pounding feet in the hallway.

I stuck my head out of the door and saw the golf-clad freshmen racing around the banister and down the center steps. They were going to get away with those pictures. Josh slid around the corner, took one look at the distance, threw his legs over the banister, and jumped. He landed right in front of the freshmen.

My breath caught and couldn't seem to catch back up.

"Give me the fucking camera." He snatched it away, ripped the SD card out of the side, and threw it back at them before they could sputter another protest. "If I ever catch you taking pictures of any females without their consent again, you won't have to worry about making it as a brother. You won't have to worry about taking another breath. No arguing. No second chances. Understood?"

The three nodded their heads, their eyes downcast. "Yeah."

"Clean the damn kitchen."

"Ah, man! Walker!"

"*Now.*" He didn't have to shout, they got his meaning and scurried off. He glanced up at me and gave a tight-lipped half smile, holding up the SD card. I took my first full breath.

I couldn't find my voice. How could I tell him what that meant to me? I mouthed the words, "Thank you."

He nodded, his eyes softening.

April pushed past me, fully dressed and yanking on her coat. I stepped forward, catching her arm. "Oh no, you're coming with me."

She raised an eyebrow. "Or what?"

"Or I tell Mom."

Her mouth snapped shut with a clicking sound. I led her around the banister and down the steps. Josh took point and led us out of the party, Sam in our wake. The music pounded and the crowd had grown, but the guys moved out of Josh's way. The girls were another story. They all stepped into his path, touching his arm or calling his name to get his attention. He nodded politely and smiled at each one of them but didn't slow our exit from the house.

The cold air hit me as we stepped onto the front porch. Josh threw his jacket around my shoulders. When had he picked that up? He kept his hand on the small of my back as we got to my car. I spotted April's car a few spots over.

"I'm not going with you," she argued.

Sam rolled her eyes. "I'm not sure you're in a position to argue."

"What, like you get to tell me what to do?"

"Sam saved your ass." Josh's tone said he'd had enough, but his eyes were soft when he looked down to me. "Do you want me to take you home?"

I shook my head. "I think I need a minute with my sister."

He nodded and glared back at April. "Give your keys to Sam."

April sputtered, and I nearly lost it. "Give them to her now, April."

She cursed, but she did it.

Sam gave us a mock salute as she headed off toward April's little coupe. "See you at home."

April crossed her arms and leaned against my car.

Josh handed me the SD card. "I'm sorry about how tonight turned out."

I shook my head with a small smile. "Not all of it."

"Not all of it," he agreed, a wicked glint catching his eye in the moonlight. "Do you want my help getting her home?"

April scoffed and raised her eyebrows.

"I've got this. Don't worry."

Something flashed across his eyes, like he was remembering my bitchy tirade last week. But he wasn't one to bear a grudge, and the look passed with a sigh. He skimmed his hand over my cheek and slowly, giving me time to decline, brushed his lips over mine. "Tomorrow?"

"I'll see you at practice," I said against his lips, wanting to stay just a moment longer.

"I can't wait." He gave me a soft smile, and went back to the party.

I watched him walk away and felt a twinge of jealousy. We weren't exclusive. Hell, we weren't even dating, but something ripped apart in me at the thought of him finishing what we'd started upstairs with some other girl.

But I had to take care of April; I couldn't follow him back into the party no matter how badly I craved being around him.

Freaking April.

"Pictures?" I held up the SD card for punctuation. "Do you know what these could have done to you? You can't get away from crap like this once someone puts it on Facebook."

She dropped her gaze. "I didn't know they had a camera."

"You shouldn't have been here in the first place!" I threw the SD card to the pavement and crushed it beneath my shoe, breaking it into pieces under my heel.

"You're not my mom!"

"You're acting like you sure as hell need me to be." I couldn't escalate her temper tantrum. "You want to get drunk and laid?" I threw my arms out, palms up. "Be my guest! But you have a boyfriend, or did Brett just morph into Tyler? Is that who you are now?"

"I told Brett I needed some space, and he understood. It's not like I'm a virgin, or like Tyler is the only guy I've been sleeping with!"

Horror nearly froze me. "What is going on with you, April? This isn't you."

"Like you'd even understand!"

It felt like she'd slapped me. "What do you mean?"

She tucked her red hair behind her ear, a nervous trait we both shared with our mother. "Dad died, Ember."

If she'd wanted my defenses up, that was the way to do it. "Yeah, I remember."

"You…" Tears welled in her eyes. "You just picked up and went along perfectly! Everyone else is falling apart and you're just…perfect little Ember! I don't expect you to understand how this feels or why I'm here because I'm not… perfect!"

A ball of frustration worked its way into my throat, nearly choking me. "You really don't think I know what you're doing, April? You're here to forget."

Her head snapped up, her gaze meeting mine, but she didn't speak.

"You want to forget everything that hurts. You don't want to think about the fact that Mom can't seem to function, or that Gus doesn't have a dad…that we don't have Dad." Now it was my eyes that were blurring. "You're sick of crying, and worrying, and the fucking pain! So you lose yourself in someone, and you give over to those feelings because for those few moments, there's nothing in your head or your heart but the way he's making you feel. Yeah, April, I get it."

She shook her head, her mouth hanging open like a fish sucking air. "You do? How?"

I leaned back against the car next to her, freezing my skin where it met with metal. "Because I've done the same exact thing."

"No way."

I looked away, toward the frat house where Josh was doing God-knows-what with God-knows-who. "Not my finest moment, but Riley put me back into a tailspin, and Josh…"

"OMG! You slept with Josh Walker? Details!"

"No, I did not sleep with him!" A heavy sigh escaped me. I couldn't blame her for what I'd done, too. "But that's only because he is a really, really, exceptionally good guy. He knew what I was doing, and he…took care of me, watched out for me."

"I'd like to take care of him," she muttered.

I smacked the back of her head. "Knock it off. I'm just saying I know what you're feeling, because I am, too. But you can't sneak into a strange guy's bed and sleep around. You're giving away all these pieces of yourself, and if you don't stop, there's not going to be anything left of who you really are."

She sniffed and rested her head on my shoulder. I leaned my head on top of hers. "April, I'm not perfect. I'm a train wreck, and I have been since long before Dad died. I only stepped up because I was the one who could. Mom wasn't functioning, and Gus needed someone. You needed someone. I couldn't let it in, I couldn't let the pieces fall. I still can't. Why do you think I'm here, going to this school we both know wasn't even on my fallback list?"

"I thought you wanted to go to Vanderbilt? Whatever happened to that?"

"I clung to a plan because it made me feel better, a plan that had nothing to do with what I wanted. I let myself get sucked into someone else's dream. What you call being perfect is actually me treading water with every ounce of strength I have so I don't drown."

We stood there quietly for a few moments, both staring up at the crystalline Colorado stars. They were clearer here than at any other duty station we'd been to, and definitely one of my favorite parts of living here. I made out the shape of Orion in the sky and waited for April to speak, content to stay as long as she needed me to.

"I'm kind of glad you're as much of a mess as I am," she whispered.

I closed my eyes and sighed. "I'm so much more screwed up than you could ever be, April. But it would really help my shit pile if you could keep yourself together just a little."

She nodded against my shoulder. "Can we go home?"

"Sounds like a plan. I can't feel my knees as it is." We both burst into laughter for a moment before she grasped my hand.

"Thank you for getting the SD card."

"It was all Josh." Gus and hockey, April and the card, me and...whatever we were doing. One by one, he seemed to be saving every member of my family.

"He's pretty amazing."

"Yeah, tell me something I don't already know."

"I wouldn't mind 'forgetting' for a while with him. As a matter of fact, for Josh Walker, I'd consider temporary amnesia."

I gave her a light push and then hugged her back. "Ugh. No more talking about Josh."

"Just sayin', I've seen that picture of him on your wall at home. The newspaper clipping from when they won state when you were in high school. You had a huge thing for him." She tilted her head back at me. "You still do. There's nothing wrong with getting over Riley, Ember. Or Dad."

"It's too soon. I don't know what the hell I'm doing with myself. I can't bring someone else down with me."

"Then what are you doing?"

"I don't know." Panic choked my voice as I realized I'd just shamelessly sent Josh more-than-mixed signals. What the hell was wrong with me?

Sunday afternoon, the doorbell chimed as I walked into my favorite creamery, ready for a fix. I hadn't seen Josh since Friday, and as hard as I was trying to distance myself and take it slow, I missed him. I'd thought of a dozen reasons to go over to his apartment yesterday, from the mundane, "can I borrow a cup of sugar?" to "our garbage disposal broke." I'd debated chucking a wrench into it just for the excuse. By this morning, I'd been jonesing for the taste of Josh, so strawberry ice cream, like the night I'd apologized in his apartment, would have to do.

If I hurried, I could grab Gus a cone and get it home before it melted. It was still early enough that Mom wouldn't flip that I'd spoiled his dinner.

"Next!" the black-aproned attendant called out.

Two scoops of strawberry in a sugar cone and two scoops of mud pie in a waffle cone later, I paid the clerk. Strawberry ice cream filled my mouth, and I smiled. I could almost feel his hands on my face, and his voice in my ear. As I rounded the corner near the register, the rest of the store came into view, and I about choked on my ice cream.

I could hear him laughing from here and the smile that lit up Josh's face was breathtaking. It was mirrored by the enormous grin on my little brother's chocolate-covered face as he sat across from him, his arms waving in the air like mad.

"And then guess what? Mrs. Bluster said my volcano was the most awesome volcano she'd ever seen! And then I got to start it up! And then guess what? It exploded!" His hands went wild in animation. "And then everyone's like, 'cool!' but I don't think Mrs. Bluster thought so. I mean, there was red stuff all over the white board and the floor!"

I laughed out loud, imagining the scenario he painted so vividly.

"I'm sure she thought your volcano's unpredictability was awesome. All the best ones are, you know," Josh answered.

Gus waved when he saw me. "Ember!"

I crossed the room, keeping my eyes locked on Gus. "I was going to surprise you with this." I handed him the cone. "But it appears you've already been kidnapped."

He grinned up at me, sporting another lost tooth. "Cool! Double ice cream! Thanks!" Gus dug in, and I prayed I didn't just cause him a huge bellyache.

I glanced at Josh, who looked as happy and surprised to

see me as I was to see him.

"Hey." He pulled out a chair, and I took it, sitting between them. "Gus, you lied," Josh accused, mock shock on his face.

Gus's brow furrowed. "No, she doesn't like strawberry. She likes cookies 'n' cream."

I took another swipe at the ice cream so I wouldn't have to talk. Josh wasn't fooled. "Funny." He laughed. "Strawberry's my favorite."

I knew I was turning shades way darker than the ice cream. "I just wanted to change it up," I lied. No, I'd wanted to taste Josh, and he knew it.

"So, what am I supposed to do with this?" he asked playfully, pointing to the hand-packed quart of cookies 'n' cream.

"Oh, I'll eat that, too," I promised. He'd bought me ice cream!

"Good to know you have a weakness besides coffee, Miss Howard."

He didn't know that he was my other vice, and he stared at me in a way that made me picture more Sunday afternoons and ice cream stores. "I have a ton of weak spots, Mr. Walker."

"Done!" Gus shouted like he'd won a race.

"Gus, man. You're a mess."

He was right. Gus's entire mouth was covered and most of his cheeks assaulted, too. He'd put away two scoops faster than I'd managed one. I pointed to the bathroom. "Clean it up, buddy." He gave me a mile-wide grin and slipped into the bathroom.

"You really bought me ice cream?" I asked Josh.

"How else was I supposed to find an excuse to see you? Borrow fake sugar?" My cheeks burned. He leaned forward on his elbows. "Besides, you really bought *my* ice cream?" He dipped forward and took a mouthful of the strawberry, leaving some around his mouth.

"Yeah," I whispered. "I missed you, I guess."

He ran his tongue over his lower lip, catching the rest of the pink ice cream. "If your brother wasn't with us, I'd kiss you."

Yes, please. I was ready to crawl across the table, ice cream and all, for it. "Yeah, you're probably right."

"When are you going to put me out of my misery?" he asked with a smile, biting into my cone.

"You don't look miserable to me." I wiped away a drop of ice cream from his lip with my thumb, and licked it off.

He groaned. "Trust me, I am. When are you going to let me take you out?"

My eyebrows raised. "Like an actual date?"

"Yeah, you know, like pick you up, we go out, have a good time, I steal a good night kiss?" He leaned back across the table and whispered, "I get to tell people you're mine?"

Could I do that? Was I ready? First dates weren't exactly commitments, right? Gus saved me from answering by walking back in, clean face and all. We stood, tossed our trash, and headed for the parking lot.

"Want me to take you home, Gus?" I asked as we stood halfway between our cars.

"I've got a better idea," Josh interrupted. "What do you say to laser tag?"

Gus lit up. "Heck yes!" He scrambled into Josh's Jeep.

Josh turned back to me in question. "Ember? Want to shoot at each other in the dark?"

He was giving up his Sunday afternoon for ice cream and laser tag with my little brother. "Where is your flaw, Josh Walker?"

He laughed. "I keep it in the closet."

I slid next to him as he told Gus to move to the backseat and reached on tiptoes to whisper in his ear. "If it's dark in there, does it mean I get a kiss?"

He turned around so I was against his chest. "I have half a mind to tell you no more kisses until I get a date."

"Oh?" I stepped back so Gus wouldn't get the wrong... ahem, right...idea.

"Yeah, but you see, that's my flaw, December Howard." He helped me into the Jeep and reached across to buckle me in. He slid back, stopping to whisper in my ear. "I have no self-control when it comes to you."

Problem was, I saw that as a virtue, not a flaw.

Chapter Sixteen

I adjusted the gold scarf around my neck and waved to Mom down the stands. She was holding an entire row of seats. April gave me a smile and patted the chair on the other side of her. Coffee in hand, I started toward them. Today was the semifinals round of playoffs for Gus.

The tingles in my fingers weren't from the chilled temperature of the World Arena, but from knowing I'd see Josh. Every day for the last two weeks, he'd asked me out, and for the last two weeks, I'd avoided answering. He'd borrowed cups of sugar, found "lost" mail, and tapped out Morse code on our shared bedroom wall. I saw him in class, at practice, and ran into him at home, but I was never, ever alone with him. Being alone with Josh always led to me being naked. Not allowed. Besides, he'd held true to his threat and hadn't kissed me in fourteen very long days.

What the hell was holding me back? Just the fear of the risk, of letting him all the way in and getting destroyed when I'd barely put myself back together.

Walking into class yesterday, I'd slid into my seat at the

same time a leggy brunette perched on his desk. I kept my eyes on my notebook, pressing the date deeply into the paper as her giggle nauseated me. "Josh, I can't wait to see you play tomorrow night. I bet you'll score a goal just for me, huh?"

Vomit. This would be it. The moment I realized he'd finally grown tired of waiting for me to get my act together.

"I'm hoping to score a lot of goals, Scarlet." Double vomit.

Her giggle was even more obnoxious than the first one. "Of course." What the hell was she? Part hyena?

"And there's only one girl I'm thinking about." Why did he have to use that tone of voice? The one without flirting or chauvinistic shimmer? Why did he have to use the low, seriously sexy one he reserved for me, the one I couldn't ignore...at her?

His hand reached across the aisle and captured mine. My gaze flew toward his, and I found him staring. My smile must have told Scarlet everything she needed to know, because she hopped right off his desk.

"Sorry, Ember! I didn't realize...well, yeah!" She bounced back to her seat.

He didn't drop my gaze. "I meant every word."

"I know." And I did.

"Gus is starting tomorrow."

"Yeah, you've done amazing things with him."

"He's an amazing kid," he countered. "December, about tomorrow—"

"Don't." My fingers cut into my palms around the pen. "Don't ask again, not yet. There's something in me that can't tell you no, so just don't."

He kissed my hand, a quick brush of his lips against my palm, and dropped his hold.

I wanted him with a desperation that threatened to overwhelm my common sense, and I never allowed that to happen.

"Ember!" April's voice snapped me back to the present.

I slid past Mom and took the seat next to April. We were two rows behind Gus's bench, but the ice was empty. The boys had already warmed up and were in the locker room getting their pep talk. The arena was about halfway full, not bad for a pee-wee hockey tournament. If they won this game, it was on to the league championships.

"You didn't bring me coffee," my sister pouted.

"I didn't realize you were coming." I offered her mine, but she shook her head.

"It will give me an excuse to sneak out during second period and find a Starbucks." She laughed and went back to playing on her iPhone.

I sipped my mocha and smiled at Mom, who returned it. Her skin was flushed, her eyes bright with excitement. She'd been looking forward to this game all week. Sitting with her on those wooden chairs felt like nothing had changed, almost like she had never left.

Her eyes drifted past me, and a wider smile graced her thin face. "Gwen! I saved you a seat!" She waved up to Mrs. Barton, and I cringed.

Riley's mom slid past me, patting my shoulder. "So good to see you, Ember!" She gave me a little wink. "I brought you a present. Maybe you two could have a little talk?"

Oh no.

She did not.

April kept her head pointed at her phone, but slid her eyes my way with raised eyebrows. Her gaze landed above my head briefly, and her indrawn breath told me he was here. "You okay?" she mouthed at me.

I swallowed and tried to find a little bit of that grace Mom preached so heavily about within me. Be the better person, my ass.

"Hey, babe."

Riley's voice drenched me in familiarity. I didn't bother looking up. Besides, the ice was fascinating, right? "Don't call me that."

He sat next to me. "Sorry, old habits and everything."

"Right, and everything."

"Ember, can we at least be civil?" He angled toward me.

"I'd tell you to fuck right off, if I were Ember, but I'm allowed to say those things, seeing as I'm all grief-stricken and whatnot," April answered from next to me, still engrossed in her phone.

Mom shot her a death glare.

I checked my watch. They'd take the ice any second now, and I'd be stuck next to Riley for hours in crappy, uncomfortable silence if I didn't swallow my pride and make nice. The high road sucked. "We can be perfectly civil, Riley."

He reached across the cup holder and held onto my hand. "I've missed you."

I yanked my hand away from his. "I said civil, Riley. Don't touch me."

"Can you at least look at me?"

I turned, expecting my heart to break all over again, but oddly enough, it only twinged like a splinter. "Happy?" Not that he didn't look good, because he did. Abercrombie perfect as usual, but there was something in those blue eyes that wasn't normally there. Remorse?

"Not really, honestly. Not since you left."

The announcer spared my speechlessness. "Your Colorado Tigers!" Cheers erupted around us as the boys skated out, raising their arms to the roof like they were already NHL stars. I jumped to my feet, calling out Gus's name and clapping. He'd worked so hard to get here. I couldn't be more proud of him.

The boys skated around the goal and back to stand in

a straight line. Jagger walked onto the ice and into the box, followed by the head coach, and then my breath caught. Josh came out onto the ice and turned into the box. His black suit draped over the powerful angles of his body, complete with black shirt and gold tie. I had the most ludicrous vision of winding that tie over my hand and pulling him toward me.

His eyes skirted over the crowd before they locked onto me. I met his private smile with one of my own. One thing I craved almost as much as Josh himself was the peace, the serenity I felt when I was around him. Everything else melted away. Seeing him brought to mind all those horrible analogies in romance novels, like water in a drought, sunshine in winter, color in a world of gray. Yes, yes, yes. He was all of that and more.

Josh eclipsed Riley, and the twinge at seeing Riley again after these six weeks was no more. Could I really be over it?

"Is he…What's going on with you now?" Riley asked, his voice dropping just like his face.

I nodded. "Yeah, I think he is."

Josh's eyes moved to the right, over Riley, and his smile faltered. He gave me a head nod, like he finally had something figured out, and turned his back on me. Shit. He thought I was here with Riley.

I didn't have time to dwell on it when the puck dropped.

The first period went by in a blink, and the Bears were up on us two to nothing. Gus skated his heart out, but man, the other team was good.

The kids headed back to the locker room, and the coaches filed out after them. Josh glanced up at me, but his eyes held none of their usual warmth.

"Hungry?" Riley asked.

My stomach answered for me. "Sure."

"You kids have fun." His mom winked at us.

Once we were at the top of the stairs, entering the

rotunda, I had to ask. "Your mom has no clue why we broke up, huh?"

Riley shook his head and ran his hand through his hair in a gesture I knew all too well. "No. I told her we'd grown apart, and you needed to move down here for your family. She's secretly plotting with your mom to get us together."

I laughed. "Yeah, I haven't told Mom, either, otherwise she'd know this was never going to happen."

Riley stopped in front of the snack bar and ordered me a slice of cheese pizza and a root beer. That's what being with someone for three years did; he knew the mundane details about me. "Never?"

I stared up at him for a long moment, absorbing the light in his eyes, the way his hair lay, the familiar worried purse of his mouth. A feeling of peace came over me, and I managed to let it all go. "Never, Riley."

"But we have a plan, and it's a great plan. You in teaching, me in law. Everything is mapped out so perfectly." He took our pizza from the cashier and handed me the soda. "How can that all just be…over?"

We chose a spot to the side, sitting at a tall table tucked away in an alcove. "It just is, Ry."

"But I love you. I'm not just saying that. I've known since our junior year that you were my perfect partner. I know we can work past this if we fight for it."

I chewed my pizza slowly, turning over the phrasing in my head before I swallowed. "That's just it. I don't have any more fight in me. Too much has happened to go back, and the things you've done make it impossible to go forward." I sighed, letting the last of my pain over Riley go with my words. "I want to be angry. I want to scream, and kick, and tell you what an asshole you are for what you did, but the truth is I'm not mad anymore. I just don't have the energy for it." There was no bluff, no lie. Out of everything that had happened the last six weeks, he was something I was actually over. Saying it aloud only drove it home.

"Is it this thing with Josh Walker? Is that why you won't give me a second chance?" I knew from the strain on his face what this was costing him. Riley didn't lose. It wasn't in his nature.

"No. Yes. I don't know, I guess." I laughed, feeling free for the first time since December. "I can't be with you because I can never trust another word that comes out of your mouth, not after what you did to me. Maybe if you had loved Kayla…" That thought spun around my brain, blurring it. "Did you? Love her?"

"No. She was just…there. Convenient."

I concentrated on the drops of condensation that formed on the outside of my root beer. "I thought that would make it better," I shook my head. "But it doesn't. It just means you traded what we spent years building for sex. Just sex. I can't be in a relationship with someone who values sex over love, especially when I offered you both."

Silence stretched between us. It wasn't awkward as much as it was final.

"I can't give up on you, Ember. I've never pictured my life without you." He reached across the table for my hand, but I pulled it back into my lap.

"It's time to start. You're going to do amazing things with your life; I know that much about you. But I won't be a part of any of it."

He picked up our empty plates and tossed them into the trash can behind the table before turning back around for me. "I'd gone through this a hundred times. I pictured you hitting me, cursing at me, crying, and every time, I convinced you how much I loved you and won you back." He lifted his arms out, palms up. "What I did to you was selfish, and wrong, and…fucking awful. I can't make up for it."

Part of me wanted to feel moved by his honesty, but instead, there was only a lingering sadness in my heart for what we had lost, and what he hadn't given up on yet. Asshole or not, I'd loved Riley for three years, and it wasn't easy to see him hurt, even if he'd been the one to destroy us. I walked into his open arms and tucked my head against his shoulder, where it had always fit. "You can't make up for it, Riley. Not now, not ever."

His arms closed against me, enveloping me in the smell of his familiar cologne, and the embrace I'd always thought would hold me for the rest of my life. "Can we be friends?"

"I don't know. Not now, it's too much."

He pulled my face back gently, looking into my eyes like it was the last time he'd see me. "I'm going to miss you so damn much."

"I know the feeling." I gave a half smile and dropped my eyes, ready to step away when I looked over his shoulder.

Josh stood in the middle of the walkway like he had paused midstride. His look of surprise quickly fell as he shook his head at me. His jaw clenched, his eyes narrowed, and he turned on his heel, disappearing back into crowd.

"Josh," I whispered, pulling away from Riley at a dead run. I slammed into the crowd, unable to get past the hungry spectators milling about, like I was fighting against the tide. I know what that embrace had looked like, but it couldn't be further from the truth. I had to make him see, to understand.

I only wanted him.

Like my emergency brake had been thrown, I jarred to a dead stop while people pushed past all around me. Oh shit. I wanted Josh. Not just as a distraction, but as mine. I'd fought so long and hard against it because I knew what kind of guy he was, the kind that slept with every girl in the near vicinity. But that wasn't who he was with me.

He'd been so good to me. Over and over again I'd been

a raging, slightly psychotic whack-job, and he'd stuck by me. Except for now, when he was walking away.

The loudspeaker barked the announcement of the next period, and I knew I'd have to catch him after the game. I backtracked to our section and headed down the stairs. The boys were already on the ice, ready to rock it.

Riley stood so I could slide past him into my seat. "He's not good for you," he whispered after we both sat.

"You don't know anything about him, and you don't get a say. Besides, you weren't good for me, either." I could remain peaceful with Riley as long as he didn't attack Josh. My line was drawn there.

"Please be careful. The guy still has a reputation up in Boulder, and he left three years ago."

"Reputations aren't exactly all they're cracked up to be. Yours was pretty stellar, remember?"

He sighed, and I knew the conversation was over.

At the second period, the score tied up.

The boys played hard that last period, but when it came down to the wire, they were beaten three to two. There would be no league championships for them this year.

By the time we got to the locker room to pick up Gus, Josh was gone.

Guess he got tired of waiting.

Chapter Seventeen

The World Arena felt a lot different a few hours later as Sam and I showed our tickets to the night doormen and had our purses checked for contraband. Gone were the hockey moms and dads, the fussy little brothers and sisters, and the general camaraderie that filled pee-wee hockey. Oh no, this was college hockey.

Raucous laughter and noise filled the promenade in a mix of CU Springs blue and gold, and Air Force Academy blue and white. Nothing like a little hometown action to bring out the crowds. "I could totally score a hot cadet!" Sam announced as she raked her eyes up an unsuspecting Air Force Academy cadet ahead of us in the popcorn line.

"Keep it in your pants, Sam. Not sure about you, but I have no desire to live the life our moms do." Or did, rather. "There's zero chance in hell I'd chase after a military guy."

She cocked her head to the side as if deliberating. "Maybe you're right." She turned around with our popcorn as she caught the eye of another cadet, shamelessly flirting. "Then again, I wouldn't mind a piece of that."

He tipped his hat at her with a wide grin, and I pulled her toward our entry. "Don't. All that comes out of that are knocks on your front door. Not worth it."

She stopped me at the entrance to our section and grasped both my shoulders. "Ember, it doesn't always end like it did for your dad. And don't tell me your mom wouldn't say it wasn't worth it. You can't think like that."

But I did. I turned my head away, thankful it wasn't a choice I had to make. "Let's just find our seats."

We made it down the stairs just in time for the puck drop, then slid past a few annoyed spectators before we found our seats, which were awesome, and totally unaffordable. "Sam, where did you get these tickets?" We were on the blue line, right on the ice.

"Jagger. He said he had a few, and I was more than happy to take them from him."

"He seems like a pretty good guy."

A wicked smile came across her face. "I don't know. I mean, he's not as dangerous to a girl's heart as Josh, but something tells me Jagger is a bad little boy in his own right."

"Josh isn't dangerous!" I tossed a piece of my popcorn at her.

She gave me a look, accusing me of insanity. "Josh Walker is most certainly dangerous to every single female around him—except for you, that is."

If she only had a freaking clue. "He is a huge danger to me. Just not in the way you think." My eyes locked onto his frame skating forward with the puck into AFA territory. "What if I decided he's worth the risk?" I asked softly.

"Seriously?" Her smile could have lit the arena. "I think that's the best idea you've had in, like…ever!"

Giddy excitement raced through me, and in that moment, it was like we were back in freshman year of high school, gossiping about hot boys and skipping class so I could watch

Josh Walker play. Except now I knew what his kiss tasted like, what his hands on my body felt like, and I wanted more.

With Josh, I always wanted more.

Watching him on the ice was hypnotizing. I lost my thoughts in the glide of his skates, the turns and switches. Ten minutes of the game passed, and I barely noticed, entranced by his sheer determination, drawn into everything about him. He was relentless, pushing through the defensemen to shoot and SCORE!

We were up out of our seats, yelling and cheering as he lit the lamp and was engulfed by his teammates. "Goal scored by senior forward Josh Walker at eleven minutes twenty-three seconds." The announcer brought out another wave of cheers.

The crowd died back down enough for me to hear the two girls sitting right behind us. "He's so fucking hot."

"I know right? I wonder if we can catch him after the game."

Ah, yes, puck bunnies. I laughed out loud. He may have been just a hot hockey player to them, but he was so much more to me. They could sleep with him, hell, maybe they already had, but something told me I had more of him than they ever would, and that was without the sex.

Sam giggled, and I knew she'd heard them. Not that they were being overly discreet. A quick glance behind me showed what I already knew: it was Tweedledee and Tweedledum, and they both had his number painted on their cheeks. Then again, I couldn't get too judgmental. After all, I was trying to catch him after the game, too.

Josh scored one more goal in the third period, and the Mountain Lions won, three to one. From the look of the hugging melee when the final buzzer sounded, he'd be in a good mood. Sam pulled me up the stairs before the puck bunnies could make it out. "You need a head start!" she called over her shoulder with a laugh.

Give Sam a good pursuit of a guy, and she became a female 007, ready to seek and destroy.

We made it up to the promenade as it was filling. "Sam, can I catch you at home?"

She hugged me close with a little more exuberance than usual. "As long as you're catching Josh Walker!"

I pushed her away with a laugh. What, was I sixteen again? Because it sure as hell felt like it. "I'll see you later!" With a wave, I ran across the promenade and down the stairs to the locker room entry. There were benefits to my little brother playing hockey in the same arena I was stalking a guy in.

I slipped out the west doors and huddled my jacket to me against the February chill. The path was well lit to the locker room entrance as I hurried along the back side of the arena.

I fell in with a small group of mostly girl fans as we bottlenecked at the door. Guess I wasn't the only one with this idea. We filed into the hallway, and I snagged one of the only bare spots against the wall. Girls pulled out compacts, checking their makeup or applying more as they giggled about what party would be hot that night, and who had dibs on which player. Josh's name was called out more than once.

Holy shit. I was hanging out with groupies.

To affirm my guess, Tweedledee and Tweedledum sauntered in and brazenly approached the pimple-faced security guard to attempt to get into the locker room. Although it appeared he highly enjoyed their attempts, he stood his ground.

Atta boy.

Heads turned as the locker room door opened and the first players emerged. Cheers echoed through the hallway, reverberating off the painted cinder block walls. Once those players made it down the hallway, bags of gear slung over their shoulders and a girl on their arm, the others filed out.

It felt like the entire team exited before Josh made his appearance. He nodded to the security guard with a smile and zipped up his black Columbia coat before turning toward us. His hair was damp from a shower, and he rubbed his hands over it with a look so broken I nearly lost it. A quick shake of his head, and a fake smile appeared on his face. The two puck bunnies raced forward, and Josh held out his arms, making room for them under each.

He was certainly no stranger to female adoration.

For a split second I debated running, just taking off and saying to hell with this plan. He looked happy enough, right? He would never lack for a girlfriend; it's not like not having me was killing him. Yeah. I would just leave.

My grip tightened on the strap of my purse, and I glanced up at him one more time before escape. He was looking at the floor, laughing with the girls as he came down the hallway, but the smile faltered, and I saw it again, the broken part of him that I somehow knew I was responsible for. I had to try to fix it.

"Josh." I stepped out and said his name so softly I barely heard it over the noise in the hallway.

His head snapped up like he'd been struck. "Ember?" Everything I needed to know was in the curt snap of his voice. Instead of the smile I longed for, his eyes narrowed in suspicion. "What are you doing here?"

I looked at the Tweedle twins, who both threw me mocking smiles. "Can I have a minute?"

He blasted that fake smile at me, which hurt more than anything he could have said. "Not sure." He kissed one of the puck bunnies on the cheek. "What do you think, ladies? Should we bring Ember along to the party?"

Heather took a peek at my casual jeans, vest, and Henley, compared to her short skirt and shorter neckline, and giggled. "Why not? She looks like she needs to loosen up."

Josh shrugged. "Come on, if you can keep up, Ember."

He walked right past me, assuming I'd follow in his wake. Mean, spiteful comments crept up my throat, itching to worm their way across my tongue and out of my mouth, but I choked them back down. Whether or not he was being an ass, it was my fault. I owed him an explanation. He owed me a chance to explain. Right?

The girls giggled as he opened the doors to his Jeep. Tweedledee jumped in the back, and Tweedledum took the passenger side, leaving me behind Josh. He reached in and lifted up his seat. "After you."

"Josh, really, I just need a minute." I looked up into those brown eyes and almost forgot what I needed the minute for.

He caged me between his arms, pressing me against the back quarter of the Jeep. "Really? I can think of a lot to do in a minute, Ember. Then again, I bet Riley wouldn't like to know what I'd be doing with you, would he?"

"That's what I'm trying to talk to you about." It took everything in me not to kiss him, to pull his face to mine and make him see. If he'd been irresistible when I was determined to stay away, what would he be like now that I was ready to jump?

He brushed his cheek against mine, his breath tickling my ear, so much warmer than the air. "Maybe I'm not quite ready to hear about how fucking perfect Riley is, and how you've forgiven him and worked it all out."

"Josh—"

He placed two fingers across my lips, silencing me. "You want to talk? Fine. I'll give you five minutes once I have enough alcohol in my system to hear it. You want it? Get in."

Our eyes were locked in a silent, heated battle. "Fine."

He gestured with his hand toward the open door. "Your chariot awaits."

I swallowed the sarcastic remark that lingered on the

edge of my tongue, took the hand he offered, and climbed into the Jeep. He leaned over me, fastening the buckle just like he had the night I'd found Riley with Kayla. I couldn't fight off my need to touch him and brushed my hand along the bare skin of his neck. He jerked back with a hiss like I'd burned him. His eyes flashed to mine for an instant before he shut my door.

If I still had that kind of effect on him, I had a chance.

Once his gear was stored in the back, he climbed in, and we started the drive up to campus. Catching his reflection in the rearview mirror, I gave myself time to soak him in. His concentration on the road was fierce, but the way he worried his bottom lip between his teeth told me there was more on his mind than traffic. God, I wanted to steal that lip away from those teeth and kiss it free.

When we stopped at a red light a few minutes away from campus, we locked eyes in the mirror. Electricity passed between us, threatening to turn me to ash. Would it always be like this with him? Would this infatuation wear off? Something told me no, and that was scarier than the thought that one day we'd be complacent. If we ever reached a "one day."

"Josh, which party are we headed to?" Tweedledee asked.

"I figured we'd head to the house, if that's okay with you ladies."

The girls squealed. Sweet mercy, they were freaking loud.

"I'll take that as a 'yes.'" He chuckled. "Ember?"

I locked onto those brown eyes again and stuck to the plan. No more hiding, no more fighting it. "I want to be wherever you are."

I felt the girls both turn and stare at me, but I wasn't letting go of his gaze long enough to acknowledge them. If this was a fight for his attention, I was winning. Period. His breath left his chest in a ragged sound as the light turned green, and he broke our stare.

Three minutes and a lifetime later, we pulled in front of the Kappa house. It wasn't as packed as it had been for the Snow Bash, but there was still more than a decent showing. People scurried out of the way as Josh sped into his spot, threw the brake, and bolted from the car like he was on fire. The girls climbed down, pulling their skirts to cover their asses as they hit the ground.

"Walker!" his brothers called out from the porch, lifting red solo cups in salute. "Great game!"

Josh gave them a head nod and helped Tweedledee and Tweedledum over the roped markers that separated the parking lot from the sidewalk in front of the house. I climbed over on my own.

With one girl under each arm, he walked up the porch steps. Another set of puck bunnies, this time of the brunette variety, met him at the door. "Josh! We wanted to catch a ride with you!" one pouted, sliding her fingers up his chest.

The urge to hurl nearly overpowered me. Could they be any more pathetic? It seemed like the more desperate they were, the smaller their clothes got. "Don't worry girls." A cocky smile made his face less austere, more boyish. "There's plenty to go around, and I'm feeling good tonight."

The girls slid up next to him, giving Tweedledee and Tweedledum a run for their money, and exasperation nearly choked me. Who the hell *was* he tonight?

Then I realized, this was the Josh Walker everyone else knew. The one who scored the goals on the ice, and the girls off it. This was the Josh I was warned against, and here I was chasing after him like a naïve freshman again. Five years hadn't changed much.

My feet hit the first steps and stopped as my hand clenched the thick porch railing. Who was I to call those girls pathetic? Sure, they had on less clothes than I did, but we were all there for the same reason: chasing Josh Walker. He was being an ass, and I was being pathetic.

"You coming, Ember?" The mocking look on his face pushed me over the edge I'd been walking.

He wanted to play games? Fine.

"Yep." I skipped up the steps ahead of him and headed in the house, not looking back at him.

The house was packed. Speakers blared 50 Cent, and I pushed my way to the pool table, where Jagger leaned over the green felt with a cue. "I need a drink."

His eyebrows shot up, and he sank the shot. "My pleasure." He stood, stretching the cue above his head, the movement lifting his shirt to reveal a set of seriously cut abs. But as gorgeous as Jagger was, he didn't have me desperate to run my tongue up his stomach. "Beer?" He handed his cue off to one of his brothers and walked me to the bar. A minute later, he popped the lid off and handed me a bottle. "You're a cherry wheat fan, right?"

"Yeah, thanks for noticing." I offered him a smile, took a long pull of the beer, and leaned back against the bar.

"You're not exactly dressed for a party."

A wry laugh bubbled out of me. "Yeah, well, I didn't know I'd be competing for Josh with the rest of the crowd here."

His gaze transferred from me to across the room where I knew Josh was already dancing with the bimbo brigade. "You know what you're doing, there? Josh is...Josh."

I slammed back my beer and peeled off my Henley to just my blue lace camisole, cut low enough to bare my cleavage but not my bra. Catcalls erupted around us. I tossed my shirt on the bar and ran my fingers through my static-ridden hair. Freaking arid air. "That's better, don't you think? Dance with me."

His eyes widened. "I think Josh has his damn hands

full." He pulled me onto the floor so I could dance, but kept a junior-high-dance space between our bodies. No doubt the last thing he wanted was to piss off his roommate.

I locked eyes with Josh from a few feet away, looking over the Barbie rubbing up against him. *Get a freaking room.* Ugh. The thought sent slices of agony through my chest. His hands may have been on her body, but his eyes were on me, following each move I made with the beat. Energy thrummed through me, not from the music, but from watching Josh move and remembering what it felt like to have him pressed against me.

Barbie turned in his arms and whispered in his ear. He gave her a seductive smile, and she took his outstretched hand. She slid by us first, pulling him through the crowd toward the stairs. Josh cocked one eyebrow up at me in question, but I couldn't bring myself to look him in the eyes. If all he wanted was an easy piece of ass, then he was right to take Barbie upstairs.

But I knew that was a lie the moment I thought it. Sure, he'd taken me farther than any guy had, but he'd stopped before sleeping with me. That kind of guy wasn't only about an easy piece.

He shook his head with a self-deprecating smile, like he was disappointed, and kept his eyes locked on me as he whispered something to Jagger. Jagger nodded, and Josh threw me one last inquisitive look before taking Barbie upstairs.

"Let's get a drink," Jagger suggested. I nodded my head absentmindedly and followed him back to the bar. "Beer?"

"Tequila." Beer just wasn't going to cut it.

Lick. Slam. Suck. The alcohol slid down my throat like fire, and the cool lime soothed the numbing pain. But the flavor put me back in Breckenridge and the taste of Josh's tongue in my mouth. Watching him walk that girl upstairs wrecked my soul and tore it down, threatening to bring me lower than Riley ever had.

"I need air," I forced out, stumbling over a barstool. I wasn't even drunk. Just devastated. I wiggled my way through the crowd and onto the front porch, which was remarkably empty, and gripped the chain on the porch swing as I lowered my weight into it. Josh was upstairs, touching another girl, kissing her. I took deep breaths to keep from puking.

Jagger followed me out and leaned against the porch railing, watching me silently as he nursed another beer.

"I don't know what the hell I'm doing," I admitted, staring up at the stars.

"Neither does he."

"Oh, I think he's pretty well-versed at taking girls upstairs during these parties." God, it hurt. "Why does this hurt so badly?" It was a rhetorical question, but Jagger answered.

"Love's a bitch."

That brought my gaze to his. "I don't love him."

"Really? Then why do you care who he takes upstairs?"

I didn't owe Jagger an explanation. Hell, I barely knew him, but maybe he could understand. Someone in this situation had to, right? "I-I-I don't care who he takes."

"You cared when it was you." Josh's smooth-as-velvet voice came from the doorway.

I turned to see him leaned up against it, arms crossed in front of him casually. He looked so damn sexy. Had she tasted good to him? "Done already? You know, it's not about scoring the fastest, right?"

Jagger took one look at the tension in Josh's face and excused himself. "Yeah, just let me know when you're ready to head home, man."

The swing rocked slightly as Josh took the seat next to me. "What are you doing, Ember?"

I bit back the fury that choked me and let honesty rule. "I

have no idea. Why would you do that? Take her upstairs with me watching?"

His eyes took a hard glint. "Like it matters? Last time I checked, you have a boyfriend, right, Ember? You choose to be with an asshole who doesn't deserve a single one of your kisses, and I choose to sleep with vapid girls."

"I'm not with Riley. That's what I've been trying to tell you."

His mouth hung open momentarily. "You're not?"

"No. We had lunch at the game and both got the closure we needed. You don't walk away from a three-year relationship without taking a minute to let it go, Josh."

"But I saw you in his arms." His brow furrowed, and I desperately wanted to smooth the lines in his forehead with my fingers.

"You saw me hugging him good-bye, yes. I tried to catch you and explain, but you were gone, and then you wouldn't take my calls." I shifted my weight toward him, making the chains of the swing squeak.

"You're not with Riley?"

What was he, a parrot? "No."

"Why not?"

I bit my lip, gnawing on the possibility of letting him in, all the way in. Just a few words, that would be all it took for him to know what he meant to me. But those few words opened me up to all the hurt I'd been trying to protect myself from.

He reached over the distance that separated us and stroked his fingers down my cheek. "December, why not?"

I savored the sound of my name from his mouth.

"Please, tell me?"

His plea broke me. "Because he's not you." The confession slipped past my lips in a whisper before I could use my better judgment.

A ragged sigh burst from his lips a second before he claimed mine. Without preamble, his tongue swept inside my mouth and took me in a crushing kiss. With what sanity I had left, I pulled away. "Why aren't you upstairs with Barbie? She's a pretty little package."

He rested his forehead against mine. "Because everything I want is wrapped up in you, Ember."

"Everything about me is...just messed up. You have no idea what you're getting into."

"You. I'm getting into you, December. That's all I need." He finished his promise against my mouth, and I lost myself in him. "Just give me a chance."

Chances meant vulnerability, and I knew I couldn't survive another loss, especially if it was from Josh. But my other option was not to have him. So there was only really one choice.

"Okay, let's give this a chance."

Chapter Eighteen

Three knocks sounded on the door. Josh was right on time.

I checked my makeup in the mirror, like I hadn't already done it a dozen times or more. Yup, my face was still there. I let out a deep breath and tried to slow my racing heart as I opened the door for our Friday night date.

The slow smile that spread across his face sent my heart rate flying again. "Hi."

His teeth bit into his lower lip a scant second before he shook his head at me. "You can't wear that."

Ouch. "You don't like it?" I looked down at the short, flirty skirt Sam had talked me into, paired with leggings and a low-cut sweater. This was her idea of "helping" the situation along.

"Oh no, I like it." His eyes darkened. "You look edible, Ember. But you'll freeze that cute little rear of yours off if you wear it."

"What do you want me to wear?"

"Pants."

I laughed. "These are pants."

"Those are glorified pantyhose." He took three steps, backing me against the entry-hall wall. My breath hitched as he reached down my left leg and lifted it, curling it by the knee around his waist. One move, and he had me so turned on I was ready to forgo the date and skip to the good-night kiss, or more. Or something. He ran his hand from my exposed ankle up my legging-clad calf, across the back of my knee and up my thigh, stopping where the skirt began. He brought his forehead down to rest against mine. "I can feel every curve of you under these, December, just as if my hand was on your naked skin."

I arched up for a kiss and he pulled back, his eyes dark with familiar desire. "If I kiss you now, there will be no date."

"I'm okay with that."

With one last stroke of my leg, he released it from his waist and gently set it back to the ground. He lifted his hands like he was under arrest and backed away slowly. "Pants. Now."

I pushed off the wall and headed back to my bedroom to change with an uncontrollable smile on my face. I had Josh Walker close to losing control.

Thank God for the stupid pants.

"I cannot believe this is your idea of a date." I looked up at the ceiling of the Honnen Ice Arena for the fifth time this hour from my back. I'd been down so often that the cold had seeped through my vest, shirt, and into my skin. At least I'd worn gloves to spare my fingers.

Josh laughed, pulling me up yet again. "I guess it's a pretty good way to get you on your back."

"Ha. Ha." My feet slipped out from underneath me, but he had a firm enough grip to keep me upright. It was the first time in his arms that I wasn't thinking about taking his clothes off. "I can't believe you find this fun."

He skated me toward the goal and made sure I was steady before he skated around me. "This is where I live. Everything else is just breathing to get by."

"So basically you brought me here to show off?"

He skated backward away from me, his grin drawing me in like nothing else could. "Is it working?"

"It's making my butt sore."

His laugh echoed around the empty hall. I skated out a few yards, forgetting my precarious position, and lost myself in watching him. He turned so quickly, I couldn't believe he didn't fall, and cut back toward me. It was true: this is where he lived, not just existed. There was vitality in him that didn't exist anywhere else but on the ice. He'd had it in high school, but it had increased since then. He skated more powerfully, and yet had more control now. He was more skilled and more comfortable with it, more daring when the situation called for it, and more patient when daring wasn't the way to go.

Where did I live? Where was I vital? Did I have anything that made me feel as alive as Josh looked right now?

"Hey, where are you?" he asked, gliding forward and bracing me before I fell. "You went far away just then."

I forced a smile. "Nothing, no worries."

"Don't pull that crap with me. If there's something on your mind, I want to know about it. Don't shove it to the side."

I couldn't put it into words, not really. "It's stupid."

He came around my side and, with one hand around my waist, guided me smoothly around the ice. "I didn't mean to push. It's just that I don't want you faking stuff around me. Don't treat me like I'm someone else."

We both knew who he was talking about. We made another turn, and I was careful to watch his feet, mimicking his smooth motions with my own. "You're really happy out here."

"Yes."

"I don't have anything like this. I can't remember the last time I had something of my own. Something that made me feel driven, alive."

He turned so he was skating backward, pulling me while I faced him. "If I remember correctly, you were a spitfire on the debate team."

I would have tripped if he hadn't kept me steady. "Debate team? That was eons ago. Like freshman-and-sophomore-year eons." My eyes narrowed. "I don't remember seeing you anywhere near the debate team." If I had, I wouldn't have bothered to look at Riley.

His grin nearly undid me. "I seem to recall a certain argument over school uniforms. You handed the opposing team their asses, and that paper was brilliant."

"Hey! School uniforms are an equalizing measure that takes away a lot of the peer pressure to spend tons of money on clothes for stupid social status...Wait. You were actually there? You read my paper?"

"Yeah." His thumb grazed across my cheek, and he took my hand. "I was Andrusyk's TA, so I entered all his grades. What were you planning to do with all that fire?"

I braced myself for the oh-she's-a-dork look. "I wanted to write history books, finding the other side of the story, kind of like Howard Zinn." I quickly changed the subject before he could think I was an insane library-stalker. "Besides, you entering my grade was one thing, but actually being there to watch?"

His smile faded into a look of brutal intensity. "I had a thing for this girl, but she was way too good for someone like I was."

The silence of the rink was only broken by the sound of our skates on the ice. "I had the biggest crush on you."

The confession tumbled and tripped from my lips. "I used to daydream about asking you to Sadie Hawkins, or that you'd notice me, but you were Josh Walker, and that was never going to happen."

He swallowed. "I'm glad you didn't. I wasn't the right kind of guy back then."

"But you are now?"

"That's the beautiful thing about time. No one stays who they were in high school. You wrote the most amazing history papers, looked at issues with such fresh views. You'd be a great historian. Why did you quit?"

It took less than a second to think back and remember. "Riley." It came out as a whisper, and I stopped moving my feet. We coasted for a few feet until Josh stopped us, waiting for me to continue. "We got together and made all these plans. I mean, they were good plans, but they were his, I guess. I decided to become an elementary teacher instead, and everything else just went away. Besides, quitting gave me more time for other things, and Dad was gone that year, so Mom needed help with Gus."

"Do you ever think of yourself first?"

I laughed. "All the time. Don't paint me as some kind of martyr, Josh. There are just certain ways that things run. Everything has a system, a schedule, and whatever doesn't help that run gets eliminated. It's logic, not selflessness."

"And now that Riley isn't in the picture? Are you still planning to teach?"

The pit of my stomach dropped out, threatening to take me with it. "Yes." I shook my head. "No." I closed my eyes and my breath rushed out as vapor in the air. "I don't know. It wasn't losing Riley that hurt the most. It was losing the plans we made. Everything was set, and straight, and perfect. Now everything is just a jumble, and I don't know how to clean it up without him telling me."

He nodded slowly. "Just make sure you're doing what you need, Ember. Find what makes you happy. It's out there."

I shuffled the inches that separated us, bringing me up against his chest, and wound my arms around his neck. "The only time I really feel alive anymore is when I'm with you, and that scares the hell out of me." I whispered the admission.

His lips met mine, cool and firm. The kiss was chaste, sweet, and more tender than any we'd shared before. He pulled me in even closer and rested his forehead against mine. "Everything about you scares the hell out of me, December."

I didn't have a chance to respond. A herd of elephants headed our way, coming through the locker-room entry to the ice hall. It was the hockey team from Colorado College, the Tigers, Gus's fantasy come to life. When it came to hockey, Colorado College was the place to be.

"Hey! You can't be here!" one of the players shouted, skating over. "We've got practice."

"Yeah, man, sorry. We stayed a few minutes late. We'll get out of your hair. Thanks for loaning us the ice. "

A peculiar expression came across the Tiger's face before surprise. "Hey, you're Josh Walker!"

If I hadn't been watching Josh so closely, I would have missed the quick jaw clench. "Yeah. Nice to meet you."

The guy turned around, revealing his last name of Cedar on his jersey. "Lugawski, Hamilton! This is Josh Walker!"

"No way!" the other players skated over.

"Dude, you were, like, phenomenal! We've watched your tapes!"

I cringed at the "were." Crowded by three padded hockey players, I suddenly felt very tiny, but very defensive of Josh. "He's still pretty phenomenal."

Josh backed me out and nodded to the guys. "Thanks again for the ice."

"You still play?" Cedar asked, skating over as Josh moved

me toward the door.

"Yeah, for UCCS," he answered.

"Man! If Coach had known you were all healed up, he would have come calling. He's always been a big fan of yours. How did he lose you to Boulder?"

Healed up? When had Josh been hurt? I'd never heard anything about him being injured during a game, but he'd left Boulder the year before I got there. His hand tightened around mine like he was holding something back.

Josh laughed. I wondered if anyone else realized it wasn't a real laugh, or if I was just that tuned to him. "Full ride to CU. I couldn't afford you guys, and your roster was too stacked my freshman year to afford me. Stars just didn't align."

Cedar shook his head. "Man, we would have been lucky to have you. When did you start playing again?"

"Just this last year."

"Damn shame about your leg. But thank you. You're a hero to the rest of us."

Josh took his outstretched hand and shook it. "Nothing to thank me for. Just doing my part." His voice dropped so low I had to strain to hear what he'd said.

"Still, it's fucking amazing."

Man, these guys had a serious case of hockey-player hero worship.

"Cedar!" Another player called him back.

"Yeah!" He turned back to Josh. "Listen, if you're ever at a game, let me know."

Josh gave a tight-lipped smile. "Absolutely. We're going to get out of your hair. You guys look good this year." With another handshake, he pulled me off the ice, and I walked toward the bleachers with awkward, clunky steps. Skates did nothing for my poise.

I barely had my skates untied when Josh knelt in front of me, tension coming off him in radioactive waves. With more gentleness than I expected, he brushed my hands aside and had my skates off before I could blink. He was so intent on his task, I didn't bother to tell him I could put on my own shoes. He slid my flats onto my feet and helped me stand.

"You ready?" he asked.

"Yeah." I tossed one more glance at the black-and-gold clad team warming up. "Man, they're good."

Without looking back, he gently led me out of the ice hall. "They're the best."

Something was incredibly wrong with him. I hurried my steps to match his, coming in under his arm. He pulled me in.

Outside the rink, the cool air hit my face, and I took a deep breath. Josh opened my door and saw me safely inside the Jeep, but he didn't get in right away. He walked around to his side, but then leaned back against the door, tugging his hair through his hands for a moment before leaning over. My first instinct screamed to go to him, but the vibe he was putting out said it was best for me to stay where he put me.

His head came back up, and he rested it briefly on the window before taking what looked like a huge breath and steadying himself. Then he opened the door, slipped inside, and gave me a smile. "Good first date?"

"Don't do that."

His eyes flashed a warning that I sailed right by. "Don't treat me like I'm somebody else and hide from me."

He gave a half sigh, half laugh. "I deserved that."

I pointed to the arena. "That's what you wanted."

"Yes." His hands dug into the soft leather of his steering wheel. "You weren't the only one with plans." I reached over and laid my hand on his thigh, needing to touch him. He closed his eyes, something akin to pain wracking his features.

He threw open his eyes, turned the radio up, and pulled out of the ice arena. He held my hand between changing gears, but didn't speak the whole way home. God, I had been so self-absorbed. Yes, I had lost my father and the plans I'd made, but while I had been wrapped up in my family and my own life, I hadn't paused to see that my tragedy wasn't the only one around me. People lost their dreams every day.

He pulled the Jeep into his parking spot and hurried around to open my door. We both knew he didn't have to, but he lowered me from my seat to the ground carefully, like I was something precious.

"You wanted to be a Tiger?" I asked, trying to get him to talk to me. I couldn't be the only one to give away my secrets. I wanted to know everything about him, especially the parts he kept so carefully hidden from everyone else.

He unlocked the door to our building and waited until we were inside to speak. "Yeah. One of the happiest days of my life was when I was accepted to CC. But we couldn't afford it, and CU gave me a full ride. So I went to Boulder."

"And you were hurt? I never knew about it."

He punched the elevator button with his finger. "It was off-season and not very big news."

"Was that when you came home?" Shit. I knew next to nothing about Josh Walker.

He shook his head. "My mom told me she had breast cancer the day after winter finals my sophomore year. It's just the two of us, not like she had anyone else to take care of her, you know? I transferred to UCCS."

"And you call me selfless?" He was so lucky UCCS had honored his scholarship, especially since their team wasn't on the same level.

Ding. The elevator opened, and we stepped inside. "That's why I didn't give you crap for transferring here. I know what it's like to be the one your family depends on." He twined my fingers with his and kissed the back of my hand.

"Your mom? Is she…"

"Mom's great. She's a fighter. Once she was in remission,

she moved back to Arizona to be near my grandparents, and I stayed here."

"But then you were hurt?" He was like a puzzle where every piece was black, and I couldn't tell what went where.

His jaw clenched again. I wondered if he knew that I could spot his tell. "Yeah, right around the same time Mom's scans came back clean. I wasn't eligible my sophomore year, since I caught the tail end of their season, but I rocked my junior year, and Colorado College came to talk to me about a scholarship. I was hurt a few months later, and the rest—"

Ding. We were at our floor. We headed down the hall and paused in the middle of our doors, our hands still linked.

"It took you a year to heal?"

"It took me that long to get back to hockey, but I'll never be as good as I used to be." He looked deep into my eyes. "That's the thing, though. Plans change, you adjust the sails and go with it. Just because I won't play for CC doesn't mean I won't do something else equally amazing."

"But it still hurts you."

"Yeah, but it's better bit by bit. It sucks to get it tossed in my face, but it's not like I can change the past or what happened."

Sure, he was talking about himself, and it wasn't some back-handed lecture, but still, his words cut through me, leaving me raw, bare. I couldn't change what the last few months had brought. I couldn't bring back Dad, and I wouldn't take back Riley, but I could step forward.

"One day, will you tell me what happened to you?"

He took a moment to answer, and then nodded. "Just not right now. I'm not ready."

His honesty was more soothing than knowing about his injury. "Thank you for tonight."

His hand brushed my cheek, cupping my face and sending a thrill of electricity down my neck. "Sorry. It may have been a little heavy for first-date material."

"It was perfect. Then again, I've been dreaming of a date with you since the first day of my freshman year, so we probably could have done something atrocious and awful, and it would have been perfect. Don't ever apologize for showing me who you are."

"There was another reason I was happy about you transferring," he admitted.

"Oh?"

"Selfishly, I wanted you near me."

"Josh—"

"Listen for a sec. Yes, I wanted you near me, and I still do, but there's something I have to give you, and then you can choose what to do with it. Wait here." He disappeared into his apartment for less than a minute and came back with a manila folder, rubbing his fingers along it nervously. "This is because I know what you're capable of, even when you don't."

He gave me the folder, and I opened it slowly, sucking in my breath. "An application for Vanderbilt?"

He smiled. "Some dreams aren't dead, just sleeping. I need you to know every option you have, and not to be scared of them. More than this craving to have you near me, I want you happy."

That was the moment I fell in love with Josh Walker.

Everything clicked into place, mending the broken parts of my soul enough to finally breathe freely, to soak in everything about him, and the beauty of what we were together.

He leaned down and brushed his lips over mine, still holding my face. I arched up for more, wanting everything I knew he was capable of giving. That was the problem with kissing Josh. The guy had some seriously addictive kissing abilities. He gave me another lingering kiss and pulled away.

"First date, remember?"

My jaw dropped. "Seriously? After everything we've—" He was like a high school girl, forcing me back to halfway-to-first-base at the start of every date.

He feigned shock. "Why, I've never! December Howard! Whatever would you think of me if I let you steal my virtue on the first date?"

"Right. You're so virginal." He oozed raw sex, the kind I knew would be a little bit dirty and a whole lot to handle.

"Everything with you is new to me." He let go of my face and turned me toward my front door. "Get inside before I change my mind, December."

"Oooh, am I getting to you, Josh?"

He reached around me, opened my front door, and gently pushed me inside. "More than you'll ever know. Now be good. Go to bed."

"It's nine o'clock."

"Doesn't matter. Go to sleep. Fully clothed. Or study. Or something."

I turned around and saw him leaning against the top of the door frame, his hands braced on either side of the door. He was so damn beautiful. "Are you thinking about a second date?"

His smile was breathtaking. "Hell yes."

"Then you'd better give me a kiss good night worth it."

In a millisecond he pulled me into him. My heart jumped, and my lips tingled in anticipation of what I knew had to come next. I was going to go mad if I couldn't get his mouth on mine.

He leisurely took my face in his hands, brushing back the stray strands of auburn hair. He examined every curve and line of my face, his eyes skimming over my cheekbones, pausing at my eyes, lingering on my mouth.

Then he took my mouth the way I needed him to.

His lips moved in delicious ways that had me instantly

ready for him. He slanted my head to gain better access, and all I could do was concentrate on not collapsing. He kept his hands on my face, but I craved them on every inch of my skin.

Once my knees wavered, he retreated. If I hadn't seen the desire raging in his darkened eyes, I would have thought he was completely unaffected. "May I call you for a second date, Ms. Howard?"

"Yes, please, Mr. Walker." My breath sounded like he'd just led me out of the bedroom. I wished he had.

"This evening was my pleasure." He kissed my hand and backed away, closing the door behind him and leaving me braced against the wall.

Shit. Crap. Shit. Crap. Yeah, that. Every fiber in my body was calling out for him, and now I had to go to sleep knowing he was only a wall away? I wanted to scream in frustration. Instead, I picked up my purse and the application from where I must have dropped them and headed down the hall into the living room.

April sat huddled on my couch, her eyes red and puffy.

"She got here about half an hour ago," Sam explained, dressed for the club. "She wouldn't explain what was wrong, and I didn't want to leave her alone."

"I got it, Sam. You head out."

She gave me a quick hug and after throwing a sympathetic look in April's direction was out the door. Friday night was calling.

I tossed everything on the end table and sat next to my sister, pulling her into my arms. "April?"

"He left me. Brett found out about the other guys and said he was done." Her sobs racked her tiny frame.

I held her to me and rocked her back and forth. I promised her everything would be okay and sent up a prayer to God that He would not make me a liar.

"What am I going to do?" Her warm tears soaked my

neck. "I love him, Ember."

I cupped her face in my hands and pulled her away so I could get a good look at her. The tears she cried were real and ugly. "You really want him?"

She nodded her head and bit her lip through the tears that tracked down her red cheeks.

"Then you apologize. No reasoning, no excuses. You were wrong, no matter what you've told yourself, and you're going to have to own up to that." She didn't need my judgment, but she needed the truth.

Something had to give.

"Okay, I can tell him I'm sorry. I was wrong. I just—"

"No. No excuses, April. Not even to yourself. And apologizing doesn't just mean you're sorry, it means you won't do it again, and unless you're ready for that, you leave him alone."

Her shoulders straightened, and I watched my sister grow up a little.

Chapter Nineteen

Crap. It was six thirty at night. The puck dropped in forty-two minutes, and I was easily a twenty-minute drive away. I hopped on one foot, trying to pull off the black boots so I could put on the brown ones that matched better with my cream-colored sweater. With an enthusiastic tug, the left one flew off my foot, and I landed on my butt, banging my head against the bookshelf.

"Ow!" I shouted. The bookcase shook from the impact, and I flung my arms over my head to catch what was sure to be an avalanche. A moment later, an envelope hit. Overreact much?

Dad's letter stared up at me from my lap. I traced my name in his familiar handwriting with my finger, like that could somehow bring him closer.

For the hundredth time or so, my fingers flirted with the seal, tempted to rip it open and hear from him one last time. But what would he say if he knew everything that had happened? If he knew I'd transferred? If he knew all my carefully laid plans were nothing but a pile of ashes waiting to be swept away?

What could he have left to say to me that he hadn't already told me in person? What had he held back? I turned it over in my hands again, determined not to leave anything unsaid in my life. There would never be a reason for me to write a letter.

Josh needed to know I loved him. Tonight. No waiting. No regrets. No worrying about consequences or debating if I'd grieved enough to move on.

I stood and put the envelope back on the top shelf.

I slipped on my brown boots. "Sam! We've got to go now!"

"Hold on!" she shouted back from the bathroom. "You can't rush perfection, and I'm about to go man hunting."

"Where the hell are my keys? Can't you put anything back where it goes?" I threw my arms into my coat and started tossing Sam's coffee-table mess around.

"Don't get your panties in a wad, Ember. We can't all have super-organizational OCD around here."

"Not helping, Sam!"

She laughed and kept applying her makeup.

Four minutes, three curse words, and a set of keys later, we were on our way.

Traffic wasn't bad until we hit the World Arena. Add in the five minutes to park, and we flirted with missing the puck drop.

We raced down the concourse, rudely shoving our way past people until we reached our section. A quick glance past the usher at the open ice confirmed we'd made it in time. We slid into our blue-line glass seats as the team took the ice. Perfect timing.

Like I had super-Josh-radar, I found him the moment he skated onto the ice. My smile erupted as I heard the arena burst in applause at the team's arrival. My eyes couldn't leave

Josh.

"Holy shit, girl, you've got it bad."

My smile spread wider, accepting the riot of emotions within me. "You have no clue." I loved him. But more than that, I wasn't just proud of the player out there, I was in awe of the man he'd become. "Did you know he got hurt?"

She nodded her head. "Yeah, he was out last year, but I didn't really talk to him. I mean, he was on campus and at the parties, but it's not like we ran in the same circles, even living next door. Did he tell you what happened?"

I shook my head.

"Rumor is he got shot that fall, but there's like ten thousand different versions of how it happened."

Shot. Holy shit, he'd been shot? "What's the most popular?"

"I heard everything from stopping a robbery to a pissed-off girlfriend."

Tweedledee and Tweedledum took their seats behind us again. What were the odds? These were the seats Josh had given us…Josh. I glanced back at the blondes with a smile. "Nice to see you, ladies."

Tweedledee glared at me. "Yeah. What's the deal with you and Walker?"

I gave my best go-to-hell smile. "He's just my whatever. You guys enjoy the game, okay?"

I turned around and ignored their scoffs and comments about how hot Josh was. I couldn't blame any of the population for fawning over him. Hell, by the end of the first period, he had me reduced to nearly drooling with want. When he checked someone into the boards, I flashed back to feeling him press me against a wall, undoubtedly his signature move. When I watched him skating backward, I remembered him pulling me down the ice, so careful with me. When he took a shot, I saw his fist flying through Riley's face, ready to destroy him for hurting me. When he adjusted his grip on the stick, I swore I could feel his hands on my body. The temperature in the rink called for a coat, but I was on freaking fire.

He scored, his arms raised in victory, and he met my eyes with a joyful smile before being assaulted by his teammates. It was me he was searching for.

There was no way to deny it, and I didn't want to. I was in love with him.

By the end of the third period, I was ashamed to admit that I didn't care they'd won, or that Josh had scored two of the five goals and assisted one. I just wanted him alone. The buzzer announced the end of the game, and the arena exploded in applause.

"Hey, can you take my car home for me?" I asked Sam as we waited for the crowd to clear the concrete stairway.

"Planning on catching a ride with a certain player?" She winked.

"Something tells me he'll bring me home." I laughed, and it felt good. I could do this, be happy, if that's what this ecstatic feeling bubbling through me was.

I might have skipped down the back of the arena to the player's entrance for all my feet hit the floor. I had to tell him. He needed to know. I didn't even care if he reciprocated. Well, that was a lie. Of course I cared, but it was more of an epiphany that I could feel this way again and not hide it. It wasn't about what he felt for me as much as it was what I was now capable of feeling for him.

The hallway was crowded, but I found a spare piece of wall and waited while the Tweedle twins glared from near the entrance. I understood their infatuation, but they didn't know him. No one knew him like I did. To them, he was a hot hockey player and a great lay. To me...he was everything.

Anticipation made the wait seem like forever, but the first players finally trickled out, shaking hands and giving high fives down the lined walkway. I didn't have to wait long.

Josh burst through the locker-room doors and the hallway was filled with thunderous approval. He gave his cocky smile, the one that had girls flocking around him, touching him, but he cut through.

His eyes swept up and down the corridor before locking onto mine. The smile that came across his face was anything but cocky. It was the slow, sexy one he reserved for me. It made me think of peeling his clothes off his body right where he stood and made me bolder with every step he took closer to me.

I reached for his hand, and he brought mine to his lips, kissing the back. "Thanks for coming."

"I wouldn't miss it."

Our moment was interrupted by Tweedledee and Tweedledum. "Hey, Josh, give us a ride to the after-party?"

They slid up against him, one on the side, one on the front, doing their best to push me out of the way. How aggressive could two girls get? He expertly turned, sliding me past the girls. "Ember? Do you want to go to the after-party?"

I shook my head slowly, ready to burst with everything I needed to tell him. I couldn't contain it, or it was going to come shining out of me like I was some dysfunctional Care Bear.

He gave a nod. "Want to end the night? I'll take you home, babe."

"Walker! You ready to go for that division trophy?" someone in the crowd shouted.

"I've already got my trophy!" he called back with a heart-stopping grin. He lifted me by my hips, holding me above his head. "I'd better put you back in that glass case," he teased.

Other players pushed through the hallway, making the noise level unbearable. I slid down his body and brought my mouth to his ear. "I want you to take me home with *you*."

He pulled back. A dropped jaw and wide eyes met mine. "December?"

My smile was so bright it felt like it belonged to someone else. "I'm in love with you, Josh Walker. Take. Me. Home."

The stunned glaze over his eyes lasted all of two seconds before his mouth descended on mine. We might as well have been alone for the way he kissed me. He was fierce, unyielding, demanding everything I had to give. My fingers tunneled through his hair as he slanted my mouth over his.

"But, Josh! The party?" one girl called out.

"Ember is my party." He called back before returning to my mouth. He carried me from the building without breaking the kiss, enormous bag of gear and all.

The metal of the Jeep's frame chilled through my jacket as he leaned me against it, kissing the very breath out of me in the icy night air. He paused long enough to unlock my door and open it; then he was back to kissing and lowering me into the seat at the same time. How could he be in complete control? I was ready to knock him to the ground in the parking lot.

A *click,* and he'd locked my seat belt into place. I grasped the back of his neck and held him to me, desperate to drink him in.

He moaned against my mouth. "You have to let me go."

"No." I'd finally given myself permission, and I wasn't backing down.

I ran my hand along his coat, unzipping it and then skimming my hand under his shirt to trace the line of his abs. I had his muscles memorized, and tonight I was going to lick every ridge of them. "I can't wait to put my mouth here." My fingers pressed into his skin.

"December." He breathed my name like a prayer. "Let go. Now." He pushed my hands down, but his eyes told me it was the last thing he wanted to do. "Let me go now before I fuck you in my Jeep in the middle of a damned parking lot."

"Maybe that's what I want." Any flat surface sounded great. Scratch that. Any surface would do.

He bit his lip in the way that drove me mad and took a ragged breath. "My bed. That was the deal, remember?"

Memories flashed. "God, yes, I remember everything about that night: your hands on my body, the way you drive me insane." I arched into him, pulling his mouth to mine. "You want me in your bed, Josh?"

His eyes were impossibly dark against the black sky. "Yes." He bit out the word. "I've never wanted anything more in my entire life."

"Then you'd better drive fast."

Weaving expertly through traffic, he got us home in fifteen minutes flat. Impressive, considering he'd dealt with demolition-derby-style traffic getting out of the arena. Even more impressive considering I used the time to become intimately acquainted with the skin of his neck. He gave the most delectable gasps when I took my teeth lightly to his earlobe. I couldn't wait to hear the sound again.

The Jeep jolted to a stop in his parking spot, and I had my door open before he could get around to my side. I flung myself into his arms. He caught me easily.

I lost myself in the feel, the texture of his mouth. He tasted like strawberries and Josh. I became the aggressor as we stumbled inside, running my tongue along the line of his teeth, craving every bit of him that I could get.

I heard a *ding*, and I was against the wall. My head lolled back, and Josh nipped at my neck. Chills raced down my body, followed by streaks of heat that ran straight to my thighs.

Another *ding* and he lifted me into his arms. His breathing was ragged, but he walked normally as he kissed me. He wasn't winded from carrying me; he was just as lost in lust as I was. The thought turned me on to an impossible new level. I was going to catch fire at any moment.

I let his mouth go once we reached his door, only to run my tongue down the salty skin of his neck. Whatever this man wore made him freaking edible. I heard a *click*, and we were moving again, stumbling to turn on lights. "You can put me down," I suggested.

"Not until you're in my bed." His open mouth rested against my neck. "God, December, you can't know how long I've dreamed of having you in my bed." That earned him another soul-destroying kiss. Or earned me one, rather. Hell, we were both winners in my book.

Chapter Twenty

We made it through the living room and into Josh's bedroom. He flicked on the bedside lamp, illuminating the room in a soft glow. I would have looked around if I'd really cared at that moment, but the only focus in my mind was how fast I could get him out of his clothes.

He slowly lowered me to the bed, and I wanted to squeal in victory. His weight pressed me further into the soft down comforter, and I was surrounded by the feel and scent of him. I slipped my legs from his back, and he rested in the cradle of my thighs, pressing into me.

Heaven.

"Slow. Have to slow down," he muttered to himself as his eyes raked up my body.

His hands slipped off my boots before he ran them up the outsides of my thighs. He squeezed my waist as his mouth captured mine again, intoxicating me. His hair threaded like silk through my fingers. He broke away from my mouth, skimming his lips down my neck. Chills danced along my spine, and I arched, giving him better access as my fingers bit into his scalp. "Josh," I moaned as he traced the sensitive path toward my collarbone.

"So sweet," he whispered against my skin. He slid against my body with delicious friction, running his tongue along my navel as he slowly raised my sweater. He glanced up with questioning eyes and waited for me to nod my assent before he slid it over my head, kissing me again as it passed my mouth.

Then his lips were back on my stomach, teasing, tracing the hollows and planes of my abdomen. He made me feel beautiful, desired. As my back bowed off the bed, driving my hips up to his, he slipped his hands behind me and removed my bra with a flick of a few fingers. He slipped the straps down reverently, his breath catching as my breasts were bared to him. "I've never seen a more perfect woman."

As turned-on as I already was, his words were like gasoline on a fire. I wrenched myself to sit as he kneeled between my thighs, gripped his shirt at the waist, and tugged it over his head. His body was even better than I remembered. I ran my fingertips over the hard planes of his stomach, and the fuck-me lines that framed his washboard abs and trailed into his jeans. I couldn't help it; I sank my fingers into his waistband and brought him to my mouth. There wasn't one spare ounce of fat on him, no give, no softness.

I worshipped the carved ridges of his stomach with my tongue, and quickly became addicted to the taste of Josh Walker. He sucked in his breath through his teeth, and when I raised my eyes to meet his, they were focused on me. His hands delved into my hair, holding me lightly to him, but clenching and unclenching his fists as though he was unable to control his own motions.

I did that to him, made him lose control, and I loved every bit of it. In a matter of seconds I had his jeans unbuttoned and sliding off his perfectly round ass to pool at his knees.

"Ember," he growled in warning. Men with asses like his shouldn't be allowed near the female population. My hands grazed over the elastic of his boxers, but I couldn't bring myself to pull them down, no matter how badly I needed to touch him, see him.

I met his eyes and nearly forgot what I was doing. The intensity radiating from his gaze sent a surge through my stomach, and I knew that without any other foreplay, I was ready for him. I'd never wanted something so badly in my life.

My hands explored his thighs, barely brushing under the legs of his boxers. I loved the texture of his skin, the crisp hair, the incredible way he smelled, like rain and sandalwood and…Josh. When my fingers caught the raised portion of his skin, I slid the leg of his boxers up to see the scar on his left leg.

"This is where you were shot?" I asked.

He didn't deny it, or ask how I knew. "Yes." His answer was gruff, his voice thick with what I hoped was desire.

"Are you ever going to tell me what happened to you?" It wasn't the right moment to ask, but I couldn't help it. I was about to surrender my body to him, and I deserved something of his in return.

His warm hand stroked over my hair and slid forward to cup my cheek as I fell into those eyes. "Just in the wrong place at the wrong time, baby. But I guess it led me to you, so it's more like the right place at the right time."

I fell even harder, if it was possible, letting go of the disappointment of not knowing yet what had happened to him. I leaned forward and kissed his scar, hating what it meant, the end of his dreams, but hoping I could help him figure out what his new ones would be. Then I reached around and firmly grabbed his beautiful ass.

"December, you have to stop, or I'm going to snap. I'm trying to go slow for you," he growled, retreating.

Gathering every ounce of courage I could muster, I pulled his hand from my cheek, turned the palm to my skin and drew it down, through the valley between my breasts, over my stomach, and into my jeans. He sucked in his breath, and I held mine as I brought him under my panties to feel the warm, wet folds underneath. He stroked across my clit once, and my hips bucked. "Snap already, Josh. I'm on fire for you. I don't need you to go slowly; I need to know what you feel like inside me."

In one motion, he discarded his jeans and was working the fly of mine. I lifted my hips as he slid the denim over them and down my legs. The ache between my thighs intensified to torturous as he looked over me like a buffet. "Fucking perfect. Every inch of you."

Before I could reply, his head was between my thighs, breathing on me through the thin silk of my panties. I couldn't even be embarrassed that they were drenched through; I was too caught up in my desperation for him. My hips lifted to his mouth of their own accord. My body knew where it belonged. "Josh…"

He breathed against me again, sending a ripple of need straight through me. "What do you need, baby?"

"You." My hips bucked against his mouth.

"Me?" He laughed seductively. Oh yes, he knew exactly how to twist a girl into knots.

I brought myself up on my elbows. "Joshua Walker, if you don't put your damn hands on me in two seconds, I'm walking out that door." I wasn't putting up with his teasing. He had to be as lost as I was.

Before I could count to two, he dragged my panties down…with his teeth. I moaned at the sight.

Once they were lost to the oblivion of Josh's bedroom, he was back on top of me, stroking my skin, relearning every curve and plane. "Jesus, I can barely control myself around you, December. You're so fucking..." His voice drifted as his hands covered my breasts, pulling lightly on my nipples, rolling them until I thrashed beneath him.

"So. What?" I managed to get out.

Where I expected to see that slow, sexy smile was the fiercest glare I'd ever seen. If I didn't know him so well, I'd have been afraid. "Mine." He growled, his hands stroking up to cup my face. "You're so fucking mine."

He took my lips in an intense kiss, and as if I'd heard it snap, I knew his control was gone. I clenched his hips like a vise as he stroked himself over me, his erection gliding just enough where I needed it to wreck me, but not enough to get me off. I could only whimper and take what he gave as he controlled me, stroking his tongue into my mouth at the same speed he was thrusting against me. But I wanted more, eager to feel his skin against mine with no barrier.

Desperation made me do the one thing I thought I never could: I pulled down his boxers.

He groaned against my mouth, and with his free hand lost the boxers. For the first time in my life, I was in bed with a naked man, and it was glorious. I angled against him, knowing that if he moved the slightest fraction of an inch, he'd be inside me. God, I needed him there. I needed him to stop the ache, to quell the burn.

"Josh—" I rolled my hips against him. "Please..."

His breath ragged, he ripped his mouth away from mine, reaching for a foil packet in his nightstand.

A wave of reality rolled over me. He kept condoms in his nightstand. How many girls had he brought to this bed? How many times had he torn panties off with his teeth? How many girls had been right where I was at this moment? Worse, what did it mean about me that it didn't change what I had decided to do?

"Ember?" He stilled above me.

I shook my head and feigned a smile. "I'm just glad you're prepared."

Something almost intangible flickered through his eyes, and his lust-sharpened features softened in a smile. "December Howard, you're the first girl I've ever brought into this bed."

"But you, and all those girls…"

He shook his head. "Never here. I have never brought any other woman into this bed. You're the only one I've ever wanted here. This is *my* space, and you're a part of me. No one else ever has been."

I was the first woman in this bed. A possessive smile graced my face, and I stole the packet from him, ripping it open, and then stared at it. Opening it was all well and good, but putting it on…

He took it from me and rolled it over his length, protecting us both. Then his mouth was on my breasts, and his fingers stroked into my folds, bringing the fire to a raging inferno. He knew just where to touch, just where to give, just where to take away. As he licked and sucked at my nipples, my head thrashed, my body reaching for his fingers as he slid them slowly inside me. Everything in me coiled tight, drawing inward until the pressure became unbearable. "Josh!" I screamed out as I came, my back arching off the bed.

As I drifted down from the high, he angled above me, bracing his weight on his arms. "Gorgeous, Ember. I could make you come every hour of every day just to see your face when you climax."

I stretched my arms above my head, feeling warmed up like a purring engine. I ran my fingers down the smooth expanse of muscle and skin on his back until I gripped his ass and pulled him against me.

His breath left in a gush as his erection stroked me, but he still didn't move, just kept staring into my eyes like he was waiting for me to retreat, to put a halt to this. "Josh..." I swiveled my hips until he nudged my entrance. My moment of naïve fear of his size lasted all of a second before I remembered he would never hurt me.

Every muscle in his body was rigid with the effort it took to maintain his control, but he still didn't move.

I slid my body up, taking him inside me not even an inch.

He squeezed his eyes shut for a moment, and when he opened them, they were so dark I couldn't tell iris from pupil. "You're mine."

I was panting, desperate to get him inside me. "Yes," I promised.

His jaw clenched. "Tell me you want this, that you won't regret it tomorrow. I'm not taking your virginity if you're not sure."

"Please, Josh. I'm yours. I've been yours since I was fifteen. I want this, I want you. I love you." I pulled on his neck, bringing him down to me, and thrust my tongue into his mouth at the same time he brought his body into mine. He swallowed my gasp.

He laid his forehead against mine, a fine sheen of perspiration covering his skin, making him glow. Any sting I felt dissolved after a few seconds, and I wiggled my hips. "Don't. Move. Jesus, December. You're so fucking tight, perfect."

I gently bit into his lower lip. "Because you were made for me."

"I love you," he whispered, as though the confession had been ripped from him.

Thank you, God. Everything in my world fell into exquisite alignment. "And I love you," I answered.

Something in him broke free, and with a primitive sound, he began to move, stroking my body with his in equal, measured thrusts, angling my hips just right so he pushed within me exactly where I needed him to. This. Was. Amazing. Pleasure radiated through me as I brought my hips against him by instinct, meeting him as he slid into me again and again.

He kissed me as he thrust, claiming my mouth the same way he was claiming my body: fully, completely, with no extra inch or give. There was not one part of me that didn't belong to him. I vaguely wondered if he'd always own me like this.

He reached between our bodies and stroked me to insanity. A few moments, and I was spinning out of control. "More! Yes!" I demanded in a voice I didn't recognize as my own. He grasped my hips in his hands and pushed deeper, harder, pounding into me without control, and I reveled in it.

My orgasm slammed into me, splintering me into tiny pieces just to further rip me apart and put me back together in a glorious moment of release. I called out his name and opened my eyes to see his face contort beautifully as he climaxed. "December," he whispered in a strangled cry. Then he collapsed on top of me, his weight deliciously oppressive. I could barely breathe, and I wouldn't have wanted to.

He raised his head and kissed me tenderly. "You okay?" His brows puckered. "I didn't mean to lose it like that."

"You're unbelievable."

Now he smiled, and my heart flipped in my chest. "We're unbelievable together. I've never felt that before. You stripped my soul clean."

I smoothed the lines of his forehead with my thumb and teased him. "Since I have nothing to compare it to, I guess it will have to do. I mean, all first times are awkward right?" An impish grin spread across my face. "Besides, I'm sure you'll do better for round two."

He raised his eyebrows at me before claiming my mouth in a kiss. "Smart ass! Round two it is!" My laughter didn't last past his mouth trailing down my stomach. Perfect.

Chapter Twenty-One

Sunlight streamed in through the windows when I peeled open my eyes. The bed next to me was empty. A single calla lily rested on Josh's pillow with a note propped up on its stem. I smiled as I stretched, luxuriating in the delicious soreness of my body.

So that was what everyone raved about. Why had I waited twenty years for that? His scent still clung to the sheets, and that was my answer. Because Josh was the one I was waiting for.

Josh, who loved me.

Happiness flowed through my veins, and I reached for the lily and brought it to my nose. No roses or daisies; Josh didn't do anything typical. I unfolded the note.

Good morning my gorgeous December,

I wish I could be here to wake you up the same way I put you to sleep, but you looked too peaceful to wake. I had to leave town, but I'll see you as soon as I'm

*back tomorrow night. Sleep as long as you like, I love
knowing you're in my bed. Thank you for the best
night of my life.*

I love you,
Josh

It had been the best night of my life, too. I felt free for
the first time in years, free and empowered, like the choices I
made were mine, and right, and for the right reasons.

I rolled into his pillow, pulled the soft sheets to my face,
and breathed him in. I couldn't see him until tomorrow night.
Not exactly the morning-after glow I was hoping for, but it
must have been important for him to leave so quickly.

I found my bra, pants, shirt, and located my pink panties
hanging on the corner of his dresser like I had won Where's
Waldo. The memory of him taking them off was enough to set
my skin aflame again. I made his bed and tossed the clothes
he'd left on both sides of the bed into the hamper by his door.

Then I shamelessly scoped out the pictures he had
framed on the wall opposite his bed. There was one of his
motorcycle, matted and framed like a piece of art. The
majority were hockey, starting with one from when he looked
barely old enough to walk and with a woman who I assumed
was his mom, all the way through to the team picture from
this year. He had played all of his life.

He hadn't let getting shot keep him down, though he still
wasn't ready to discuss it. He was stronger than a gunshot.
Even if it had killed his dream, he still found a way to live
it. I smiled when I caught the picture of Gus's team, Josh
standing by as a proud coach. He didn't just lick his wounds
and go with half a heart, he found a way to give back, to bring
up the next generation if he couldn't star in this one.

There was a picture of him perched on the side of a

hospital bed, his arms wrapped around a delicate, beautiful woman with striking features that mirrored a few of his own. She had to be his mother. Love radiated from his face, almost as exquisite as the bare skin of his head that matched his mother's. I swallowed back the lump in my throat. He must have shaved his head when she'd lost her hair from treatment. Could this guy be any more freaking perfect? He'd transferred colleges to be with his mother. That was why he understood how much my family meant to me, what I was willing to go through for them; he felt the same about his.

My eyes drifted back toward the high school years, and I gasped when I saw it. It was the picture that ran on the front of the sports section, the one I had pinned on my bedroom wall. I pulled the frame off the wall and couldn't contain my smile. It was from the school assembly after they'd won state. Everything about that assembly lingered in my mind, from the sheer noise of the gym to Josh's ecstatic face as he carried the trophy high above his head.

The picture captured that moment in perfection, from the deep maroon of his uniform to the blissful look on his profiled face with the trophy hoisted. He was beautiful, dangerous, and young, exactly how I remembered him. But even as gorgeous as that picture was, the high school version of Josh couldn't hold a candle to the one I loved now. Now his beauty and danger were tempered with maturity, which made him all the more amazing.

I lingered over the lines of his face, joy and pride emanating from him. I'd studied this picture so often and always found something I hadn't seen before. I loved that he wasn't just happy, there was something deeper there, a longing. I loved that we both had the same picture on our walls. I loved him.

But this wasn't the same version the paper had printed. That one had been cropped, apparently. I caught the details behind him now, the ones left off the print I had. In this picture, the crowd of students was visible behind him in beautiful detail. I had always wondered what he had been staring at, longing for. I traced my finger over the glass, following his line of sight.

It was me.

I was sitting next to Sam, laughing at something she said, and Josh's eyes were focused on me. Everything in me melted. He had noticed me, and after last night, I knew that look. He wanted me. I may have been gangly, awkward, and fifteen, but Josh Walker noticed me. I shook my head and smiled to myself as I rehung the picture. I'd definitely need this version.

I closed Josh's door quietly and breathed a sigh of relief when I saw my purse on the kitchen cabinet. I grabbed it from the counter and almost made it out the door.

"Walk of shame?" Jagger joked from his bedroom door.

My skin flushed hot, but I threw him a jaunty salute. "Jagger."

He laughed, his head thrown back in abandonment. Yeah, I could see why the girls went for him. He screamed reckless in a way that caught the eye. Just not *my* eye. "Ember, you have nothing to be ashamed of. Josh is fucking crazy over you."

Joy beat through my embarrassment. "I'm pretty crazy about him, too. Where did he skip off to this morning?"

Jagger's face dropped all expression for the barest of moments, but I caught it before a smooth smile took its place. "Scholarship stuff."

"Scholarship stuff? What do you mean?"

His eyes fell away, and my stomach went with them. "It's just something he has to do for his scholarship. He'll be home tomorrow."

What could Josh be doing that Jagger wouldn't want to tell me about? "Right," I muttered absentmindedly and turned for the door. My feet caught a stray bag of hockey gear, nearly sending me tumbling to the ground. Thankfully, I caught myself. Hockey gear. "Wait. Don't you have a game tonight?"

He reached over and pulled the bag out of my way. "Yeah."

"Josh is missing a game? That's not like him. Why would he miss a game?"

Jagger cleared his throat. "Coach is fine with it. He knows how Josh's scholarship works."

"But why would he miss a game if he's on a hockey scholarship?" Nothing made sense, and the way Jagger purposely dodged my questions didn't make me feel any better.

He closed off his expression and stepped back, cracking his neck in a stretch. "Yeah, so anyway, Josh will be back tomorrow night. I know he'll be dying to see you. He really cares about you, Ember. I've never seen him like this, not with any girl."

I melted. Was I really going to let whatever was going on with Josh's scholarship kill my morning-after buzz? Hell no. If something was wrong, he'd tell me. *Just don't let him be injured.* There was no way he'd take it if they took him off the ice for an injury. Was his leg more hurt than he let on? I'd have to ask him tomorrow night.

"Thanks for not making this all awkward, Jagger." He gave me a smile and a wave. I waved back and let myself out of the apartment, turning to mine. I reached into my purse for my keys. Shit. Sam drove my car home last night. Right. I knocked on the door, and she answered a few minutes later.

"Wow. You look..." There were simply no words for Sam's appearance. Or smell.

"Don't even. You went home with Josh-freaking-Walker and I decided, after I got home, alone, that I was going back out to have a good time. No lectures, I took a cab." She waddled like a penguin back to the darkened living room. I smiled at the drawn curtains.

"Medicate and hydrate?" I tossed my purse onto the counter.

She saluted me with a Dasani and nodded to the bottle of Excedrin next to her. "Besides, I may look like crap, but at least I'm not wearing what I went out in last night." She wiggled her eyebrows at me. "So dish, because if you spent the night in Josh's bed, I want freaking details."

I threw up my index finger at her and slid into my bedroom, tossing yesterday's clothes into the hamper and pulling on comfy pj pants and a tank. From the looks of Sam, we weren't going anywhere today.

The chair made a *whoosh*ing sound as I plopped my full weight into it, throwing my legs over the arm. "Yes. I spent the night with Josh."

Sam squealed and then grimaced, pushing her fingers into her temple. "Stupid tequila. Is he as yummy in bed as he looks?"

The smile that spread across my face may as well have been its own entity for all that I couldn't contain it. "He is perfect. Everything."

"I'm so freaking jealous!"

I laughed. "I just can't believe it happened, you know? I mean, Josh! He makes me forget everything. I don't need a schedule with him, or a plan, and things can be insane, and wonderful, and out of control because I know he's not going to let me fall." The words tumbled so quickly from my lips, but Sam interpreted my rant with a gleeful laugh.

"You love him!" She clapped her hands together with a smile that lit the room. "You trust him, and for once you're not molding yourself into whatever some guy wants."

That sweet feeling hit my heart again, like it was

reminding me it belonged to Josh. "I don't have to be anyone else. He loves me, and I love him."

She jumped across the coffee table, scattering magazines to the floor, and lunged at me in a bear hug. "I'm so happy for you!"

"I'm happy for me, too!"

We collapsed into a fit of giggles for a moment before Sam winced. "Ugh. My head. Let's talk about your new love life in soft tones the rest of the day. I want to know how that body of his stacks up."

My neck was crimped when a knock on the door sounded. I threw my history book on the table. So much for getting studying done; I'd fallen asleep with the book on my lap. The clock read 4:45 p.m. Sam was racked out on the couch with a Diva-embroidered sleeping mask, sleeping off her hangover. She'd be screwed if she wasn't recovered by tomorrow morning. Those kids she tutored in math Sunday afternoons could be brutal even when she wasn't hungover.

I checked the peephole and pulled back. What the heck was Mom doing here? I opened the door, and Gus came flying around her, tackling me with a sticky hug. "Ice cream?" I laughed.

"I totally ate yours."

I ruffled my fingers through his curls. "I'm totally cool with that."

Mom looked me up and down. "Late night?"

I raised an eyebrow. "Afternoon checkups never happened at Boulder."

She bowed her head with a smile. "Touché."

I motioned her inside, and she stepped in, dressed, hair and makeup done. She was healing. "It's nice," she said, her eyes sweeping over our apartment.

"Thanks, Mom."

"Mrs. Howard," Sam mumbled as she sat up.

"There's your late night," I whispered at my mother.

Mom laughed quietly. "Her mother would definitely not approve."

"Here's the deal, Mom." I crossed to the refrigerator, pulled out a Sprite, and pushed it toward Gus. "You show up on the weekend, you keep the secrets."

"Deal." She fidgeted with her phone. "I have an appointment for your sister. Do you think Gus could stay with you for a couple hours?"

"An appointment on a Saturday?"

"We thought it best that she start seeing someone, especially after I found those credit card bills you paid off while I wasn't quite myself."

I cringed. "I didn't know how to tell you."

"You did just fine. Better than I could have ever dreamed. I confiscated everything she bought. She's buying it back a bit at a time, and seeing the psychologist is part of that. It wouldn't hurt you to, either, you know." She forced a smile, like she hadn't just suggested I go to therapy.

I blatantly ignored her and turned to see Gus staring at Sam's glittery eye mask. "Gus, you want to hang with me for a bit?"

"Yeah!"

"He's cool, Mom. Sam, there's no point trying to sleep. He'll start poking at you in five minutes."

"Rawr!" she growled at Gus and pulled him down, locking her arms around him as he struggled playfully to get away.

"Thank you, Ember."

"No problem. That's why I moved back here, Mom. To help out."

Her cool hand stroked down my face like I was five again, and the light caught the diamond of her wedding set. "I want you to live your life, too."

I thought of Josh, and the way he'd worshipped my body last night. Mom would die if she knew. "I am. Don't worry so much about me."

"I never have to worry about you. You're more put together than half the population. Gus! I'll be back in two hours. Don't you dare act up."

"Bye!" he managed through his laughter.

Mom gave me a hug and headed out the door.

I snagged Gus out of Sam's arms. "Sam, if you're going to attack my baby brother, you at least have to smell decent. Shower. Now. Before child protective services gets called on us."

She flipped me the middle finger when Gus ran into my room and went for the shower.

"Can we watch this?" He held up a DVD of a horribly gory movie he took from the bookcase in my bedroom.

"Nope."

He grabbed the envelope from the top, and his expression puckered. "You haven't read Dad's letter yet?"

I shook my head. "Not ready, yet. I will."

He nodded. "It's okay to do things at your own pace." My brother, the sage.

"Did you like yours?"

He nodded, his head stuck further into my DVD collection. "He loves me, but I already knew that. He said he sent me my own soldier-guardian almost-angel. At least, that's what he called him. How cool is that?"

Sometimes I just didn't speak seven year old. "Awesome, buddy."

"*Iron Man*?"

"Sounds like a plan." We popped it into the player, and

I pulled him back onto my lap. I breathed in the sunshine scent of his hair, like taking a shot of pure joy, and smiled as it raced through me.

Sam came back in, freshly showered and perky, with a towel wrapped like a turban around her head. "That shower sure helped you."

"Well, I figured we'd have to get ready for the hockey game, right?"

Gus slurped at his Sprite, but I didn't bother to correct him. That's what moms were for. Big sisters were for movies and contraband soft drinks.

"I don't think I'm going tonight."

"What?" Sam dropped her jaw. "You're like the girlfriend of the star player, and you're not going? What's he going to think? I'll tell you what. He's going to think that he's awful in—"

I threw a pillow at her face before she could finish the sentence. "He's doing something for his scholarship and won't be back until tomorrow night."

"Well, that sucks. What do you think he's doing?"

"Not sure." As I shook my head, my chin rubbed across Gus's head. He leaned further against me, more engrossed in Tony Stark and his soda than anything. "I'm just hoping it's not his leg. I don't know what he'd do if he lost his scholarship."

"You and Coach Walker? That's cool. Gross, but cool. He got shot, you know," Gus announced. "Coach Walker did."

I hated that Gus had already been exposed to so much of the ugliness in the world. "Yeah, buddy, he did. But he's okay."

"It almost killed him, but he was super lucky."

Apprehension raced up my spine. "Did he tell you that?" Josh was really private about his injury. So private he hadn't even told me the full story.

"Dad did."

I turned him in my arms to see his face. "He what?"

"Chill out, Ember. I'm not crazy." He craned his neck back, but couldn't see the movie. "Dad took me to hockey, so he knew Coach Walker. He talked about him sometimes."

Don't be a moron. Of course my brother wasn't talking to dead people. "Yeah, sorry, buddy." The movie sucked him right back in.

Sam took a seat on the couch next to us. "So what do you really think is going on? Do you think he's hurt again?"

"He's at drill," Gus answered with a huge slurp.

My stomach fell through my body and a gaping hole opened up that cried out desperately to be filled with any piece of logic. "Drill for what, Gus? Like construction?"

His head swiveled, and he gave me the my-sister-is-dumb look. "No, like *drill*, Ember. You know, for the army. That's why Dad liked him. Josh is a soldier like he was." Gus turned back around like he'd announced that his hair was red. So matter of fact.

"Drill? Soldier?" No. No. No.

Gus sighed and stood up. "Seriously? You're going to have to rewind the movie if you keep talking, Ember. I'm missing the good parts."

Sam grabbed the remote and hit the pause button. "He's in the army, Gus?" she asked softly.

He nodded. "How do you think he got shot?"

Where the gaping pit in my stomach had been, now was a sense of crushing, of everything imploding into me like a black hole had opened up in my soul. Once a month. He disappeared for a weekend a month. Drill. "He's in the Guard," I whispered.

"Yup! Sergeant Walker!" Gus plopped down on the floor in front of the TV.

Sam pressed play and then pulled me into my bedroom,

shutting the door behind us. "Talk to me, girl."

It all made sense now. *Wrong place, wrong time.* He'd only failed to mention that the wrong place was half a world away and he'd been in uniform. He'd been lying to me from day one.

Oh God. I was in love with a soldier. I couldn't love a soldier. I swore I never would. I would never put my heart in the hands of someone who threw his life away in a foreign country, fighting for people who didn't even want us there, and left for months at a time.

I couldn't love a soldier. I couldn't sit home and wait and wonder if he'd ever come back. I wouldn't answer the door when strangers knocked. I wouldn't fall apart. I wouldn't hang a gold star in my window.

I wouldn't be my mother.

"You're not speaking, Ember."

I snapped my focus back to Sam. "He's wrong. He's wrong! Josh would have told me. He knows how I feel about the army. He would have told me!"

I was on my feet before I realized I'd wanted to stand. I had to know. "Gus, stay with Sam!" I flew out the door, not bothering to shut it behind me as I pivoted and pounded on Josh's door.

"Hold the fuck up!" Jagger shouted, ripping the door open. "What the f— Oh, Ember. Hey, did you forget something?"

I shook my head and pushed past him, stumbling through the apartment like a drunken crazy woman. Maybe I was.

"Ember?" He followed me into Josh's room.

"He's not right. Gus can't be right," I muttered, opening Josh's drawers. "He's just a kid. What would he know?"

"What are you looking for? Right about what? Josh isn't seeing anyone else, if that's what you're worried about. Hell, he's barely looked at another girl since you showed up in December." He closed the drawers once I was done rummaging through boxers, jeans, shirts, and socks, trying to find something that would prove Gus wrong.

"Gus, he told me..." I glanced up at the photos. There were no pictures of him with other soldiers, or deployments, or in uniform. Uniforms.

"Where is your flaw, Josh Walker?"

He laughed. "I keep it in the closet."

Right. I sidestepped Jagger and opened the closet door, flipping the switch just inside.

"Ember, no!" Jagger yelled.

He was too late.

My eyes skipped over the various hockey jerseys and sparse dress clothes and were drawn to the ACUs like a magnet. Two steps and a reach, and I could touch them. The fabric was as foreign and familiar as it came, the backdrop of my whole life. "No, no, no," I whispered, praying I was wrong.

The uniform slid from the hanger, and I held it out in front of me. On the left shoulder was the patch for the Colorado National Guard, on the right, signifying he'd been deployed, his combat patch was identical. The stripes of a sergeant were fastened across the chest, and across from the US ARMY tape was the word that froze up the love and hope in my heart.

"Walker." The whisper left me broken. I crushed the fabric in my fists, wishing I was strong enough to rip it at the seams, to shred the future I knew it stood for. The one I refused to be a part of.

"He wanted to tell you," Jagger said softly. "He just... couldn't. He couldn't lose you."

"Get out."

He sighed, and his footsteps retreated.

The room spun, or did my racing heart make it seem that way? How could something so perfect, so exquisite be so damned? This wasn't how it was supposed to go. I wasn't supposed to live like this!

A primal scream ripped free of my throat. I tore the remaining two sets of ACUs off their hangers, unable to cope with them in my sight, and slid down the back of the closet onto them. Pain lacerated me, shredding the joy I'd had just an hour before and replacing it with an overwhelming feeling of hopelessness. Maybe this is how all love ended up, crushed beneath the weight of something darker and stronger.

Maybe the tears would come and release me, prove I was processing what I'd learned. But there was nothing. I'd cried so much in the last three months that maybe there was just nothing left to give. I was hollow and empty.

I kneeled, scooping up the uniforms, but my hand hit a hard object toward the back of the closet. The light caught the dark green case folder, one I had seen too many times to count. It was an award.

I pulled it off the stack of abandoned binders and opened it. "Order of the Purple Heart, awarded to Specialist Joshua A. Walker for wounds sustained in combat in the Kandahar Province of Afghanistan."

Exactly where my father had been killed. Wrong place. Wrong time.

Just like me at this very moment.

I brought it all up into my arms and carried it into his room, leaving the uniforms on the bed and propping the award on top. He'd been the one wounded, but somehow I'd taken a fatal shot straight through my soul.

The state championship picture mocked me from the wall, so I pulled it down and left it next to the award. I had been wrong. We hadn't been fated since I'd been fifteen; we'd been doomed.

Chapter Twenty-Two

My phone *ding*ed, announcing yet another text message. In another twenty-nine seconds, it would ring four times and then go to voicemail. Another ten minutes or so later, it would begin again.

"You gonna answer that?" Sam asked as she passed me a plate of spaghetti over our bar.

I spun the noodles on the plate, but I couldn't manage to eat them. "Nope."

She let out an exaggerated sigh. "Ember—"

"Don't. Just...don't, because I can't." I spun another bite and let the spaghetti fall off the fork.

Sam sat on the stool next to me and studied me thoughtfully as she chewed. "You haven't eaten since yesterday. You're not crying. You're not talking. What am I supposed to do with that?"

Everything was numb, chilling me from the soul outward. There was no hurt because I couldn't feel anything. At this rate, my arm could have been ripped off, bleeding pints onto the floor, and I wouldn't have noticed. All the color had drained out of my world, taking with it my ability to feel... anything.

I played with my food and watched the digital clock on the oven changing. Six more minutes. Five more minutes. Four. Any minute now he was going to call again, and I still wouldn't know what to say. Who was I kidding? There was nothing left to say.

Fists struck our front door three times, and I cringed. "December!" His voice was rough, strangled.

Sam raised her eyebrow at me, but I couldn't do it. I shook my head without raising my eyes from the red-checkered plate. How nice that the spaghetti sauce matched it. She sighed purely for my benefit and scraped the legs of the stool across the floor as she scooted back.

I heard the door open. "She doesn't want to see you, Josh." She sounded sad, like she was siding with the guy who'd just broken my heart.

"Please, Sam. I have to see her."

I closed my eyes against the pain I heard in his voice. Letting it in would lead to madness.

"I can't." The door shut with a *click*, and I let out the breath I hadn't realized I'd been holding.

"December!" he shouted, the sound slightly muffled by the closed door. "I have to talk to you! I will pound on this door and scream your name until security arrests me or you come out!"

Sam sat back down and shoved a bite in her mouth. As she chewed and I spun the noodles on the fork, he continued to shout. Pain ripped through my stomach at the misery in his voice, but I quickly shut it down. The moment I acknowledged it, the rest would overwhelm me, and I wasn't ready for it.

"December!"

"For fuck's sake." Sam grabbed my hand and squeezed. "Before he gets arrested?"

I couldn't let him get in trouble, not over something as trivial as me. I slid from the bar stool, wearing the same tank top and pajama pants I had been since yesterday, and made my way to the door.

"I'm not opening the door," I spoke to the wooden frame.

"God, December. Please, we have to talk."

I shook my head like he could see me or something. "There's nothing to talk about."

"There's everything to talk about!"

He was angry. Good. It was good that one of us still had emotions.

"One question."

"Whatever you want." Something knocked against the door, and from the position and sound, I guessed he'd leaned his head on it.

"Are you in the army?" I reached my hand up and pressed it to the door, where I knew his head was on the other side.

A long moment of pause passed, condemning him more than the uniforms had. "Yes. National Guard." His reply was soft, broken.

I didn't realize how much I wanted him to deny it until he said it. "Then we're done talking, Josh. There's nothing you can say. We're just done."

"December, please!"

"Go. There's absolutely no chance for us." I managed to keep my voice flat, unemotional.

I waited several heartbeats until something slid along the door. His hand? "I love you."

"Good night, Josh."

The door to his apartment opened and shut, and I leaned back against our front door for the barest of seconds before I slid my back down it. Once my butt hit the floor, I drew my knees up to my chest. There were no tears, no anger, just an overwhelming sense of weariness.

I wanted one thing: Joshua Walker.

But I wouldn't do it. I would never become my mother. I would never love a man whose love could destroy me.

Monday morning wasn't any easier. Wasn't it supposed to get easier? This hurt worse than losing Riley, but maybe I was so lost in my grief over Dad that I hadn't really noticed Riley's loss? That wasn't true. Riley hurt, but I didn't love him like I loved Josh.

"Good morning, Ms. Howard." Professor Carving nodded to me as he walked in the room just ahead of me. Perfect timing.

I slid in behind him, skipped my eyes right over where I usually sat, and spotted an empty chair in the back of the room. Bingo. I studied the tiles on the floor and dodged backpacks on the way to the back and claimed the seat.

One Mississippi.

Two Mississippi.

Three Mississ—

"Ember."

My body physically reacted to his voice. Chills swept down my arms, and my throat tightened. I shook my head and reached for my notebook.

Josh beat me to it, pulling the purple spiral out of my bag and laying it on my desk. Before I could protest, he'd lined up one pencil and one pen exactly how I liked them. "You have to talk to me. Let me explain."

Heads pivoted in our direction. The only thing more gossip-worthy than going home with him was our obvious break-up. I couldn't speak. Hell, I was lucky to still be breathing with this pressure crushing my chest.

"Ember, please?"

"Mr. Walker?" Professor Carving said, saving me. "Could you take your seat?"

Josh sighed. "We're not done, Ember."

But we were.

I took meticulous notes, like always. Other than the gaping hole in my soul, everything on the outside was as normal as could be. The clock gave me another ten minutes to make it through this class. Then I could beat Josh to the door, run to my car, and get out of here before he had a chance to confront me. Yes. If I grabbed my stuff immediately, I could escape before everyone else had packed up.

As Professor Carving wound down his lecture and started to talk about our assignment for Wednesday, I slipped my notebook and pens into my bag and pulled it into my lap. I was half off my seat when he dismissed us.

As quickly as I could, without looking insane, I passed by the other students in my row and threw open the door in my exit. "Ember! Wait!" I didn't turn around, didn't pause, but instead launched into headlong flight. Well, extremely fast walking.

The halls filled with students, and I wove through the crowd. I would make it to the car. I wouldn't have to see him, or face everything I couldn't have. I could hold it together for one more day. The early March sunshine hit my face, and I took my first deep breath. I'd made it out.

"Ember! What are you going to do? Run forever?" Josh yelled out.

Half the students turned to gawk. My cheeks stung as blood rushed to my face, but I kept walking, picking my way down the path between the academic buildings to the quad. *Keep it together. Stick to the plan.*

The moment he touched my arm, I knew it was all about to fall apart. I stopped, took three breaths, and focused on anything else. The snow had melted, and the grass lay brown and bare. It was the ugliest time of pre-spring, when the pristine white had faded, but nothing had come to life yet. Everything was still cold and numb.

"Ember." His voice was soft, pleading.

"Don't." It was all I had in me.

He stepped around me, but I refused to look up into those eyes. "Please. I didn't mean to keep it from you. I just didn't know how to tell you."

Pieces of me cracked into a fault line, and every word he spoke expanded it. The blissful, numb feeling that kept me together was melting, leaving me bare. I swallowed back the need to look at him, to reach out and touch him.

"You have to talk to me about this. I'm not going to lose you over a job."

I broke, snapped in half, my logic and reason flying away. "A job?" I stepped back, needing the distance. I finally looked up at him, but the misery on his face didn't dispel my anger. He looked like shit. Good, that's how I felt. "It's not a *job*! And you hid it from me! You know how I feel about it!"

"When I saw you burn the West Point gear? I knew you would never accept it, that you'd push me away as soon as you knew, and I couldn't let you go."

"You selfish fuck!"

He paled. "Yes. I needed to be near you. I had to."

"Why? Why the hell are you in the Guard? You had a full ride! And you just join up and go over to get yourself killed?" The idea, the word struck me with nausea. Josh in uniform. Josh in a cold box draped by a flag. No.

"Mom got sick. I transferred here to take care of her. UCCS hockey is small; it didn't have the funds to give a full ride midseason. Some of us don't have rich families and doctor dads, Ember. I did the only thing I could think of to put myself through college. A weekend a month seemed like a damn good deal to be near my mother. I don't regret it. Not any of it, and not you!"

My eyes glanced down to the scar I knew ran through his leg. "You don't regret losing the one thing you love? God! You were shot! Wounded! Nearly killed, and you just stay in? Do you have some kind of fucking hero complex, or something? Let me tell you, Josh. Heroes die!" My voice caught, and I sucked in a strangled breath. "They die."

The muscle in his jaw flexed. "I haven't lost the one thing I love, Ember. You're still standing in front of me, and I'm fighting like hell."

"Don't. I'm not going to stand by and watch you die like my father. I don't care if you're almost done with college, nothing is worth that wait, that pain."

"Your dad believed in his mission. He saved a lot of lives. I knew him, Ember. He was proud of what he was doing. He was proud of me!"

Jealousy stabbed deep. Josh had been friends with my dad because of Gus. He'd talked to him about things I never could, about why he chose the path he did. Josh knew my dad intimately in a way I never would, because I had been too scared, too angry with Dad's choices to understand.

"Look what he got for it. A doctor in a hospital, not a soldier on the front, and he's dead! Don't try to rationalize war."

Silence enveloped us, and I noticed the crowd gawking as they passed by at the same time Josh did. He pulled my messenger bag by the strap, gently guiding me under the nearby tree so we stopped entertaining the masses.

"Please fight for this, Ember. We are worth the fight. I love you, and that's something I've never said to any girl. I love you more than hockey, or the air I breathe. You love me, too!"

That felt like a giant slap to the face. "My love? You want to use my love in this?" The tears burst free, streaking my face. "I never would have gotten close to you if I knew! I hate what you do. I hate that you lied to me. But mostly, I hate that you let me fall in love with you when you knew! I *hate* that I love you, so you don't get to use that." The tears drained my anger into a pit of misery.

Pain radiated from his eyes. "I love you enough for the both of us. I can't regret anything that brought us together."

His eyes, his words, they all started to melt through my resolve. "You should have said something."

He took a tentative step, reaching out to run the backs of his fingers down my face. "I should have given you the choice and told you, but I couldn't. You are this miracle, something I never thought I was worthy of touching, let alone calling you mine. I've wanted you since I was eighteen, but I was never good enough, not for someone like you."

"Because I had a doctor daddy?" I threw his words back in his face, trying to hang on to the last vestiges of my anger. Anger would keep me alive when Josh had the power to break me.

"Because you were kind, and smart, and seemingly unimpressed with me. Oh, you'd watch; believe it, I noticed, but you had way more self-esteem than to throw yourself at anyone. I had too much respect for you to pursue you. I would have wrecked you back then."

"You're wrecking me now." The confession was soft. I'd known from the picture that he'd noticed me at fifteen, but hearing him say it, the longing in his voice, brought me another notch closer to insanity. I had to be crazy to even entertain the idea of staying with him.

"I love you. You are everything, and I'm not going to let you walk away over a uniform." He pulled on my waist, bringing me flush against his body. My traitorous nerves misfired, remembering all too well how it felt to be in his arms. "Just let me love you, December, because I can't stop anyways. I've been at your mercy since I was eighteen."

The fight bled out of me as I melted against him. His brown eyes shone in the patchy sunlight. It didn't matter in the long run really. He only had a few months left until graduation. I did my math. "You enlisted for the typical three years, and those are up soon right?"

His jaw flexed. "Technically."

My eyes narrowed. "There's no technically. Don't you dare hide anything else from me."

He glanced around for a moment, like he was searching for his answers in the trees, the buildings around us. "I'll be done with my enlistment the day I graduate."

I breathed a sigh of relief. "Three months. I can do three months."

His grip tightened on my waist, a little desperate. "My enlistment is up on graduation day because I'll be discharged from service. A few minutes later, I'll be sworn in and commissioned as an officer. I've been in ROTC since I was wounded. It paid my scholarship, and the guard paid my rent."

Where was the numbness, the icy feeling that kept me distant? Instead, raw pain, gaping and ugly, clawed its way up and seized hold of me. "You're commissioning. You're going career." Twenty years. The best years of his life given in service, risk.

His eyes said that he wanted to lie, but he didn't. "Yes. That's my plan."

I nodded and smiled, swallowing the lump growing in my throat. Before he could say anything else, I reached up on tiptoes, wound my arms around his neck, and melded my mouth to his. I kissed him with abandon, pouring all of my love, my sorrow, my desperation into him.

As he responded, I found the tree at my back, his tongue moving with mine. His hands left my waist and held my face like I was something delicate, as he kissed me with obvious relief. Everything in my body called out for him and I gave in, angling to get closer to him, reveling that I could be so swept up in someone else.

Everything with Josh was so perfect, and yet so fucked up.

I kissed him once more, gently, drawing onto his lower lip as long as I could, savoring the taste and feel of him against my lips. "I love you so much," I whispered against his lips. "Thank you for getting me through losing my dad. Thank you for protecting April and loving Gus. Thank you for being exactly what I've imagined love would really be like."

He smiled against my lips, but pulled back startled when my tears flowed against his cheek. "December? Don't cry."

I shook my head and stepped out of his arms. The cool air immediately took away the sweet warmth he'd left. "I love you," I whispered once more.

Denial drew his eyes wide. "Don't. Don't do this."

I cupped his gorgeous face in my hands and smiled through the tears. "Good-bye, Joshua Walker."

I clutched my messenger bag as I walked away, needing something, anything to feel real. Gravity was gone. I'd just lost the one person who'd been holding me to the earth.

Chapter Twenty-Three

The clock made me nervous. Two minutes left in sudden-death overtime and the Mountain Lions were tied up and down one player. Jagger never could hold his temper. From our seats, Sam and I had a clear view of him across the rink, and he looked pretty pissed.

"He's hotter when he's angry," she noticed with a *click* of her tongue.

"Seriously?" I laughed her off.

"Defense! Defense!" the crowd yelled as Western State raced toward the goal.

My fingers dug into my vest as they shot and missed. The defenders swept out from behind the net and fired it up to the forwards. "Come on, Josh," I whispered, afraid to say his name too loudly. Every time I'd heard it in the last three weeks I nearly destroyed the ground I'd gained.

Everything hurt. Breathing moved the lump in my throat. Sleeping on the other side of the wall from him meant I couldn't sleep. Thinking about him shut me down for hours.

Thank God for the pain; it meant I hadn't gone numb.

It meant I was processing, albeit slowly, but still. I hadn't vanished into myself. I pushed through the pain and acted as normally as I could with a broken heart. After the first day in class, when I'd only smiled politely at him and focused on Professor Carving, Josh stopped trying to talk to me.

I was thankful. I was devastated.

I knew better than to come tonight, but I couldn't manage to stay away, not when the game was this important to him. It would be the last hockey game of his collegiate career.

Josh flew toward the Western State goal, passing up the other defenders so he was one-on-one with their goalie. My body coiled in tension. He would do it, he would win his team the league championship here. I knew it as certainly as I knew I missed him.

Deke one. Deke two. My heart stopped as he shot…and made it!

The arena jumped to its feet, screaming out his name. "Walker! Walker!" He'd done it: captained the League Championship team, scored the game-winning goal. I couldn't stop the smile that consumed me any more than I could stop wanting to claim him, to say that amazing man was mine. My heart swelled with pride for what he'd accomplished.

The team cleared the bench, swarming onto the ice. He dodged the melee and instead skated over to where I stood against the glass. There was no victorious smile on his face, just those intense eyes staring out at me from under his helmet. He ripped off his glove and placed his palm to the glass where I stood. Helpless against him, I lifted mine and matched it across the glass. I heard a flash, a snap, but I didn't care. Everything I had wanted to say to him—my pride and my happiness too—was there for him to see.

I was still in love with him. We both knew it.

A faint smile curved his lips, but it didn't reach his eyes. They dulled in sadness, resignation.

He pushed backward off the glass, but before he turned to where his team was ready to engulf him, he looked back. He pointed to me, and brought his hand to his heart. Then he was swallowed up by his team, and I begged Sam to take me home.

"You sure you want to miss the party?" she asked as we pulled up to our apartment building. "It's going to be awesome over at the house."

I shook my head and stepped out of the car. "Not tonight. I just can't." I was too weak. Five minutes alone at the house with Josh and I'd be in his arms.

"Okay, baby girl. Get some sleep."

"Be safe." She waited until my key opened the front door and then took off for the after-party.

I dressed in my pajamas and climbed into bed, flipping the light switch off. In the darkness, I ran my fingers across the screen of my phone and got stupid.

Ember: *Hey, please don't reply. I just need you to know how incredibly proud of you I am tonight.*

What didn't I say? That I loved him, that I'd been miserable without him these last three weeks, that he consumed my mind in a way that reminded me of drug addiction and I was going through withdrawals.

Josh: *You were in my head the whole game. You're in my heart every minute I'm awake. I love you December Howard.*

That damn lump was back in my throat, and tears threatened. I should have put the phone down. I should have tucked it into the nightstand. But I didn't, blurry eyes and all.

Ember: *I know. And you know that I love you, Joshua Walker.*

Josh: *I wish that was enough to change your mind.*

Ember: *Me, too. Night, Josh.*

Josh: *Night, Ember.*

I swallowed back the pain, refusing to let the tears come.

I couldn't spend my entire life crying, there had to be a stopping point. I curled up with my phone on my pillow and drifted off to sleep.

Rhythmic pounding on the wall behind my head woke me up in a haze. I glanced at the clock: 2:57 a.m. What the hell? The sound continued, shaking the wall in time. What could he be doing? The only thing on that wall was...

Oh, fuck. His bed.

My heart shattered into a million tiny pieces, which then shattered again. It's not like he was cheating on me, right? I turned him down, broke up with him, hurt him. He'd just won the league championship tonight, what the hell did I expect from a playboy like Josh Walker? It was only surprising he'd waited this long.

But that didn't mean I had to listen to it.

I scooped up my pillow and comforter and headed out to the couch. This time, as I lay down, I didn't bother to stop the tears; I just let them consume me.

Monday morning, I slid into my seat in history and pulled out my notebook without looking at Josh. I couldn't. I already envisioned him in bed with that other girl, I didn't need to see his face to do it.

"Great game, Josh." Mindy slid past him, running her hand along his shoulder as she claimed her seat. Maybe it was her.

I bit my lip and kept my eyes on my blank paper.

"Calm down, everyone." Professor Carving pulled his notes onto the lectern. "Oh, and congratulations, Walker. That was quite a shot."

"I had some great inspiration."

I nearly gagged on my coffee.

"You must have," Professor Carving agreed. "Now, we're onto the end of the Battle of Gettysburg, and I'm assuming you've all done the required reading?"

A few muttered assents greeted him.

"Oh no? Pop quiz it is." A collective groan went up. "Easy peasy. Just write your name on the top and, to the best of your recollection, write down your favorite line from the address."

I scrawled my name across the top line and brought out of memory exactly what had stuck in my mind. Like I'd ever forget it.

He waited a few minutes before ending the quiz. "Okay, now everyone pass your paper to the right."

I stuck my paper out at Josh without looking at him. His fingertips brushed against the back of my hand, scalding me, destroying me all over again.

I took Patrick's paper from my left. He was quiet, unassuming, and, unfortunately for his sex life, kind of acne-ridden. But he was sweet as could be.

"Who wants to read the paper they have? Mindy?"

She cleared her throat, sounding like a porn star. "Forescore and seven years ago—"

"Ah, easy way out! Who else do we have?"

"I will," Josh answered.

No. I didn't want to hear his voice, but since plugging my ears and rocking back and forth wasn't an option, I had to listen.

"Mr. Walker, let's hear it."

Josh's voice was clear and strong. "That from these honored dead we take increased devotion to that cause for which they gave the last full measure of devotion—that we here highly resolve that these dead shall not have died in vain."

There was no sound over the erratic beat of my heart.

Professor Carving leaned back against the podium. "Ms. Howard? Why did that passage come to mind?"

I opened my mouth to speak, but nothing would come out, not without breaking down in front of the entire class, which sure as hell was not going to happen.

"Ms. Howard?"

I shook my head and closed my eyes, wishing my seat would consume me and let me out of this situation where I couldn't manage to complete a simple task like talking.

"Ember's dad was killed in Afghanistan a few months ago," Josh answered softly, reaching across the aisle and leaving my paper on my desk.

I opened my eyes and looked into the surprised eyes of Professor Carving. "I can see how that would draw you to this passage."

I nodded my head, but he didn't get it.

The rest of the class passed in a blur, then he dismissed us. I gathered my things at the same time Josh did. "Ember?"

I braced myself and turned, still blown away by how impossibly gorgeous he was, but his looks had nothing on his kindness, his warmth. Any girl in this school would have been grateful for just a shot at Josh, let alone his heart on a plate. "Yeah?"

He raised his hand like he wanted to touch me, but lowered it slowly. "Your dad, he didn't die in vain."

I pulled the loose piece of paper from my bag, folded it in half, and handed it to him. "What made you think it was meant for Dad? You're the one resolved. What's your full measure of devotion?"

I walked away before I had to listen to his answer.

Chapter Twenty-Four

March faded after another snowstorm, bringing April and three more storms over the greening grass. May, however, was finally gorgeous.

I pulled on a pair of black capris and a soft, pale blue blouse for Sunday dinner. I hadn't realized how much I'd missed the dependable routine of our house until it was gone. Now everything seemed to be in place again; we were just missing Dad.

I turned his letter over again, rubbing the ink so frequently I was amazed it hadn't worn off. The lines were softer now, smudged from my trifling. Four and a half months had passed, but holding that letter made it feel like I was still standing at the front door, opening it to disaster. I put the letter back up on the shelf and headed out.

The cemetery was already covered in flowers; the grounds crew had taken a jump on spring. I spent as much time with Dad as I could without breaking into a heap of useless mush, and then continued down south to the house, as was my routine. Life had become all about routine again.

Only one thing could change it, and I was still waiting to hear from Vanderbilt.

Gus was out of the house before I even parked my car in the driveway, launching himself at me. "Ember! I missed you! Come see my science experiment. It's totally rad!"

"Like, totally!" I ruffled his curls and was enveloped by the smell of roasted turkey as we stepped into the house.

"I was so worried, because Dad had all the plans. We'd talked about it so much."

I dropped down to his level. "But you found them, right?"

"Yeah, they were in his e-mail."

My grip tightened on his shirt unconsciously. "You can get into his e-mail?"

He nodded, his curls bouncing. "Yeah. Just his personal one. His security question was easy enough because Mom said he'd had the same password for like *ever.*" He skipped off, leaving me stunned in the foyer.

Mom looked the part of the fifties housewife as she came through the dining room. A quick hug as a greeting, and she was racing back for the ringing phone. Gus showed me his giant spaghetti bridge, which took up a huge part of Mom's desk in the kitchen. "Good work, bud!"

"It's the coolest thing ever. I can't wait to see how much weight it takes to break it!" His eyes lit up.

Mom made the universal quiet-while-I'm-talking-on-the-phone hand gesture that looked like she was conducting assault maneuvers. Gus and I both stifled a grin and complied.

"Sure, that's not a problem, Chloe. We're just having some turkey. Why don't you bring the boys over and eat with us?" Mom paused, listening. "Oh, we could care less what you're wearing. Just drive over." She leaned back to check the time on the clock. "I'm expecting you in fifteen minutes. No excuses." With a smile, she hung up. "Gus, add three more places to dinner."

"Mrs. Rose is coming?" I pulled down the plates from the higher cabinet for Gus.

Mom smoothed the lines of her apron, a habit I'd learned meant she had more on her mind than what she let on. "She doesn't sound well." Distracted, she went about the kitchen, stirring gravy and pulling the turkey out to rest.

I jumped in to help Gus, who asked, "Who is Mrs. Rose?"

I readjusted his fork to the correct side of the plate and centered it. "You remember. Her husband was with Daddy?"

Recognition lit his eyes. "Yeah! Carson and Lewis's mom!"

"Exactly."

April danced into the dining room as we set the dishes on the table. Thank God that outfit wasn't new. She'd quit shopping once Mom had put her into therapy. "Nice to see ya, Ember." She smiled and took her seat.

"Nice to show up and help, April," Mom sang back.

April shrugged at me. "How are things up at your place?"

I knew what and who she meant. "There's nothing new to report."

"Damn shame that is, to let someone like him just walk—"

"April." My voice was sharp even to my own ears. "No."

"Someone needs to set you straight." She ran her hands down her hair.

"What, like you're a relationship expert?" She'd barely been back with Brett for two weeks. I was shocked he'd taken her back at all.

"You're unhappy." Her eyes bored into mine, resolute to getting her point across. "You deserve to be happy."

My voice softened with my temper. "I don't need a guy to make me happy. I haven't been single since I was seventeen. These last few months have sucked, yes, but I've learned so much about myself that I wouldn't have." She arched a skeptical eyebrow. "No, really. I can repair a garbage disposal, and change a tire, and spend Friday night with my girlfriends or alone. I have missed Josh; I still miss him every day, but I have to be okay alone before I can ever be with someone else."

"So good to see my girls getting along." Mom tossed a skeptical look our way and handed me the bread bowl.

"You know us," April chimed in with a wink, dispelling the last of the tension.

In that moment, everything seemed so normal, so peaceful. I thought about telling Mom about Vanderbilt. It was on the tip of my tongue for the next ten minutes while we listened to the details of Gus's science project and April prattle on about prom. When Mom asked me what I thought about my classes, I opened my mouth.

The doorbell rang, and Gus was out of his seat, anxious for his friends and yanking open the door with all of his body weight.

"Gus! Cool! Did you see the new Bakugan we got?" The boys were immediately lost in conversation.

They looked…unkempt, which was saying something for the normal Pottery Barn look the Rose kids sported. Dirt covered their shirts and holes consumed the knees of their jeans. Their hair had grown long enough to brush out of their eyes.

"Chloe?" My mom gasped, standing.

Mrs. Rose wore a pair of yoga pants with a torn Colts sweatshirt. Her hair frizzed every which way until it culminated in a knot on top of her head, and her makeup ran down her face. For someone who normally looked like she just stepped out of Ann Taylor, seeing her like this scared me.

She walked in, her dead eyes searching for Mom. "June."

Mom rushed around me, taking Chloe by the arm. "What's going on?"

"God, June. It's supposed to be next week, and I don't think he's coming home!" She crumbled, Mom only slowing her descent as they fell together to the floor. Ugly sobs tore through the room, ripping a hole straight through me to the part that hadn't healed yet from losing Dad. "I just kept pushing through...I never realized..." Her words were punctuated with hiccupping cries in my mother's lap. "The unit comes home next week. When those planes come in, he won't be on one. He won't be on one! It's supposed to be over, but this is never going to end because he's not coming home!"

April covered her mouth with her hand. I shuddered through a deep breath and forced a smile to my stricken face. "Boys! Let's have a special dinner in the den! *The Avengers* looks great on that big TV!"

Carson and Lewis looked at each other with wary eyes, and I recognized that look all too well. It was the same one April and I had just exchanged, the glance between siblings that spoke without words. They were so small, only Gus's age, and they didn't have bigger siblings to look out for them.

"Gus, why don't you take them to the den?"

Gus's somber eyes dragged away from Mom and Chloe, who was still sobbing on the floor, leaving wet, dark streaks down Mom's chevron apron. "Yeah, it's really cool." He faked a smile that didn't reach his little eyes and pulled the boys away. "I love Iron Man!"

I sighed at the sheer perfection of Gus's heart.

"Captain America all the way!" Carson answered as they raced the opposite way into the den.

"Hulk! Dude, he like tears off his clothes he's so massive!" Lewis added from a distance.

Mom moved Chloe to the couch, cradling her head against her chest as the younger woman let out sobs that ripped through the scar tissue I'd grown over my grief. Chloe had held everything together, and I'd been so jealous that she was functioning while Mom was basically catatonic. This was nothing to be jealous over now.

April and I gathered up plates, making open-faced hot turkey sandwiches instead of the traditional fare Mom had intended. She carried them in to the boys while I traded their glasses for juice boxes. Comforting another widow or not, Mom would flip if they spilled open glasses of juice on the den carpet.

We situated the boys, turned on the movie, and left them to their Marvel heroes, softly shutting the door behind us to lock them into their world. April sagged against the wall just outside the room. "Jesus, Ember, is this ever going to be over?"

I leaned next to her, drawing her under my arm. "I think it's always going to hurt. It's always going to be there." I blinked back tears. "But we're getting better at living with it every day."

"Just when I think I'm getting past it, something happens and it jumps in my face again, as bad as that first day." Her voice broke.

"I know." I looked up at the family pictures hung along the opposite wall, a collage of school years and events that made our family what we were, and it hurt because we wouldn't be that way again. "It still floors me, too, April. I promise."

Chloe's sobs echoed through the house, reminding us that grief had no mercy, time limit, or expiration date. I held my sister as Mom held Chloe, unable to give any advice or utter a word that could lessen the blow we'd been dealt. We were stumbling through, even all these months later. I rested my head against April's, thankful we weren't alone, that we had each other.

"I told Chloe to sleep in your room, Ember. I hope you don't mind," Mom said, tossing her apron into the hamper.

"Not at all." I slid the last dish into the dishwasher as April wiped the counters. "We put Lewis and Carson down in Gus's room."

"Good. I'm glad they have one another."

There wasn't much else to say, so we cleaned up the rest of the kitchen in comfortable, sad silence.

"I'm headed up to bed. Ember, are you going to your place tonight?" April asked.

"Yeah, I have class in the morning."

She hugged me. "Thank you. I know I don't say it enough. Thank you." Before I could respond, she skipped out of the room and up the stairs.

"She's getting better," I said.

"We all are. I think these next couple weeks might be a little rough on us, but we'll get through." Mom quirked her eyebrow as I sanitized the counter April had only used a sponge on, and straightened the knife block. "How are you doing? I don't get to ask you as often as I'd like."

I leaned back against the cabinet. "I'm okay. I feel like I'm in this excruciatingly long period of adjustment, but I'm okay, under control." She waited for me to talk, as was her way. She never pushed me; she knew better. Dad, I could open up to in a heartbeat, but Mom and I had always struggled with communication. Too much alike, I suppose. "My grades are good, and living with Sam is great."

"I'm glad you two reconnected."

"Me, too. You always think these are your forever friends on graduation day, when everyone is signing yearbooks, but only a couple really stay. Everybody just sort of…fades away."

Mom pulled two K-Cups down and turned her back to brew a couple lattes. "The people stay when you make an effort for them." Her hand paused on the coffee cup as she sucked in a deep breath. "Ember, there's been so much going on for you this year, and I'm sorry I wasn't there for you." A mocking laugh slipped free. "I'm sorry I couldn't be there for myself. If I had realized what was going on with Riley..."

"There's nothing you could have done. His mistakes were his own. If anything, his cheating showed me how much of my life I'd wrapped around him. I changed everything for him, for this plan we'd created together that I never really liked to begin with."

She handed me a cup of chai latte, and I took a tentative sip. Delicious, and enough caffeine to power me through the homework that waited for me at the apartment.

"I liked Riley," she admitted. "I liked that he fit with our family, that you two seemed to have everything worked out. If I had known what he was doing, I'd have put his balls in a vise."

I sputtered, leaving a trail of latte droplets on the kitchen island. We both burst out laughing and Mom recovered enough to clean up every spot. "In all seriousness, I never would have pushed you toward him."

"I know. On paper, he was perfect."

"And Josh?" She slipped it in so easily, but it still sent a streak of pain through me.

"Josh is in the army; well, the Guard." It had been over two months, and this was the first I'd told Mom. "If he was getting out, then maybe, but he's going commissioned after graduation. I can't do it, Mom. I won't do it."

She quietly sipped her coffee before answering. "Do you love him?"

I swallowed, struggling for words. "Yes. More than I ever thought was possible. I can't seem to get over him, but I will. Once he's gone, I will." It was more of a promise to myself than a statement to Mom. "Besides, he's more than moved on."

"You can't work through this?" A fire came into her eyes that I hadn't seen in months. She gave a damn about something. "Love isn't something you throw away lightly."

"I'm not living this life, Mom. I want stability, and roots, and one house for the next twenty years where my kids can mark the door frames as they grow. The army is a deal breaker."

She slightly narrowed her eyes, as if judging whether or not the subject was closed. Wisely, she moved on. "You sacrifice too much, December." Her eyes darted to the refrigerator, the counter, and the floor before she brought them up to mine. "I need—" Her voice sounded clogged, and she cleared her throat. "I need to say thank you. Thank you for what you did. Thank you for being here, for taking care of everything when I couldn't."

"No problem, Mom." The answer was so easy now, automatic.

"It was a problem. You gave up your school, your life, your plans. Don't you think I know what your plans mean to you? You gave up too much."

"Yeah, and it sucked. But we're family, and someone had to do it. So I did, end of story. Anyone else would have done the same."

"No, they wouldn't have!" I cringed as she raised her voice. "You carried this whole house. You carried me! No daughter should have to carry her mother." She slammed her cup down on the counter.

This had to stop. "What do you want, Mom? Do you want me to tell you I was angry? That I regret leaving Boulder? What's going to make you feel better?"

"Yes! I need to know how you felt. I never asked how you felt!" Color rose in her cheeks. "I want you as angry about it as I am!"

Something snapped, setting me free. "Fine!" My cup

clanged into the sink, my forgotten latte draining. "Yes, I was angry! I was jealous that Chloe Rose held it together for her kids, but you couldn't manage to get out of bed! I was lost, and confused, and everything went from ordered and perfect to this giant fucking mess of…shit!" My chest heaved, trying to keep up with my racing heartbeat. Oh God, I was going to be sick. "You lost your husband, but I lost my father *and* my mother. I lost my boyfriend, and my plans, and my home, and you couldn't be bothered to show up for me, for any of us."

"I know." Her admission was soft, but I was too far gone to pause my reckless tirade.

"You know why I can't be with Josh? Because I can't do this again!" I circled my arms around my head. "I can't be you! I can't open that door and see them standing there, ready to end everything I ever knew. I can't." The tears I'd fought all night, no, the tears I'd fought since December, overflowed and streaked angry paths down my face.

Mom took a step toward me, but I fended her off with an outstretched hand. "No. You don't see the worst part; that everything was to try and make up for what I did."

"What could you have possibly done?" She stepped forward tentatively.

"God, Mom! I opened the damn door! You said not to because you knew! And I opened it and let them in. They destroyed our family, and I opened the damn door!"

She closed the distance between us, pulling me against her tighter than she had since I was a small child. "No, Ember. No. There's nothing you could have done to stop this. Nothing. No part of this is your fault. I should have opened the door. I'm so sorry I wasn't stronger. So sorry."

I sobbed against my mother until there were no more tears to be had, not over Dad, Riley, the plans, the colleges, or even Josh. I cried myself clean.

Then I stopped.

Chapter Twenty-Five

I waited almost a week, until Saturday morning, before I decided the price of my integrity was hearing from my dad. I leaned forward in my computer chair, staring at the blinking cursor on the Gmail account. I typed slowly: Justin.A.Howard@gmail.com.

Password. Right. This was going to be a bitch. I typed in his birthdate and the server spat it back at me. I tried my mom's name. Declined. A little white box popped up in the center of the screen. "Would you like your hint?"

"Hell yes, I would," I murmured, clicking on the "ok" button.

The page loaded, and the hint popped up.

Glowing dim as an ember

Things my heart used to know

Chills raced down my arms and legs, as though he was standing right behind me, singing to me again. "Daddy," I whispered. I clicked on the sign-in again.

Password: OnceUponADecember

His e-mail opened and relief rushed through me, tingling

every nerve in my body. I had more of him. The letter wasn't the last piece anymore. These e-mails weren't enough, but they would do. Here were his letters, his words. A primal need to claw through the screen gripped me, crying to bury myself in what was left of him, snuggle down among the typed words and find my father.

I looked through his inbox, only glancing on the unopened ones. I didn't care what other people said, only Dad. There was Grams, Mom, Gus, April…me. I clicked on my last e-mail to him, a few days before they came to the door.

Hey, Daddy,

Everything's great, stop worrying about me. I'm headed down to the Springs tomorrow to spend Christmas with Mom, April, and Gus. No worries, I remember where you hid Mom's special present, and I won't let her fall asleep before it's Santa time. I really wish you could be here. It's not the same without you.

I love you,
December

My last words to him had been of love and our family. I was good with that. It didn't hurt nearly as much as I thought it would. He'd been concerned about me giving away all my dreams for Riley, especially the second year when I dropped my English/History double major pairing and picked up education instead.

But it's not like I could tell him he'd been right.

I scanned his sent box, my breath catching. Josh Walker.

My finger clicked it open before my conscience could stop it.

Hey Josh,

I'm glad you got the files. I'm sorry I had to scan them in, but I know how fast you needed them, and I didn't know how long they would take if I used snail mail. I'm glad you're playing again; you've always been a sight out there on the ice. I'm so proud of what you've accomplished, and you should be, too. Checking our return dates, I'll be flirting with the timing, but I might be able to make it back to commission and pin you. I'm so honored that you asked, and I would like nothing more than to see a man like you become an officer. Oh, and thank you so much for uploading the video of the game. Gus is growing too damn fast.

VR,
Justin Howard

I sat in stunned silence. He hadn't just known Josh, they'd been friends. I knew they'd chatted during hockey practices and such, but never imagined he'd corresponded with him. No wonder Josh had looked so shaken up at the funeral.

I glanced through the e-mail again, my eyes catching on the word "file." What had Dad sent him from Afghanistan that he couldn't get back here? I dropped my scruples—hell, I'd already checked them at the door—and opened Dad's "sent" file, and filtered it to Josh's e-mail.

Dozens of e-mails popped up, spanning…almost two years? They'd been writing each other for two years? The oldest one was simple, asking Josh to consider coaching Gus's team, Dad saying how great it would be for his injury to get back on the ice when he was ready. Something dropped in my stomach and then clawed up my throat, leaving a sickly sweet taste in my mouth. There was more to this, something deeper.

My breath shuddered as I scanned the right-hand side, looking for the paperclip that signaled an e-mail attachment. There were more than a few, mostly clips of Gus playing hockey. Josh kept Dad connected in a way none of us could, through the sport he and Gus loved and shared. Gratitude overwhelmed me.

I opened the e-mail with the subject "found the records," from this August, and clicked.

Hey Josh,

Here are the records I found in our system. Tell the Guard to get their act together and do a backup every once in a while, eh? Better yet, come active and forget about it. I'm thrilled to help get you back on a team where you belong. Things here are the same: long hours and tough calls. Do me a favor, run by the house and force June to let you cut the grass? That woman takes on too much. Ember's back at school now with her jerk-faced boyfriend. You know, if you'd ever like to show up and steal her away for a bit, that'd be fine with me. Hint. Hint. But really, let me know what else you need, UCCS is lucky to have a player like you.

VR,

Justin Howard

He'd tried to set me up with Josh? He had to have been kidding. Dad loved Riley, didn't he? Had he just faked it because he thought I was happy? I pushed the question aside and clicked on the document. Josh's medical records popped onto the screen. It wasn't his full records, just a collection of pages that began in early July two years ago.

Why would Josh ask my dad for his records if the Guard lost them?

I pushed back from my desk. There were too many questions, and I was done feeling confused and lost. I deserved answers.

Before I could talk myself out of it, I was walking for the

door.

"Where are you going dressed like that?" Sam laughed from the couch, lounged out in her pajamas.

My hair was pulled on top of my head in a messy knot, the result of no effort. I waved my hand to her and headed out the door in my jean shorts and layered ribbed tank. I didn't bother with shoes. I told myself I didn't care what he thought I looked like anyway as I knocked on his door.

"Hold up!" Jagger's yell was muffled by the door, the loud television, and giggles. For the barest second, I thought about running, but it wasn't an option, not if I wanted to figure this out. The door swung open and Jagger appeared, his eyebrows shooting up at the sight of me. "Hey?"

My smile was tight and close-lipped. "Is, um, is Josh here?" I could barely get the words out of my mouth. Saying his name was still torturous, even almost three months later.

Jagger smiled through his shock. "Yeah, yeah, come on in."

I followed him down the hallway and made the turn that mirrored the floor plan of our own apartment into the living room. "Walker, you're not going to believe who's—"

"Holy shit." Josh cut him off, immediately standing, which was unfortunate for the co-ed who had been perched on the arm of the couch next to him. He caught her just before she hit the floor, and then set her aside. "Ember?" His eyes raked up and down my frame, and I didn't miss the stab of desire that raced through them. Glad I could stoke the fire he had for...oh, yes it was. Tweedledee and Tweedledum both glared at me.

Jagger hit the mute button on the TV, and whatever slapstick comedy they were watching fell silent. For a moment, I couldn't speak; I was too lost in looking at him. For the last few months, I hadn't let myself meet his eyes. I'd sat next to him in class, smiled in his general direction when he said something amusing to our professor, but I'd avoided looking at him like the plague. Losing myself here was the reason.

He wasn't wearing a shirt. Neither was Jagger, but nothing affected me like Josh's bare chest. He was still cut like a dream. If anything, his muscles were larger, more defined, especially the lines that ran into his black basketball shorts. And his tribal tattoo wasn't just black anymore; it had ice and flames dancing through it and around it, all originating from the area over his heart. I tried not to swallow my tongue, or think about how badly I ached to kiss him. "New ink?"

Ten feet separated us, but we may as well have been naked together, or ten thousand miles apart, it was the same difference, really. "Yeah."

"What the hell are you doing here?" Tweedledum glared at me, crossing her arms under her breasts to shove them up through her neckline.

"Sorry, I didn't mean to disturb your, eh"—I gestured to the room—"date. I just need to ask Josh a quick question."

"You came all the way over here to ask him a question?" the girl fired back.

I looked to Josh, but he looked too awestruck to answer, refusing to take his eyes from me. My cheeks flamed. "I'm his next-door neighbor, and—"

"And she's done explaining herself to you," Josh interjected, finally coming to life. "Ember, what's up?"

The way he said it, his voice curving around the words, made me want to ask him for more than information. Then I thought about the way his bed had pounded against my wall. He'd moved on. I steadied myself with a deep breath and hugged my waist. "You didn't tell me how close you were to my dad."

His jaw flexed, and his face paled. "That's not really a question if you already know the answer." His hand raked over his head, through his short hair, a style I now knew he kept for the Guard. "But yeah, we were friends."

"What's with the records? Why would you ask my dad for them? Why not go to Evans Hospital here?"

He swallowed. "Did you read them?"

I shook my head. "No, they're yours. I saw the date and stopped."

He walked in through his bedroom door and motioned me inside, but I wasn't sure I could walk into that room. "Come on, Ember. I won't take advantage of you." The smile he gave me was small and didn't reach his eyes. It was gone almost as quickly as it came.

"You can take advantage of me!" Tweedledum sang after him. Then she leaned in close to whisper so only I could hear. "The body on that man is just…"

I shook her off and walked toward him before she could finish. If I had to choose between the lion's lair and the snake pit? Well, at least I knew the lion. I glanced around, noting that nothing had changed. He'd even put the picture from state back on the wall. I thought twice about sitting on the bed and instead chose to stand while he rummaged in his closet. Finally, he came out with a gray handled filing case.

He rested it on the bed, opening it with a *click*. "I have to say, I never thought I'd get you in here again, but if I did, I never imagined it would be like this."

I concentrated on the movement of his fingers and the play of muscles up his arm. "Could you put on a shirt? It's a little distracting." My voice sounded breathless, even to me, but I couldn't slow my pulse, not with him standing three inches from me.

He laughed, which didn't help my state; it only turned me on. "Could you put on some pants? Those mile-long legs of yours have me thinking about the way you loved to wrap them around my waist."

I sputtered, and he grinned, pulling out the records from

his file and handing them to me. "You're going to find out some day, it may as well be my doing."

I scanned the top. "You were hurt in July, two years ago?"

"Yeah, I was stupid and gave the Guard the only hard copy I had. Then when they updated their computers, they lost mine from Afghanistan. I needed them for the docs here to clear me to play for UCCS. Your dad was deployed, and I knew that hospital would have a copy somewhere. I was just lucky your dad knew where to look."

"Same hospital, right, but why would he know where they were?" There was something right there, but I couldn't put it together.

"Right. Same hospital. They did emergency surgery there before Landstuhl." I felt his gaze boring into me.

I shook my head, waving the papers. "What are you trying to tell me?"

"Look at the date."

"July sixth."

"What were you doing that summer?"

I thought back. "Um, I had just graduated high school, and Mom took me up after the Fourth of July to go to the Boulder campus because I'd decided to go to college with Riley." Instead of Vanderbilt, where I'd wanted to apply; just another concession I made for our plan. "Mom took me..." Understanding dawned.

"Because your dad was deployed," he finished.

Chills ran from my scalp down my arms.

"Look at the record, December. You know that handwriting." His voice was gentle.

I flipped back to the start, for the attending physician. Dr. J. A. Howard.

There was no panic, no sense of betrayal, or anger, just the feeling that something had come full circle, complete. "He was your doctor."

"He saved my life." Josh sat on his bed and looked through his walls, lost somewhere else. "We were clearing a building when I went down. I'd only been in Theater for a month. One grazed my arm." He pointed to the scar in his tattoo, the one I'd traced the night of the Snow Bash. "One went through my thigh and hit my femoral artery. They wheeled me into the CaSH, bleeding all over the place, and I knew I was going to die. Medics couldn't get the artery clamped fast enough. Your dad got right down in my face and told me I was going home. He would make sure I was going home." He looked back up to me, and I sank into those eyes. "After I woke up from surgery, that's when he started talking to me and realized who I was. He'd seen me play when he'd taken you to a game."

"Freshman year," I whispered, remembering how unembarrassed I was to be there with my dad. "Why didn't you tell me?"

He reached out and took my hand. I tried to ignore the jolt that went through me at having his skin touching mine again. "You were so mad that he was ever in Afghanistan. I couldn't tell you that if he hadn't been there, I'd be dead. I didn't want you to see me as the reason, your dad as the price of my life."

"Is that how you feel?" I stepped closer, cupping his face as he looked up at me. I'd missed touching him so very much.

"Sometimes. But I'm not the only one he saved, Ember. There are countless others. He was an amazing surgeon. I wanted to tell you about it; I just couldn't watch you walk away. You pushed me away for so long because you didn't want to think of our relationship starting when he died. How could I tell you that he's the reason I'm here?"

A wary apprehension stole through me. "Is that why you spent so much time with me? Being my whatever? Was all of this for my dad, to pay him back?" My heart seized in my chest, waiting to hear his answer. I needed everything to be real between us. I wasn't sure I could handle being a pity case. "Were we real to you? I mean, you went right back to being...you."

Pain lanced through his eyes before he masked it. "I have wanted you since I was eighteen." He nodded his head toward the picture of us. "I wasn't good enough for you back then. Hell, I'm not good enough for you now. You're everything I'm not allowed to want, because of the things I've done, and the things I'll potentially do. I had no right to love you, but I couldn't help myself. Your dad had nothing to do with any of that."

He pulled me into his lap, and I relaxed, powerless against him, because I wanted to be there, to steal whatever contact I could with him.

"When I saw you that day in the grocery store, you were even more beautiful than I remembered. It had been five years, and that girl who'd infatuated me grew up to be stunning and strong. I thanked fate, bowed down, and kissed her feet for bringing you my way. But when I heard you say your dad had died, I knew why I was there, in that store after a random drive."

"Because you owed my dad for saving you, so you saved me." As close as we were, my whisper was all we needed. "The funny thing is that I'm not even sure I care. You brought so much into my life, Josh. You broke me free of everything that held me back, and showed me what it was to be loved, really loved. If any part of that had anything to do with Dad, then it's just something else I'm thankful to him for."

"December, don't you understand? I didn't take care of you because I owe your dad; I went after you *in spite* of what I owe your dad. Me staying away from you for these last months? Not beating down your door at two in the morning when it's killing me that we're only separated by six inches of wall? *That* is what I owe your dad, staying away. I know you don't want this lifestyle I'm about to lead. I know that regardless of what he thought, I'm not everything you need. But I also know there's no one on this earth who can love you as well as I can, and I wish it was enough."

My fingers stroked down his cheek, memorizing the feel of his skin, the rough scrape of his day-old scruff against me. My thumb grazed across his lips, the only concession I'd allow myself when it came to his mouth. "It's not about love, Josh. It's about fear, and it doesn't matter how much I love you, or how desperately I want to be with you. I can't live in fear of a doorbell. I won't ever open a door to that again. I barely made it through losing Dad, and I know that was because you held me up. I wouldn't survive losing you; it would crush my very soul and leave me to where I'd be dead, too, only I'd still have a heartbeat." My lower lip trembled, and I lost myself to his eyes, the dark swirling depths and gold flecks that made him Josh. "You are an amazing man. Never say that you're not good enough, because you are better than any of this." I pointed to the door, where the girls waited for him. "Better than any of *them*. My fear doesn't make you any less perfect. It makes me a self-preservationist. You—God, what I would do for you."

"You still love me."

"With every piece of my soul. Love isn't strong enough for what I feel for you, Josh Walker. A few months and your headboard could never change that."

"My headboard?"

Embarrassment heated my cheeks to match my hair, no doubt. "The night you won division?" He still looked confused. "Your headboard bangs against your wall, my wall."

His eyes widened, and he had the nerve to smile that heart-stopping grin. "I wasn't here that night. After the game, I only wanted to be with you, and I couldn't, so I drove ten hours to my mom's. That wasn't me. The only woman I've ever taken to this bed is you. I'd rather burn it than sleep here with anyone else. God, I haven't touched another girl in that way since we were together. You can't replace perfection."

The weight that held me down since that night lifted. I smiled, using his words against him. "You still love me."

"Every fucking second I breathe. I will love you the rest of my life, December Howard, whether or not you're around to witness it. You may think you're weak, but you're the strongest woman I've ever known." He dug his fingers through my pulled-up hair and brought me down to his mouth.

Before I lost all sanity, I pulled back. "I can't. Loving you is so easy, and when you touch me, I lose everything about myself in you. I can't be what you need."

His eyes widened, taking on a desperate sheen, and his fingers tightened on my skin. "December, you mean more to me than this, my career, this uniform. I owe four years, and I can't get out of that, but I'll resign. Just four years and I'll come back for you."

God, yes! The carefree girl inside me wanted to grasp for it, to claim him as my own. I could do four years of waiting, especially if it was for Josh. But four years wasn't enough for him, not really. "I would never be responsible for you turning your back on this. You said you were going career, and I won't ever be the one who holds you down."

The tears that welled in his eyes, and the one that slipped down his face, were nearly my undoing. "How can we love each other this much and not make it? Why does a love like ours hurt us both so badly?"

I brushed his tear away and checked my own. "Maybe love this exquisite, this powerful isn't meant to last forever. Maybe we're meant to burn so brightly for each other right now to light whatever path we're heading down, but there's no sustaining a fire like this."

He brought my hand over his heart, where the fire in his tattoo began. "I'll carry it with me, Ember. You." He tapped my hand against the flames. "Here. Always. It's you, fire and ice; everything I know that's December." He took a shaking breath. "Will you come next Thursday? For my commissioning?"

I shook my head. "Dad's company comes home that day, and I promised Mom I'd go."

He nodded, disappointment etched in the sad curve of his mouth, the diminished sheen of his eyes. "Maybe it's better this way. I leave for Officer Basic Course two days later. I guess this is a cleaner cut, right? So why the fuck does it feel like I'm being ripped in two?"

"Because I am, too." I smiled as best as I could, knowing I had to go, knowing if I stayed one more moment I'd give in and pay for it down the road. "I guess if you put us together, we'd make a whole person."

His grip tightened almost painfully in my hair. It felt desperate, frantic, the need that clawed through me to be with him, to stay here forever. But if he had this much of me now, how much would he have in three years? Seven? The day they came to tell me he was gone? I wouldn't survive it. No. At least now I would live, even if it was halfhearted bullshit, and I'd settle for a love ten percent of this.

"At least we had this. Most people don't get to experience real love, and we did. You're not going to be a regret, Joshua Walker. You're my biggest blessing." I slipped off his lap and bent forward, pressing my lips to his incredible, inked skin where the flames and ice met. I pulled back far too soon, and way too late, leaving a piece of my soul embedded in that tattoo, as close to his heart as I could get.

I would never get over Josh Walker.

Chapter Twenty-Six

The Welcome Home Center on Fort Carson could have lit the world for the amount of energy emanating from the families there. Palpable excitement hung in the air. The smiles of children waving American flags astonished me with sheer beauty. This is what joy looked like.

I'd never come to a homecoming ceremony before. Mom had always gone alone, needing that time with Dad, and we'd waited at home, baking god-awful cookies that Dad would devour and claim were the best he'd ever had. It was our tradition.

I shifted in my seat on the bleachers, pulling my sundress down to cover more of my thighs. The wood was slowly putting my butt to sleep. I played with the clasp of the purse in my lap, knowing full well what was inside, knowing the time had come for this envelope. Well, almost.

A little girl, about a year old, toddled up the bleachers, holding her mom's hand, and sat two rows down. Her tutu was red, white, and blue, matching the obnoxiously wonderful bow in her hair. Her mother fussed with her shirt, and then began tapping her foot, releasing nervous energy.

I knew that feeling, what it meant to wait, knowing everything was about to be okay. The minute he walked through that door, life would stop being a half-existence and would start in earnest again. Despite what I was here for, I smiled, taking in some of that woman's joy.

Mom made her way around the bleachers, caught my eye, and started up. She was dressed in a simple green sheath, clothed in class and dignity.

She smiled as she took her seat next to me, patting me on the knee. "I saw Sam come in, too. You look beautiful today, Ember."

"Thanks, Mom."

We were both drawn to the noise and presence of the room, unable to look away from the joyous anticipation of the families waiting. Five more minutes.

"Are you ready for this?" she asked, concern in her eyes.

I nodded, and the words slipped out before I could stop them. "Mom, I'm sorry I was mad at you. I shouldn't have been. If Josh ever… If he… I don't know if I could go on living, let alone function, and he's not even mine. Dad and you, that was over twenty years, and I'm sorry. I'm so sorry you lost him."

She pulled me against her shoulder and leaned her head against mine. "You had every right to be angry with me. And for the record, it was you. You, Gus, April, that's what held me here. You're what made it worth it."

"I love him so much, Mom. I don't know how to get past this."

"Then don't." She pulled back, propping my chin up with her fingers. "If you love that boy, you don't get past him. Love is precious, Ember, and it doesn't come around very often. What you feel for Josh? It might never come again. Could you live your life knowing you'd let it slip away?"

"I can't stand by and watch him die. I can't." I shook my

head, my lips pursing to fight back the swell of emotions. "I can't start this in fear of where it ends."

"No one knows where it ends." Her fingers shook just enough to be noticed. "Why do you think I made you come here today?"

I shrugged, looking at all the waiting families around us, counting down their last moments before this deployment would end for them. "For closure?"

She laughed. "Oh, God, no. All you've ever seen from our life is the bad. You've seen the good-byes, the moving, the distance. You've held my hand through deployments and cared for your siblings when I couldn't. You've seen the folded flags and watched your father lowered into the ground, but you have never seen the high, what usually happens at the end of a deployment. You need to understand why it's worth it."

"Nothing can be worth it, Mom."

A sly smile graced her lips. "I'll accept my Mom-was-right moment in just a minute."

Right on cue, the loudspeaker came on. It was time. The families came to their feet, the noise comparable to one of Josh's hockey games, but more passionate.

I stood with my mother, our arms around each other's waists, an island of mourning in a sea of unbridled joy; the waves were taking us over.

The doors flung open, and the soldiers marched inside. Cries of delight filled the air, welcoming home heroes like rock stars, tangible relief in the giddy squeals. The tears that threatened me weren't ones of grief, but an overwhelming need to let out the emotions I couldn't contain: sadness that this wasn't our day, happiness for the baby girl clapping in front of me, thankfulness that my father's soldiers and friends had made it home alive. He would want this. If there was anywhere he would want to be, it would be here, now.

There were two hollow spots in the first row of the

company, and my mother let out a smile and a sigh. "They came home with them in spirit."

I stared at that empty space, imagining my father standing stoic and straight.

After a speech that seemed to last a lot longer than the thirty seconds the clock witnessed, the general ordered, "Dismissed!"

The bleachers cleared like it was the last touchdown of the Super Bowl, a stampede of love avalanching down to consume the gym floor in a melee of hugs and kisses.

I'd never seen anything more beautiful in my life.

My mother squeezed my waist, pulling me in tighter. "This is what you needed to see. There is not one moment I have ever regretted loving your father. Even after losing him, I would go back and choose him all over again, and that has nothing to do with you kids. Even if we didn't have you, the years I was able to spend with him are well worth the price of this pain." She gestured to the reunions going on below us. "These moments, these are the ones you cling to, because it may hurt to send him away, but nothing compares to having him back. It makes you more thankful for what you have, more aware of just how precious it is."

She turned to me, holding my face, so alike hers, in her hands. "Do not take love for granted."

"June!" Sam's mom called out from the floor, dressed in uniform.

"Sandra!" Mom called back. She squeezed my hand and descended, leaving me alone on the bleachers while pictures were taken and hugs were given in front of me.

Sam waved up to me, but stayed on the bottom row, somehow sensing I needed to be alone. She was good like that.

I sat and pulled my purse over, opening the latch and removing the worn envelope addressed to me. I carefully opened the seal and slid out the single 8x10 piece of notebook paper scrawled in my father's familiar writing.

Yes, if there was anywhere he'd be, it was here, and I was finally ready to hear what he wanted to say.

Oh My Beautiful December,

When your mom named you on that freezing night, it felt fitting. You were such a calm baby, patient and soft like snow. It wasn't long until I realized what a fire you had within you and knew Ember was what you always would be to me.

I can't pretend to know what you're feeling, but if you're missing me as much as I miss you, then I'm so sorry, baby. Leaving you like this was never my intention. I can't even begin to apologize for all the things I'll miss in your life. But I need to tell you a few things:

Hug your mother often, she's going to need it.

Don't spend your life making other people happy or doing what you think will fit in those immaculate plans of yours. Take a chance. If you won't do it for you, then do it for me. You weren't born to be confined to a roadmap.

Live, baby. Laugh, cry, scream, and love. Realize that every moment you have is worth every drop of sweat and tears you can give it.

I suppose, since apparently I'm dead, I can say this: ditch the jerk-face. You may think you love Riley, but one day real love will amaze you. Move on and find someone worthy.

Always remember that I love you, and have since the moment you were on your way to us.

That's it, baby. You have been one of my greatest joys, Ember. I promise that you might not see me, but I'm still there, still waiting to watch you get married, graduate college, and begin your life. I'm already so proud of you, and I know I'll be proud of whatever you choose to do with your life. You are strong, so very strong.

Thank you for making my life worth living.

I love you, December, be brave.

Daddy

My fingers trembled, but I managed to fold the letter and get it back in the envelope. For a few moments, I studied the happy reunions, the smiling faces and open laughter.

The love that filled this room was the stuff of movies and legends. It was the happy ending of every fairy tale, the epilogue of an epic love story.

Epic love stories needed epic loves.

Who would grasp onto Josh when he marched in from deployment? Who would kiss him good-bye and give him someone to come home to? Who would he lift into his arms and hold in thankfulness?

Me.

I was his, and he was mine. And I was done being afraid.

I scurried down the bleachers, checking my watch: 10:45. Shit.

"Sam!" I ran headlong into her.

"Whoa, who's on fire?" She laughed. "Girl, have you checked out some of these soldiers? They haven't seen a woman in a while, and I'm betting I'm right up that—"

"Sam!" I interrupted, grabbing her shoulders. "Can you get me up north in the next fifteen minutes?"

A grin broke across her face. "Feeling like another ceremony needs you more?"

"Yes."

"About fucking time!"

We raced to the car, avoiding strollers and duffle bags. We pivoted around kissing couples and dodged between packed vehicles ready to take their soldiers home. Sam's car was in the middle of the gridlock, locked in. "Shit!" I yelled, scaring the nearest couple.

"Take mine!" My mom raced up behind us, keys in hand and perfectly balanced on her high heels. "It's there! Take it!"

She pointed to where her Yukon was perched at the very front. A hop over the curb and we'd be on the road. I turned back and hugged her. "Thank you."

She squeezed me to her for a millisecond before pushing me away. "Go!"

Sam and I slipped past three more rows of cars, and I unlocked the doors as we ran. "I drive faster!" she shouted.

I tossed her the keys and jumped to the passenger side. She had the engine cranked and the car in gear before I yanked the door closed. We jolted over the curb and into the grass before gunning it on the road.

I slammed my seat belt home. "Faster!"

"I'm already going fifteen over, and speeding on a

military installation is a federal offense!" She cut back and passed someone illegally.

Once we got through the gate and merged onto the highway, she was a speed demon, taking the speedometer places my mother would never want to know about. There was no time to be nervous about what I was doing. I was too busy cop-spotting and praying for my life.

Seven minutes. We had seven minutes, and we were easily twice that away at normal speeds. Then again, I expected Sam to break into warp in just a matter of seconds. She took the off-ramp so quickly I grabbed the oh-shit handle, and prepared to flip, squeezing my eyes shut.

"You seriously think I don't know what I'm doing?" she mocked and merged into traffic.

"Sam, that light is *red*!" She busted through the light, tearing up the hillside to our college.

She raised her eyebrows at my shock. "What? I looked both ways!"

"Incredible. We're going to freaking die before I can even get there!" She yanked the wheel hard to the left, cutting through the resident parking to get to the building where the ceremony was.

The brakes squealed, and my body shot forward, stopped only by the seat belt before slamming back into the seat. "Sam!" I yelled.

"It's 11:01! Get your ass in there!"

I threw open the door and bolted across the pavement. "Thank you!" I called back over my shoulder before pulling open the heavy glass door. The hallways were eerily quiet.

"You here for ROTC?" a guard asked.

I smoothed back my mess of hair and straightened my shrug over my shoulders. "Yes, I am."

He pointed down the hall. "Room 114, but you're late."

I nodded to him and took off running, thankful I'd worn

flats today. I'd have been all over the place in heels. I skidded to a stop in front of the room, confirmed the number, and slipped in, blending with families as they took their seats.

He was easy to spot. I'd never wanted to see Josh in a uniform, but in blues, he blew me away. He was different, austere somehow, like by putting on the uniform, he'd matured years. I chased away the apprehension and instinct to run. *Be brave, Ember.* I could do this. I would be strong like my father, and brave like my mother.

The back of the room was lined with windows overlooking the Front Range, and the sunlight was perfect for this time of day. I sat far enough back in the room, about seven rows, that he didn't notice me. I liked the element of surprise, which caught me off-guard when I saw Jagger in uniform down the line from Josh.

The instructors gathered the sixteen graduates and lined them up with the Rockies as their backdrop. They called the room to attention and started the ceremony. I was too absorbed in watching Josh to listen to the speeches. Not once did he smile, or look happy like the others with him. Instead, he looked resigned, trapped. A stab of guilt pierced me. I had taken this happy moment from him, because he thought it cost him me.

I would never again hold this man down.

The oath of commissioning started, the deep voices of the graduates swearing to defend the Constitution of the United States against all enemies, foreign and domestic. It was a beautiful oath that touched me every time I heard it. Selfless service, it was apparent in every one of their faces.

The MC, a lieutenant colonel, explained the pinning process and how each of the graduates had selected someone special to pin on their yellow bars. "Butter Bars," Dad had called them. Josh was third from the end, and I sat anxiously as the other graduates were pinned.Crap. I hadn't watched enough of this. I couldn't remember exactly where the rank went. My sigh of relief was audible when I realized they were using shoulder boards, and I wouldn't have to freak out about getting the rank on straight.

One by one, I watched them pin, the knot of tension growing in my stomach with each passing second. Was I about to make an ass out of myself? Was Tweedledum here, waiting to pin him? Josh had no responsibility to wait for me. After I broke his heart again last week, was he going to want me?

"Joshua Walker," the MC called out.

Josh stepped forward, and I lost my heart all over again. Unlike the others who were pinned in relative silence, Josh spoke. "The man I wanted to pin me couldn't be here today. He saved my life in Afghanistan two years ago, only to fall there this last Christmas. I can honestly say that without his support, I wouldn't be here." The MC walked over, ready to pin him.

It was now or never. "His daughter will stand in for him." I stood slowly and stepped into the aisle, meeting Josh's shocked gaze. I walked carefully toward him, aware that every eye was on me. *Don't trip and fall.* Once I reached him, I held out my hand, and he gave me his shoulder boards. "On behalf of Lieutenant Colonel Howard," I whispered. I slipped the left shoulder board on. I leaned up on tiptoes, now wishing I'd worn the heels; he was so tall I only reached his collarbone. "On behalf of me," I whispered again, and slid the right shoulder board home.

I knew the routine. If I'd have been a man, I would have shaken his hand. Instead, I reached up and kissed his smoothly-shaven cheek, taking a millisecond to absorb the delicious way he smelled. "Congratulations, Lieutenant Walker."

His smile was radiant, though quickly contained as was proper in uniform, and I pulled away. I couldn't hold back my grin when I took my seat. I'd just delivered Josh Walker the shock of his life.

Chapter Twenty-Seven

Everyone stood and clapped for the newly pinned lieutenants as they were announced. Ceremony over. Real life commences.

The blue uniforms blended into the crowd as the families embraced. Cameras were pulled out and images snapped, but I couldn't move. My heartbeat sped up until it should have taken flight, lodging my heart in my throat.

Josh tunneled his way through the crowd, determination, awe, and a little worry dancing across his features. Anticipation curled in my stomach. God, that man was beautiful. Beautiful, and mine. I just had to be brave enough to hold onto him.

He stopped just short of me, unsure if he was supposed to come closer. "December."

"Hi." It was all I could say, there were too many emotions racing through me to form a more coherent thought.

"Don't do this unless you—"

I stopped his words with my mouth, wrapping my arms around his neck and pouring everything I felt into that kiss.

For a few seconds, I thought I'd made a huge error when he didn't respond.

I ran my tongue across the seam of his lips, and he came to life, swinging me in his arms and consuming me in his kiss.

"Walker!" Jagger called out.

Josh pivoted only long enough for Jagger to take a quick picture, and then he carried me out of the room, one arm under my knees, and the other behind my back.

I laughed breathlessly, happiness filling every corner of me for the first time since I couldn't remember. "This is very *An Officer and a Gentleman*."

"What is that?" His gaze dropped to my mouth, telling me his mind wasn't on movies.

A slow smile spread across my face. "It doesn't matter."

"Walker!" Another lieutenant yelled down the hall at us, laughing. "No PDA in uniform!"

"Let me know when you lose your virginity, McAfee!" Josh fired back, opening the door to a lecture hall. He slipped us inside, locking the door behind him. He walked down the awkwardly spaced steps, and didn't stop until he sat me on the professor's desk.

I opened my knees, and he slid between them, pulling me against him. "I want to know what this means, but at this second, I just don't care enough to hear it." He slammed his mouth against mine, groaning at the contact of my tongue against his. He held my head with his hands, angling my head to his perfect fit, kissing me deeper and deeper, until I couldn't tell where I ended and he began. I had missed this so very much.

"Damn," he muttered against my mouth. His muscles stiffened against me, and he pulled back slowly, leaving his forehead against mine.

"Josh?"

"I can say I don't care what this means, but I can't do

this again. I can't have you in my arms just to watch you walk away afterward. I've been dying inside since you left, and if you do it again, it will finish me off."

I cupped his face in my hands, drawing back far enough to see him, but I couldn't read his expression through his tightly shut eyes. "Look at me."

He opened his eyes slowly. His eyebrows drew together and his lips tensed. "What are we doing, December? I leave in two days."

"Do you know where you're going next?" I hated this part of army life, but this was a small price to pay for him.

"Fort Rucker, Alabama. I know it's in the middle of nowhere, and really far from Colorado." His gaze flicked back and forth, and his hands tensed on my waist, like he was preparing for me to bolt.

"I know where I'll be."

His eyes narrowed. "Oh?"

Here it was, what would make or break us. "Josh, a letter came yesterday. I got accepted to Vanderbilt to transfer. I start in the fall."

He sucked in his breath and let it out with a huge smile. "That's amazing! Your dad would be so damn proud of you."

"Yeah. He'd be proud of you, too." I stroked my thumbs over his cheekbones. "Proud of us."

"Is there an 'us'?" He started to draw back, his smile replaced by tense lines. "I'd go through hell for you, but I have to know you're in this with me."

I closed the distance between us, kissing him softly until his lips eased above mine. "I'm all in, yours if you'll still have me. I'll do the distance and the waiting."

"I thought that wasn't what you wanted? A life of waiting? Worrying?"

"It's just not much of a life if I don't have you in it. I'll worry about you whether or not we're together." His lips pursed again. *Was he going to reject me? After everything?*

He searched my eyes for a long moment and then smiled. "This time, I'll wait. You go to Vanderbilt, and I'll go wherever they send me. I'll wait until you graduate. We'll make this work. I don't care how far away you have to be as long as I know you're mine, and I'm yours."

"We can do this, be together." Saying it out loud made it real, possible.

"We *will* do this. I'll never lose you again, December." He kissed me gently, pulling on my lower lip with the slightest tug.

He lifted his head, stared into my eyes, and his pupils dilated when his gaze dropped to my lips. They parted. His breathing picked up for a few poignant seconds before he crushed my mouth to his, kissing me with the ferocity I had missed all these months.

Yes. This was where I belonged. Josh was my home. I lost myself in the taste of him, the feel of his skin against mine, and gave myself over without reservation. His hands tunneled into my hair, pulling just enough that I dipped my head back. He moved down my neck, licking and sucking in the perfect rhythm that drove me insane. "Hey," I gasped, balancing myself on my elbows. "No PDA in uniform, remember?"

Without breaking contact with my skin, he ripped off his jacket, the buttons flying. Next went his starched white shirt. I grabbed his tie and drew him down to me, laying back against the desk. He pulled me to the edge, my dress riding up to my thighs as I pressed against him. I let out a sweet sigh; he wanted me.

I gripped his white tee, pulling it and the loosened tie over his head. They both joined the growing pile of clothes on the floor. With that simple move, he wasn't Lieutenant Walker anymore, he was my Josh, flaming tattoos and all. He kissed down the skin of my shoulder. "God, December, it's been so long." His hands slid up under my dress, keeping the fabric over my thighs.

"Take it off," I begged recklessly.

"No, someone could see, and I can't let that happen to you." He groaned against my clothed breasts.

Every part of me throbbed, needing him. It had been so long since I'd been near him, let alone touched him or been touched by him. I was starved for Josh and unwilling to wait another minute. "Please?" I arched my hips against him and was rewarded with a moan.

His hands slipped higher up my dress, skimming my thighs until he dipped between them. He pulled aside my soaked panties and stroked exactly where I was pulsing. I couldn't stop the cry that tumbled from my lips, echoing around the lecture hall.

"Yes," he said into my mouth, rocking his hand against me. He stopped, resting his forehead against mine, and took huge, gulping breaths. "Shit. I don't have any protection with me. I'm clean. I just did my medical eval for basic, but…"

"And I'm on birth control. Have been since I was seventeen." I wiggled my hips against his hand, desperate for more of the sweet pressure I knew would get me off. "Josh, if you want me to beg you, I will."

A flash of something akin to anger flashed across his eyes as they bored into mine, an intense sea of brown and gold. "Don't you get it? You don't have to beg me for anything. I'm already yours." His kiss scorched me. I heard a rip, and my panties fluttered to the floor. Thank God. He unzipped and unbuckled enough to slide his pants and boxers down past his delectable ass and was back against me before I could appreciate how exquisitely beautiful he was.

Everything in me tingled and throbbed, aching for him. "Please—"

He stopped my plea with a kiss and thrust inside me with

one powerful surge, stretching me to the max. "Oh fuck, December. I've never. Without. Amazing. You're perfect." He rested on his elbows, sharing my breath.

I skimmed my hands down the silk-smooth skin of his back and brought my heels up to balance on the edge of the desk. With what leverage I had, I pushed against him, bringing him even deeper. "Not perfect, but I am yours."

Joy passed between us, the sweetest feeling of the meeting of two hearts, one soul. It was just...right. I swirled my hips around him, and his eyes darkened. Talk time was over. He gripped my hips, pulling them back into him as he slid inside, kissing me with the same desperation.

Everything about him consumed me, from his mouth on mine, to his body moving within me. Tension spiraled, coiling tighter until my muscles cramped and movement seemed impossible. He broke our kiss and stared into my eyes, his breathing as harsh and ragged as mine. He slammed into me over and over, gripping my hips so I didn't slide back across the desk. "Josh!" I cried out, hovering so close to the edge. "I-I-I..."

He kissed me softly, but didn't stop moving. "Shhh. I've got you." He held my weight with one hand, and used the other to slide back under my dress. With the first taste of pressure on my clit, I moaned. He rubbed, and I gasped, arching off the desk as everything crashed in release. He caught my cries in his mouth, and fell over the edge with me in intense shuddering waves.

For what seemed like eternity, yet not long enough, we lay there, holding onto each other and absorbing what we'd both been longing for.

Josh braced himself and met my eyes. "You're mine?"

I let loose a slow, very satisfied smile. "Yes."

"Say it once more." There was an anxiety in his eyes I never wanted to see.

"I love you, Josh. I'm yours for as long as you want me." I was laid bare, every emotion raw.

He kissed me softly. "Like I'd let you get away again?"

I laughed. "You're going to have to let me get a little bit away, before someone peeks through that window."

Like I'd said the devil himself was watching, he was off me in a second, pulling my dress back down across my thighs before putting on his uniform. Once we were cleaned up and presentable, he stood between my knees, tucking my ripped panties into his pocket with a wicked grin. It had taken more than a few minutes to find all of his buttons.

He kissed me again, but there was no rush to it this time, no desperation. He kissed me like he'd been doing it forever and would continue the same way.

"You and me." I met his lips one last time as he lowered me to the floor. "Against the world?" I couldn't help the cliché.

His smile radiated pure joy. "Always."

Epilogue

"How many clothes did you bring?" Josh asked as he huffed up the stairs to my second-floor walk-up apartment in Nashville. It was in a great area, safe and close to Vanderbilt, for which my mother left a sizeable amount of money in my account to pay for. She excused her actions by saying it's what Dad would have wanted.

"Enough," I answered with a smirk, opening the door with my foot so he could get inside. The mid-August heat had sweat dripping between my shoulder blades, and the air conditioning offered sharp relief. Josh collapsed melodramatically on my couch, throwing his head back.

"Dying. I'm dying."

Well, if that wasn't an invitation. I straddled his lap, and he immediately came alert. "Better?"

He skimmed my shorts and gripped my thighs with a playful squeeze. "I just think you have too many clothes. I like you with none."

He kissed the laughter out of me and had me relishing the perks of my own place. "When do you have to be back?"

"Tomorrow night."

Too soon. I tried not to pout, and instead ended up kissing him again. I could've lived off kissing Josh. "That means you'll be here all weekend," I whispered suggestively.

"It does," he agreed, pulling me harder against him.

"Sweet! I like my closet color- and weather-coded according to the order of the rainbow." I gave him a smacking kiss on the cheek and bounced off his lap, heading to unpack the kitchen.

He groaned. "Can't we just have lots of sex?"

"Sure, as long as everything is put away…" I laughed uproariously as he jumped over the back of the couch and chased me into the kitchen. He lifted me to the counter and mercilessly tickled me.

I wondered if this is how it always would be with him, laughter and smoking-hot chemistry, with enough soul mixed in to melt me. Whatever it was with us, I knew it would always be more than enough. Josh was my home, even six hours away at Fort Rucker.

Two more years here, and we'd both finish together; him with flight school, and me with college. And we would make it, not because we were strong, or determined, but because there was no other option for us. We simply *were.*

He ceased the tickle-assault and kissed me, stealing every last thought from my head with that wicked mouth. "What do you say we enjoy what time we have?"

It would be the motto of our lives, I had no doubt. "I can't think of anything better."

"December, there's nothing better than you."

I pulled him closer, thrilled that this phenomenal man was mine, and stole a kiss before I whispered against his mouth. "There's nothing better than us."

Acknowledgments

Thank you, God, for this beautiful life, your mercy, and the blessings I don't always deserve.

Thank you, Jason, for choosing me. For a dozen years of marriage, and never once doubting we'd make it here to hold this book. For folding laundry, making dinners, supplying caffeine to the edit cave, and being here, even when you can't be "here." Our incredible children, I love you more than life. You've put up with four deployments, thrown-together dinners, and heard "one more minute," way too often during this process, but never begrudged me a hug or kiss. You are everything exquisite about this world.

Thanks also goes to: my rock star agent, Jamie Bodnar Drowley, for standing in my corner for every aspect of this insane military life we both live. For taking a chance on me, and making my dreams come true. Karen Grove and Nicole Steinhaus, my amazing editors—for your keen eyes and fabulous comments that kept me from using "pull" 232 times. You ladies keep me on my toes with laughter and grace. To the Entangled team—I couldn't be happier with what a beautiful family you are—especially Brittany and Sarah. LJ Anderson for this beautiful cover. My critique partners and agency sisters—Nola, Lizzy, and Molly—for midnight conversations and thousands of words of encouragement. This story would not have been the same without your input and cheerleading. Mindy—for dropping everything to read. The fabulous Backspace Survivors: Sean, Monika, Malia, Alicia, Lauren, Michael, and Ulana—Thank you for pushing my limits, both in literature and Korean food, but more importantly, thank you for being my friends. I am blessed to have you.

Thank you to my friends, who put up with my moods and my hermitish ways. Emily, thank you for being my shoulder for the last seventeen years, no matter where I happen to live, and for carrying me with your strength when I'm at my weakest. Christina, for your phenomenal timing, selflessness, and understanding. Best battle buddy ever. Tami, for reminding me who I am when deployment makes me forget. Thea, for your endless encouragement and unconditional friendship. Kierstan, for always being a safe place. My fabulous military spouse sisters who have held my hand through these four deployments, and stood by my side with steadfast love and loyalty. My Drum girls, the Rucker crew, the Germany gals, and my Apache ladies, I'm humbled by all you endure, and am honored to stand among you.

My incredible family—my parents who never stopped pushing me to be what they knew I could. Mom for Godzilla, and coming when I need you, and Dad, for keeping your office in my playroom, impromptu German road trips, and always making me your priority. My brothers, Chris, Matt, and Doug, for your inspiring enthusiasm, and always, my sister, Kate, for being my friend, confidant, hair-curler, and constant during our army-brat upbringing—love 'ya, mean it.

Lastly, to Jason again, because you're my beginning and my end. From Colorado to Capri, you are the inspiration behind every hero, because you'll always be mine. I love and live you.

About the Author

Rebecca Yarros is a hopeless romantic and lover of all things chocolate, coffee, and Paleo. In addition to being a mom, military wife, and blogger, she can never choose between young adult and new adult fiction, so she writes both. She's a graduate of Troy University, where she studied European history and English, but still holds out hope for an acceptance letter to Hogwarts. Her blog, The Only Girl Among Boys, has been voted the Top Military Mom Blog the last two years, and celebrates the complex issues surrounding the military life she adores. When she's not writing, she's tying on hockey skates for her kids, or sneaking in some guitar time. She is madly in love with her army-aviator husband of eleven years, and they're currently stationed in Upstate New York with their gaggle of rambunctious kiddos and snoring English Bulldog, but she would always rather be home in Colorado.

Don't miss the rest of the **Flight & Glory** *series!*

EYES TURNED SKYWARD

BEYOND WHAT IS GIVEN

HALLOWED GROUND

THE REALITY OF EVERYTHING

Also by Rebecca Yarros

WILDER

NOVA

REBEL

THE LAST LETTER

GREAT AND PRECIOUS THINGS

THE THINGS WE LEAVE UNFINISHED

Discover more New Adult titles from Entangled Embrace...

Until We're More
a *Fighting for Her* novel by Cindi Madsen

Chelsea is the best friend I've ever had. Ever since she left, I've been a wreck, focusing only on keeping my family's MMA gym afloat. But now she's finally back, and things are weird between us. By weird, I mean I can't stop thinking about her in *that* way. Even stranger, I'm pretty sure she's feeling the same. And this time, I'm not going to stop fighting until we're more.

Not So Happily Ever After
a *British Bad Boys* novel by Christina Phillips

Two years ago, I accidentally, yeah maybe on purpose, crossed that line with my best friend and it ruined everything. I haven't seen him much since. But now he's standing at my door. And then he gives me that half smile, and I know I'm about to agree to do something I'm going to regret. I've got to spend two months with him now...and that's not the worst part.

Rush
a novel by Shae Ross

Priscilla Winslow has a mouth that spits fiery sarcasm faster than I can throw a touchdown. But I've wanted her ever since I saw her in that Bo Peep outfit on Halloween. Yep, I'm a sheep who will follow that little hottie anywhere. There's one problem... she hates me. Just because we ended up in jail and quite possibly ruined both our futures...

The Summer of Jake
a novel by Rachel Bailey

Life is just dandy for aspiring fashion designer Annalise Farley... until her best friend's older brother, the guy who broke her heart at sixteen without realizing it, saunters back into her life needing her help. Helping Jake Maxwell land his next girlfriend is the last thing Annalise wants to do, but Jake's makes her an offer she can't refuse. Is that the sound of her life cracking at the seams? It's hard to tell with Jake smiling at her like she's the only thing that makes him happy...